Mr. Darcy's Twelve Days of Christmas

A Pride and Prejudice Variation

MJ Stratton

Mr. Darcy's Twelve Days of Christmas
A Pride and Prejudice Variation
Copyright 2025 by MJ Stratton
Edited by Ree Hudson
Cover design by https://regencyromancecovers.com/
All rights reserved.

This book is a work of fiction. Any person or place appearing herein is fictitious or is used fictitiously.

All rights reserved, including the right to reproduce this book, or portions thereof, in any form. No portion of this book may be reproduced in any form without written permission from the publisher or author, except as permitted by U.S. copyright law.

NO AI TRAINING: Without in any way limiting the author's exclusive rights under copyright, any use of this publication to "train" generative artificial intelligence (AI) technologies to generate text is expressly **prohibited**. The author reserves all rights to license uses of this work for generative AI training and development of machine learning language models.

This eBook is licensed for personal use only and may not be re-sold or given away to others. If you would like to share this book with another person, please purchase an additional copy for each person. If you're reading this book and did not purchase it, or it was not purchased for your use only, then please purchase your copy.

Thank you for respecting the hard work of this author.

Contents

Dedication	V
About This Book	1
Foreword	3
1. Chapter One	5
2. Chapter Two	14
3. Chapter Three	25
4. Chapter Four	35
5. Chapter Five	45
6. Chapter Six	54
7. Chapter Seven	62
8. Chapter Eight	74
9. Chapter Nine	84
10. Chapter Ten	94
11. Chapter Eleven	105
12. Chapter Twelve	115
13. Chapter Thirteen	125
14. Chapter Fourteen	135
15. Chapter Fifteen	146

16.	Chapter Sixteen	156
17.	Chapter Seventeen	168
18.	Chapter Eighteen	178
19.	Chapter Nineteen	188
20.	Chapter Twenty	199
21.	Chapter Twenty-One	209
22.	Chapter Twenty-Two	220
23.	Chapter Twenty-Three	229
24.	Chapter Twenty-Four	239
25.	Chapter Twenty-Five	249
26.	Chapter Twenty-Six	259
Epilogue		270
Mr. Darcy's Twelve Days of Christmas Poem		274
Other Books by MJ Stratton		278
Acknowledgements		280
About The Author		281

Dedication

*For the Christmas lovers,
particularly those who had no idea that the
Twelve Days of Christmas song was so old!*

About This Book

Fitzwilliam Darcy never meant to fall in love—not here, and not with her.

Fitzwilliam Darcy is relieved to leave Hertfordshire behind. The temptations of a certain spirited miss have grown too strong to ignore, and if he remains at Netherfield, he knows he will propose and make what he believes to be a most unsuitable match. Yet when his friend Charles Bingley cannot be persuaded to stay away from Jane Bennet, Darcy feels compelled to return to the countryside to prevent what he sees as a potential folly. When the chance for happiness presents itself, he seizes it in the only way he knows how—through quiet devotion, heartfelt gifts, and a love that speaks louder than words.

Elizabeth Bennet is delighted by Mr. Bingley's return, especially as he resumes his courtship of Jane. But she is far less pleased to see the proud and aloof Mr. Darcy again. To her surprise, the gentleman appears changed—more thoughtful, more kind, and far more agreeable than she remembers. Then, as the Twelve Days of Christmas begin, a mysterious string of lavish and meaningful gifts starts to arrive at Longbourn. Elizabeth is intrigued and increasingly convinced the sender is the only man whom she could ever be prevailed upon to marry.

As each day passes, Mr. Darcy struggles to show the woman he loves that he has changed. For Elizabeth, the mystery deepens, and she finds her heart beginning to soften toward the man she once dismissed. In this heartwarming Regency romance full of mystery, charm, and Christmas magic, true love just might be the greatest gift of all.

Darcy's Twelve Days of Christmas is a lighthearted, low-angst *Pride and Prejudice variation.*

Foreword

How surprised I was to learn just how long this particular carol has been around! The "Twelve Days of Christmas" originates from the Christian liturgical season of Christmastide, which spans from December 25 (Christmas Day) to January 5 (Twelfth Night/Epiphany Eve). The earliest known printed version of the lyrics appeared in England in 1780 in a children's book called *Mirth Without Mischief*. This version was printed as a rhyming chant rather than a full melody and may have evolved from a traditional memory game or religious catechism exercise used during the 1600s and 1700s. The familiar tune associated with the song today is of English folk origin but was not standardized until 1909, when composer Frederic Austin published his arrangement. Austin's version set the music in a minor key and introduced the now-famous extended "five gold rings" phrase.

Chapter One

November 28, 1811
Darcy House, London
Darcy

"Charles, I must insist you abandon this absurd notion of marrying Miss Bennet. I admit, she is a pretty girl—uncommonly beautiful, even—but she is not suitable for *you*. How can you not see she has drawn you in? Her entire family is objectionable, from her reclusive father to her wild younger sisters. Would you expose us to ridicule and disdain by giving your name to such an unsuitable country bumpkin? And what will happen when her father dies? You would be burdened with the whole lot of them!"

Miss Caroline Bingley's tirade went on for another five minutes. Fitzwilliam Darcy paid it little heed; instead, he observed his friend. Charles Bingley bore the mien of a man long-suffering, yet with each passing word, his expression grew more resolute. He did not interrupt nor respond until his sister had exhausted herself.

"You are mistaken, Caroline. Of all the ladies I have had the pleasure to know, Miss Bennet is the most genuine. If she owns one ounce of guile in her body, then I shall swim in the Thames. She is everything to me—*everything*. And what do I care for her family's behavior? I intend to marry her, not them."

"Do not be a fool! Everyone knows a bride's family is part of the marriage bargain. One cannot escape such an association once the register is signed. As your elder sisters, it is our duty to safeguard you and to prevent a catastrophic error."

Bingley rose and made to leave the room. Miss Bingley's look of desperation became more evident, and she rounded on Darcy.

"Do you not agree with me, Mr. Darcy?" she cried, her voice rising with urgency. "All of us hastened to London to assist you, Charles. Mr. Darcy came as well and holds the same opinion. Do you not, sir?"

Bingley halted in the doorway and turned, his face impassive as he regarded his friend. "Well, Darcy?" he asked. "Do you agree with them?"

Darcy detested being drawn into familial discord. Still, he cared deeply for Bingley and did not wish to see him ensnared in a marriage lacking equal affection. "I observed her closely at the ball, Bingley," he said slowly. "Sir William Lucas made me aware that you have raised…certain expectations. I regret to say I saw no indication of particular regard in her manner. It appears Miss Bennet's heart is not easily touched, and I fear she might accept your proposal to secure her future—and that of her family by extension."

For a moment, Bingley appeared stricken with doubt, though he swiftly schooled his features. "I shall take your…observations under advisement. For now, I will retire. I spent the day with my solicitor, and I am thoroughly exhausted." He pivoted on his heel and strode out, leaving the Hursts, Miss Bingley, and Darcy behind.

"Well done, sir!" Miss Bingley moved to his side and settled into the chair beside him. Her hand reached out to rest upon his sleeve. "How very fortunate I am that you and I are of one accord. My brother will be spared a fortune hunter, and at last we may leave Hertfordshire behind. What a dreadful little backwater it is. There is no hint of refinement among any of the natives. Indeed, they are veritable savages compared to those who frequent town. I am certain you agree."

"Their country manners are suited to their environment, I should think," he replied, drawing his arm away from her grasp and shifting in his seat to face the fire. "Quite comparable to the area surrounding Pemberley."

"But of course, those near your estate are of a different caliber. Their proximity to a great house must naturally instill sensibilities and manners not found in the wilds of Hertfordshire." She shifted in her seat, and he angled himself to look at her, striving to remain civil, though he wished fervently that she and the Hursts would take their leave.

Bingley had accepted an invitation to stay at Darcy House while attending to business in town. As Darcy had returned to London in the Hursts' carriage, they had all agreed to address the matter with Bingley openly and without delay. Now that it was settled, he longed for solitude. His thoughts were muddled and conflicted, and he needed time to set them in order.

In truth, Miss Bennet would make a most a suitable match for Bingley—if only she returned his affection. Bingley possessed ample fortune to marry as he pleased and had no exalted relations to appease. Marrying the daughter of a gentleman would elevate, not diminish, his standing. Yet, as Miss Bennet remained unmoved, quite untouched by his friend's ardor, it was best they part ways before promises were made that could not be easily undone.

There was, too, another matter Darcy had not fully acknowledged: the strength of *his* attraction to Miss Bennet's younger sister, Elizabeth. Should Bingley return to Hertfordshire and wed Miss Bennet, Darcy would be forced into Elizabeth's company time and again. He would either sever ties with one of his dearest friends or submit himself repeatedly to a most dangerous temptation.

"Caroline, let us go to Hurst House now," Mrs. Hurst complained. "We have been in the carriage all day, and I long for my chambers and a cup of chocolate." Darcy had, of course, offered them tea, and they had partaken. Still, he welcomed the remark, for it prompted Miss Bingley to rise, albeit reluctantly, and prepare to take their leave. Darcy stood to see them out.

"Thank you, Mr. Darcy, for your assistance. I am certain that, after a good night's sleep, Charles will see our point of view and resolve to give up Netherfield Park." Miss Bingley once more reached for his sleeve. "I can only trust your observations will aid him in coming to that conclusion. Then, of course, we may direct him toward a more…desirable match." Her expression suggested a specific lady, and Darcy wondered whether she had already chosen a candidate for the future Mrs. Charles Bingley.

Mr. Hurst was nudged awake, and the three were conducted to the entrance hall. Darcy's butler, Brisby, offered Mr. Hurst his great coat and helped the ladies into their cloaks, then attended them to the door.

At last, he was alone.

Darcy wandered back to the parlor, reflecting upon the confrontation and questioning whether their words had left any impression. Bingley had given no sign of distress before leaving. He had, rather unusually, adopted some of Darcy's own mannerisms—guarding his thoughts and masking his features. It was curious, for Bingley typically wore his heart upon his sleeve. He seldom concealed his emotions. Indeed, his open, amiable nature left little room for misinterpretation. He had made his preference for Miss Bennet plain to all, and his attentions had raised undeniable expectations. While Darcy believed Bingley's affections were sincere, he could not say the same of Miss Bennet's.

In his experience, few individuals were truly genuine. Most were concerned with appearances, and the most attractive and engaging among them often proved the least trustworthy. George Wickham stood as a prime example. He styled himself a gentleman, employing his education and genteel upbringing to deceive, but in all things, he was a bad bargain. In every village from Lambton to London, he had left broken hearts and ruined prospects. Darcy had paid more than enough of his debts to know the truth of it.

Miss Bennet was the handsomest woman to whom Darcy had ever been introduced. Her classical beauty was unparalleled—or so it seemed, at least by the standards held by London society. Yet he could not help but suspect that behind her lovely features lay a disingenuous and calculating nature. Given the family's circumstances, it was essential that the daughters marry men of fortune, lest they fall into genteel poverty upon their father's death. Surely, her vulgar mother had taught her to put her beauty to use in securing a husband.

But she is two-and-twenty and unmarried, the reasonable voice within him countered. Darcy dismissed it. That merely signified she had not yet caught a gentleman's interest long enough to result in marriage. Perhaps others, more discerning and experienced than Bingley, had escaped her clutches. *Their acquaintance was too brief for either party to form a true understanding of the other,* he reasoned. *I have done him a service.*

Darcy retired for the night, his thoughts still unsettled. Part of him feared he was wrong and that Miss Bennet was, in fact, precisely what she appeared to be. Another part questioned his own motives. Were they principled, or born of self-interest? If the latter, then his character required correction. Darcy was not a man to ruin another's happiness merely to spare himself discomfort. And yet, as he drifted off to sleep, he questioned himself once more, wondering whether he had seen what he wished to see in Miss Bennet, simply because he longed to be free of the temptation posed by Elizabeth.

After a restless night, Darcy rose and saw to his needs before dressing and retiring to his study. Breakfast would not be ready for another hour, and he had business matters to which he must attend. A letter from his steward had awaited reply; one he had postponed until after his return to London. One of Pemberley's tenants had recently lost its patriarch. The eldest son was but twelve years of age. Though the family continued to work their land, the yield was notably diminished since the father's death. His steward, Mr. Browning, expressed concern they might fail to meet their obligations.

The Wilsons would not accept charity, and so it fell to Darcy to find a way for them to *earn* what they lacked. He had no wish to cast them out and had already arranged for another tenant family to aid in farming the land come spring. It would take careful thought, but he felt certain he could devise a solution.

"I am going back, Darcy!" Bingley exclaimed, as he burst into the study and closed the door behind him. "You are mistaken—you and Caroline and Louisa. Miss Bennet loves me."

Darcy, striving to remain impassive, set the letter aside. "How *can* you be so sure? She smiles at everyone—the same placid, gentle smile."

Bingley's head was already shaking. "No. You are wrong. How many conversations have you held with her, Darcy? Have you spoken with her directly, or merely observed her as you stalk the edges of a room as you typically do?"

"I do not stalk," Darcy scoffed.

"Forgive me, but *yes*, you do. You skulk about, glowering at everyone in silence to discourage their company. How can you possibly know Jane as I do?"

"But I still wonder at your certitude that Miss Bennet holds you in the same regard," Darcy pushed, the question no longer solely for Bingley. "How can any man be confident of a lady's affection—especially when marriage is at stake?" His fortune and connections had made him a target from the moment he came of age. How was a gentleman to discern between genuine regard and clever pretense? The uncertainty had long plagued him.

"'Tis the little things, Darcy. I can see past the composed exterior she presents—from the demure mask—to the warm, affectionate woman beneath. She inquires after my thoughts and concerns. We speak of more than polite trivialities. But above all, it is a certainty I feel within myself. Call it instinct, if you must. Miss Bennet loves me, and I love her. 'Tis my duty as a gentleman, my responsibility, to speak of my feelings first, and I shall. Besides, you said I have raised expectations. How can I claim to be honorable if I expose her to the derision of others for disappointed hopes? If I retreat now, I shall paint myself as capricious and unstable—and leave her to bear the censure and pity of the world."

"That is a little brown, I think." Darcy leaned back in his chair with a grin, crossing his legs. "But I understand your meaning. My only fear is that you may be misled. If she truly loves you, then none of your sisters' objections signify. You are certain?" Darcy asked one final time, holding his friend's gaze.

"I am. I feel it here." He pressed a hand over his heart. The gesture was rather dramatic, yet Darcy did not doubt its sincerity.

"Very well. When shall we depart?"

Bingley blinked. "'We?' You mean to accompany me?"

"Of course. I promised to stand by you and help you to assume the role expected of a gentleman landowner. If my presence is unwelcome, then say so at once, and I shall spend Christmas with Georgiana." His sister would not travel to Hertfordshire while that reprobate Wickham remained nearby.

"Capital. I have a few business matters yet to settle. We can depart on the thirtieth of November, if that suits you. Blast! The first of December is a Sunday. We shall not be able to call at Longbourn until the second. Perhaps I can conclude my business sooner."

"Do not rush it," Darcy cautioned. "If you miss something or err, you will be forced to return to London." He well knew it from his own experience.

His friend nodded, tugging on his waistcoat. "Very well. Is breakfast ready? I shall eat, then visit my solicitor." He turned to leave, pausing at the door. "Darcy, be a good chap and say nothing to my sisters, will you? I understand now how they regard Miss Bennet, and I do not desire their interference as I continue my courtship."

"You have my word." Darcy believed it wise to keep the Bingley sisters out of their brother's affairs. Besides, he would be far more comfortable at Netherfield if he did not have to parry Miss Bingley's attentions.

After Bingley departed, Darcy sighed heavily and steepled his fingers against his lips, his elbows resting on the arms of the chair. Why had he agreed to return to Hertfordshire? The notion made no sense. Had he not fled that very place to escape Miss Elizabeth Bennet, only to thrust himself once more into her company? He had taken care not to raise her expectations. The unusual shade of her violet eyes had sparkled with intelligence and lively wit, their rare hue only heightening the force of her charm and threatening to tempt him past the limits of his resolve. Their dance at the Netherfield Ball had been his silent farewell. She had challenged him, and he had, in turn, offered a caution regarding Wickham. He had felt it was the least he could do for the lady with whom he had begun to fall in love.

A thought stirred—something Bingley had said of knowing he was certain of Miss Bennet's affection? Frowning, he searched his memory for any similar signs in his own conversations with Elizabeth. His chest tightened as he reflected upon each moment with fresh eyes. *She dislikes me!* he realized, sitting upright in sudden astonishment. Elizabeth, the object of his growing admiration, did not return his feelings.

Each recollection of her conduct toward him assumed new significance, and he reconsidered every occasion with her as though witnessing it for the first time. How had he failed to perceive the truth? The very liveliness that had drawn him in—her wit, her teasing challenges, her candor—he had mistaken for signs of interest, perhaps even an attempt to capture him as a husband. Yet none of it sought to attract. There was no clever scheme. She had merely cloaked her indifference—and indeed, her distaste for his presence—behind civility.

Indignant at being so gravely misunderstood, he resolved to improve Elizabeth's opinion by every honorable means available to him. The thought of any person—man or woman—thinking ill of him made his stomach churn. That the lady he admired should do so was worse still.

And what if your heart proves entirely lost? whispered the voice within.

Then I shall ask her to marry me, he replied firmly.

All the reasons for leaving Hertfordshire—leaving *her*—now held no meaning at all.

Chapter Two

December 1, 1811
Netherfield Park
Darcy

"I cannot believe Caroline had the servants dismissed!" Bingley's continual grumbling was beginning to wear on Darcy. He had repeated the same complaint at least four times since they had set out from London—and twice more since their arrival the day before. Mrs. Nicholls had been expecting them; fortunately, Bingley had the presence of mind to send word ahead, so the staff were not completely taken by surprise. However, neither he nor Darcy had anticipated being greeted by a skeleton staff.

"I ought to have warned you it might be so, my friend," Darcy said as Bingley took a sip of port. "I understood when we followed you to town that your sisters had no intention of returning. Logically, one might conclude she dismissed the additional servants before her departure."

Bingley muttered under his breath and rose to refill his glass. "Yes, I have instructed Mrs. Nicholls to rehire all the staff she deems necessary. Caroline did not even trouble herself to dispense their quarter's pay. Goodness, what a poor image that paints of me and my household!"

The housekeeper had made no secret of her displeasure when the gentlemen had arrived. Darcy had felt like a chastened schoolboy, skulking behind Bingley while the servant voiced her thoughts with unvarnished honesty. As an employee of the estate, she showed no fear that Bingley might remove her for speaking plainly. The scene reminded him of Mrs. Reynolds, his housekeeper at Pemberley, whose loyalty was accompanied by forthright opinions. After delivering her firm but polite reprimand, Mrs. Nicholls had cheerfully set about reinstating the staff Miss Bingley had so carelessly dismissed.

"I wish it were already tomorrow." Bingley crossed to the sideboard and poured himself a measure of brandy from the decanter. "Then we might call upon Longbourn. Heaven knows what Caroline wrote in her letter to Jane—Miss Bennet, that is."

Darcy recalled seeing Miss Bingley's note leave Netherfield just as the carriages were preparing to depart. She had claimed only to inform Miss Bennet of their removal to town. Given the scene several days prior at Darcy House, he and Bingley now suspected the letter was not so innocuous.

"Patience, my friend. The Bennets are local and will not vanish overnight. You remain within the time you gave Miss Bennet for your return, too. If your sister wrote anything improper, it will be a small matter to set right. One might even say Miss Bingley was simply misinformed."

Bingley brightened. "Yes, you are quite right. Excellent. Thank you, Darcy. As always, your good sense shows the way through the muddled mess in my mind. We shall call on Miss Bennet—and the others at Longbourn—on the morrow. You were planning to accompany me, were you not?"

Darcy inclined his head in affirmation. He, too, was impatient to see Elizabeth. A part of him wondered whether he was mistaken in his interpretation of her behavior toward him. He wished to determine the truth for himself. Perhaps he had not remembered correctly. Better it should prove so, for otherwise he had much for which to atone. Was she the forgiving sort? He did not know. He was forced to admit he had not fully discerned the intricacies of her character during his earlier stay in Hertfordshire.

His feelings regarding the eldest Miss Bennet remained uncertain. He still believed she held no strong affection for Bingley, but he could no longer ignore the possibility that his prejudice had clouded his judgment. Given his recent revelations regarding Elizabeth, he felt it was only just to reexamine his assumptions. Perhaps the elder Miss Bennet simply guarded her emotions more closely than most ladies were wont to do.

They dined quietly that evening, both still fatigued from the previous day's travels. Darcy remained with Bingley for some time after the meal before retiring to his chamber. He felt restless, and sleep eluded him for some while, but at last he drifted off.

Bingley's exuberance could not be contained the next morning. He hummed cheerfully as he served himself from the sideboard, then took a seat across from Darcy.

"Did you ride out this morning?" he asked, as he tucked into his eggs with unconcealed eagerness.

"No, I did not feel up to it." In truth, he had wished to avoid the possibility of encountering Miss Elizabeth on one of her morning walks. For reasons he did not fully understand, he preferred that their first meeting occur during a formal call, where he might observe how she received him in comparison to others. It would serve as a sort of confirmation—or, with any fortune, a contradiction—of her feelings. She had always treated him with civility, even in the face of Miss Bingley's vitriol. It might even prove impossible to discern her true sentiments.

The gentlemen occupied themselves with their respective business concerns until the hour came to call at Longbourn. Bingley called for his carriage, and they rode in silence, each absorbed in his own thoughts. The journey passed too quickly for Darcy's comfort, and he found himself still unprepared to face Elizabeth upon their arrival. A footman opened the carriage door, and the gentlemen alighted. Darcy counted the steps to the manor door and marked each second until it opened.

"Good day, sirs," said Longbourn's butler, Mr. Hill, as he stepped aside. "Please, come in."

They entered and removed their hats and coats before the housekeeper, Mrs. Hill, led them to the larger drawing room, situated on the western side of the house—ideal for the winter months, as the afternoon sun lent the room its warmth.

"Mr. Darcy and Mr. Bingley, ma'am." Mrs. Hill announced as they entered.

The ladies of Longbourn were gathered in a perfect tableau of domestic felicity. Miss Bennet sat beside Elizabeth. Darcy noted the tension in Miss Bennet's features—so unlike the serene composure she was known to display. His mien shifted, a seed of doubt taking root. The evidence of his misjudgment continued to grow.

"Mr. Bingley!" Mrs. Bennet came forward and curtsied. "We are pleased to see you, sir. We heard that Netherfield Park had been closed up, but I told Mrs. Long it could not be true. No gentleman would abandon his estate—certainly not without bidding farewell to the neighbors who had welcomed him so warmly." She quivered with excitement, her hands fluttering until she laced her fingers tightly before her waist. "And Mr. Darcy." Her tone was markedly cooler, and the look she cast him spoke volumes. "You are welcome, too."

He inclined his head, though he doubted she noticed. As the matron turned away, she directed them to sit and resumed her place, taking up her embroidery and feigning disinterest. However, it was plain that she followed their every movement.

He and Bingley crossed to where the eldest Misses Bennet were seated and took chairs on either side of the settee they occupied.

"Miss Bennet," Bingley began warmly. "And Miss Elizabeth. We are glad to be back. My business in town was not nearly so arduous as I had feared, though it seemed to occupy more time than I anticipated. No doubt the inducement to return made me most impatient." His gaze did not stray from Miss Bennet's.

Her cheeks flushed, and Darcy noted that the tension in her features eased, replaced by...

Hope, he thought. What *did* Miss Bingley say in her letter?

Elizabeth spoke, answering his very thoughts, and he wondered whether his countenance betrayed more than he intended.

"We understood you would not return to Netherfield Park this winter—indeed, it was implied you meant to give up the place entirely. How pleased I am that our informant was mistaken." She met his gaze, the challenge plain.

"Yes, well..." Bingley shifted uncomfortably. "I believe certain parties expected such a conclusion. However, I am of a different mind. Hertfordshire is the only place I wish to be at present. Indeed, I cannot recall a more agreeable time in my life than the months I spent here."

Miss Bennet relaxed further, though she still said nothing. Darcy groaned inwardly. *I shall have to assist Bingley. Elizabeth is guarding her sister. She will not allow Miss Bennet to speak privately with my friend unless she is assured of her sister's well-being.*

"A walk, Bingley?" Darcy asked. "We have been confined to a carriage far too long these past days. The weather is fine."

Bingley brightened. "Yes! Miss Bennet, Miss Elizabeth, what say you? Shall we take a turn in the garden?"

Miss Bennet agreed, and her sister did likewise. Both ladies seemed more at ease once they were out of doors, and within moments they had naturally divided into two pairs—Bingley and Miss Bennet walking ahead, while Darcy followed with Elizabeth.

They walked silently for a time, the space between the two couples gradually widening until at length neither conversation could be overheard.

Darcy decided to act with purpose. "Pray, Miss Elizabeth, forgive the forwardness of my inquiry. Miss Bennet appeared rather…discomposed this morning. Is she well?"

He thought he heard an attempt to stifle a snort before she replied. "I expect Jane's spirits will improve apace now." Her cryptic answer vexed him, though it confirmed that her sister's distress had indeed stemmed from Bingley's absence.

Darcy cleared his throat, uncomfortable. He longed to know Elizabeth's thoughts regarding the entire affair, but he remained unaware of what, precisely, Miss Bingley had said in her letter.

"I am pleased to be returned to Netherfield."

He winced inwardly at the note of desperation in his tone.

She shifted to face him. "Truly, sir? I had thought London would hold more sway over you." One impertinent brow rose, and her bright and discerning violet eyes gleamed—not with amusement, but something far sharper. He saw the irritation there; was it anger?

"I prefer the country." The words came slowly, but they were true. They rounded a corner and stepped onto another path of Longbourn's garden, though Bingley and Miss Bennet had vanished from sight.

"I wonder, then, why you were in such haste to depart after the Netherfield Ball. We, none of us, expected to see you again. Miss Bingley was quite clear that the house had been shut up and that its former residents had no intention to return. You can imagine what we thought."

Darcy's nerves threatened to betray him entirely. He cleared his throat once more, determined to speak honestly, but with care enough not to provoke her further. "Bingley always intended to return. As for Miss Bingley and the Hursts, I cannot say what they meant to do."

"Then he has no understanding with your sister?"

Her question struck him like a blow, and he halted his steps. "What do you mean? *Whom* do you mean?" Some irrational part of him feared she might speak of Wickham, but reason swiftly prevailed—she must refer to Bingley. He recovered himself.

"Georgiana is but sixteen. She has no arrangement with any man. Indeed, I will not countenance such a thing until she is at least eighteen and presented to the Queen." He took a calm, steadying breath. "Am I to understand from your words that Miss Bingley implied such an attachment existed?"

Elizabeth gave a single, solemn nod. "I am sorry to speak so candidly, sir, but I must protect my sister. She seldom reveals her true feelings. 'Tis a kind of defense, learned early—but when she does form an attachment, it is deep and unwavering. Miss Bingley's farewell note…well, suffice it to say that my sister has not been herself since it arrived."

A heavy weight settled on Darcy's conscience. Though Elizabeth had not confessed her sister's sentiments, the implications were clear. Miss

Bennet loved his friend, and he had nearly torn them apart. No, he had made every effort to do so. The shame of it burned.

"I assure you, Bingley's intentions are entirely honorable," he said awkwardly. "If his presence distresses your sister in any way—"

"No! It is quite the opposite. Or at least, I believe it will be once they have resolved the misunderstandings between them. I never truly thought he had gone without saying goodbye. They seem so well suited to one another." She fell silent, her words fading into silence. After a moment passed, she continued.

"Forgive me, sir. I am sorry for rambling. It is only...I am very relieved for Jane."

Darcy found no ready reply. He believed Elizabeth's relief on her sister's behalf had loosened her tongue; she spoke more freely than she was wont to do—at least with *him*—and he feared anything he said might cause her to retreat into formality if he blurted the wrong thing.

Before he could decide what to say, she asked, "Do you intend to remain in Hertfordshire long?"

"I am at Bingley's disposal. He is my closest friend, and I shall enjoy spending the holiday season in his company."

She was not facing him, so he could not read her countenance. Yet something in her posture suggested she found his answer lacking. There was a stillness in her bearing; it was a withdrawal so faint it might have passed unnoticed by any other but him. It signaled disappointment.

"I should wish," he added, striving to bridge the silence, "that we shall often be in company. Everyone seems so pleased to have Bingley back..." He let the sentence fall away. *Yes, they welcomed Bingley warmly—but not me.*

It was no one's fault but his own. He could not blame others for the coolness he had received; it had been earned by his own prior incivility. His recent reflections, particularly the painful realization that Elizabeth did not hold him in esteem, had led to some uncomfortable truths. His behavior, upon consideration, had not been above reproach.

Bingley and Miss Bennet reappeared just then—she looking quite pleased, and he sporting a broad and genuine smile. "Shall we return to the house?" Miss Bennet asked. "Tea will soon be ready, and I am rather chilled."

His conversation with Elizabeth at an end for the time being, they followed the others back to the house. Mrs. Bennet quickly claimed Bingley's attention, paying no mind to Darcy in favor of her more engaging guest. He did not object. He took a seat near the window and sat in watchful observation of the gathering.

Elizabeth helped her mother serve the tea and biscuits. Darcy watched her with a mixture of admiration and curiosity, pleasantly surprised when she approached and handed him a cup of tea, prepared exactly as he preferred.

"Thank you." He smiled up at her, and she blinked, a look of surprise crossing her features, and Darcy wondered what had startled her. Resolved to think on it later, he took a sip of tea, releasing a low hum of appreciation as the pleasing blend favored his tongue. She moved away, and his gaze drifted to Miss Bennet and Bingley.

How could I have been so blind? With unclouded eyes free of prejudice, the truth stood plain before him. Miss Bennet loved Bingley. When he shifted, she responded without thought, and when she moved, he mirrored her. Her eyes shone brightly, and she flushed when Bingley delighted her. Mrs. Bennet, to Darcy's surprise, seemed content to leave them to their own devices, her smile triumphant and rather smug, as though she had orchestrated it all. He found it diverting.

Elizabeth did not approach him a second time, but Darcy could feel her watching him. He could not help wondering what occupied her thoughts. Within another half hour, it was time to take their leave. Once they were safely ensconced in the carriage, Bingley revealed all.

"Caroline told her I was attached to Georgiana, Darcy. Imagine it! There is nothing wrong with your sister, of course, but she is full young, and I do not see her in that way. My sister deliberately sought to wound Miss Bennet. How very despicable."

"Miss Elizabeth mentioned something of it," Darcy confessed. "I am not at all pleased with your sister's actions. They were calculated, and her words might have caused harm to Georgiana's reputation."

"There is no need to explain it to me." Bingley shifted in his seat. "I have made things right with Miss Bennet, though I do not believe she fully trusts me yet. I shall have to prove myself all over again."

"If she loves you, and you love her, then it will be worth the effort."

Darcy fell silent then, listening as Bingley once more extolled Miss Bennet's many charms.

Later that night, sequestered in his chambers, he reflected on his conversation with Elizabeth. His thoughts turned to examining his own behavior. Darcy now recognized that he had carried himself as though he were above his company during his first stay in Hertfordshire. He had once argued that where there was a real superiority of mind, pride would always be under good regulation. But he no longer believed it. When pride compels a man to treat others poorly, can it still be deemed righteous? In all his years, Darcy had never seen his father behave so. George Darcy's pride had been quiet, dignified, tempered by kindness—a mantle of responsibility worn for the sake of those he governed, never at their expense. To measure his own conduct against that example was to feel the weight of shame.

I will be better, he resolved. *And I shall do it for myself.* While Elizabeth had inspired this resolution, true change had to come from within. It was not for her sake alone that he must improve, but because he knew he ought.

Chapter Three

December 15, 1811
Lucas Lodge
Elizabeth

"JANE LOOKS RADIANT," CHARLOTTE observed. "I have never seen her so happy. My mother said there was talk that Netherfield was shut up and its residents had removed to town. I am glad to see she was mistaken."

Elizabeth shook her head. "She was not mistaken, sadly. Jane says Mr. Bingley's sisters did everything in their power to keep him in town. They offered all sorts of reasons why a connection with my sister would be a complete and utter disaster. I placed little faith in Miss Bingley's note, but Jane did, and was truly distressed. All is made right now, however, and I shall rejoice that her heart has not been irrevocably broken."

Charlotte nodded in commiseration. Her future was secure; the engagement between Miss Lucas and Mr. Collins had caused considerable turmoil at Longbourn, and within Elizabeth herself. All her sensibilities rebelled against her dear friend entering a union of convenience. Charlotte deserved more than a mediocre existence as the wife of a ridiculous parson. She, however, seemed content with her choice, and so Elizabeth would stand by her.

"Will he make her an offer soon?" Charlotte's query drew Elizabeth back to the present.

"I expect he will. It is clear his ardor has not waned, and Jane's admiration is writ plainly on her face. Her hopes wavered until he returned, but now her faith is restored." Elizabeth gazed lovingly at her favorite sister. Jane's face was luminescent; the candlelight made the jeweled combs in her hair sparkle, adding to her beauty.

"What about Mr. Darcy?" Charlotte asked, nodding to the gentleman who stood across the room speaking with Mr. Goulding. "He seems very different from how he was before the Netherfield Ball."

"I cannot account for the change. He actually *smiled* at me the other day. Can you imagine it? The proud, haughty Mr. Darcy deigned to grant me a happy expression!" Elizabeth chuckled, though it sounded half-hearted even to her own ears. The gentleman's altered behavior had startled her. Mr. Bingley had called on Jane every day since his return, and Mr. Darcy always accompanied him. He was not gregarious, but he made an effort to speak with Elizabeth. His usual aloofness was nowhere to be seen. Yes, he remained reserved, but now in a manner more reminiscent of Jane. Why, he had even attempted to converse with Mary and Mrs. Bennet—Mary had stared at him, mute, while her mother had appeared flustered and unsure how to respond.

"See how well he gets along with Mr. Goulding." Charlotte nodded once more in his direction. "Few can tolerate his inane ramblings. Though I respect the gentleman, he makes my father's monologues seem pleasant."

Mr. Goulding was elderly—nearly eighty. He had outlived three wives and four of his children. Now, he kept to his small estate, Goldfinch Manor, occasionally attending soirees or other gatherings. His daughter and grandson resided with him. The boy, merely twelve, was to go away to school the following year. Mrs. Willis, formerly Miss Goulding, was a child of Mr. Goulding's third marriage. She had been widowed when her husband, a navy captain, was lost at sea.

"Why do you suppose he is so altered?" Elizabeth asked with curiosity. "I cannot account for it. It may be all a show."

"What purpose would he have in giving a false representation of himself?" Charlotte shook her head in disagreement. "I think it is more likely that the absence of a certain lady has helped him relax enough to be pleasant in company."

Elizabeth laughed merrily. "I can agree with that. Miss Bingley's preference for his company was hardly reciprocated. I do not believe Mr. Darcy appreciates her company at all."

Charlotte's shrewd gaze turned in her friend's direction, sharpened by a pointed look. "His affections appear fixed in another quarter," she stated calmly. "No, Elizabeth, do not protest. You choose not to see it, but his admiration is clear. Why you insist on avoiding him is beyond me. He has twice the consequence of Mr. Bingley, and many more connections."

"If such things were of interest to me, then I would not hesitate to press this supposed advantage you claim I possess. Alas, I will not marry where there is no mutual respect and affection. Mr. Darcy's own words condemn him. I believe he said I was tolerable, and not handsome enough to tempt him. He watches me only to find fault—that is all."

"Think that if it gives you comfort. Only, do not be so hasty to disregard him. It may be the worst decision you could ever make. Think, Eliza. I shall have some influence over Mr. Collins as his wife, but I could scarcely urge him to receive into his home the relations of a lady who so decidedly refused him. Your father will eventually die, as we all must, and when that happens, your family will be nearly destitute."

Elizabeth shook her head. "Jane will marry Mr. Bingley. We shall not perish."

Charlotte sighed heavily and said no more as she was called away by her mother. Elizabeth felt grateful, for she wearied of her friend's constant efforts to match her with Mr. Darcy.

I do not like him. Why should I? He has done nothing to earn my regard. Indeed, he has done everything possible to make me hate him. And how could I consider marrying a man who would destroy the happiness and prospects of a close friend? That is not honorable behavior.

She glanced about the room, determined to look anywhere but at *him*. Kitty and Lydia lingered in a corner with Captain Denny and Lieutenant Sanderson, two officers of the militia. Frowning, Elizabeth realized she had not seen Mr. Wickham that evening. He had been invited, as had all the officers. Why, then, had he not attended?

He must have heard Mr. Darcy would be here and chose to remain away. Yet even as the thought formed, another recollection surfaced—something Mr. Wickham had said:

"*It is not for me to be driven away by Mr. Darcy. If he wishes to avoid seeing me, he must go.*"

Elizabeth pondered the contradiction between Mr. Wickham's words and his actions. Had he not said until he could forget the father, he could not expose the son? Was that not what he did when confiding in Elizabeth? Mr. Wickham did not strike her as a man easily intimidated. His old friend's presence ought not to prevent him from enjoying an evening among society. Elizabeth found herself resenting Mr. Darcy for placing him in such an uncomfortable and precarious position.

Yet in the next moment, logic reasserted itself, and she acknowledged the inconsistency in his behavior. She understood his reluctance to pass an evening under the same roof as Mr. Darcy, but there was something disingenuous in his refusal to attend. She did not wish for these conflicting thoughts to spoil the evening, and so she set them aside until they could be examined more thoroughly.

Elizabeth began to make her way about the room, conversing with her neighbors. All were eager for the Christmas season. From Mrs. Long, she learned that a gathering was to be held at Haye Park on Christmas Eve. It was not commonly done, and Elizabeth suspected the Longs sought to introduce a new mode of celebration. She felt confident her mother would not object, and thus they would attend.

She became strangely aware of Mr. Darcy's presence as she moved about the room. After speaking with Mr. Goulding, he next engaged Sir William Lucas in conversation. He gave every appearance of being an attentive listener; his eyes did not glaze over, as others' often did, when the knight began to discourse on St. James's Court. At one point, from the other side of the drawing room, she met his gaze. Blushing, she looked away.

Some time later, she took a glass of punch and moved to stand by an open window. The room had grown oppressively warm, and she longed for a breath of cooler air.

"Miss Elizabeth." Mr. Darcy appeared at her side. "Are you well?"

"I am, thank you. Sir William's events are always well attended. It is impossible to avoid some discomfort, given the number of guests." She shifted slightly, allowing the cracked window behind her to come into view. "I find some relief here. Charlotte—Miss Lucas—always ensures that one or two windows remain open to permit a breeze."

He shifted, his manner uncertain; whether it was from nerves, discomfort, or some other cause, she could not tell.

"Will you and Mr. Bingley receive other guests for Christmas at Netherfield Park?" she asked, attempting to make light conversation. *Why can I never converse with him as I do so easily with others?* Her glass of punch trembled slightly in her hands, and she set it carefully upon the windowsill.

Her palms were damp within her gloves, and she longed to remove them and cast them aside.

"I do not believe Bingley has invited anyone besides myself," he replied. He tugged at his cuffs and cleared his throat. "It has been peaceful at Netherfield Park, but neither of us minds. There is ample amusement and opportunity for society in Meryton and the surrounding area."

Elizabeth could not resist a pert rejoinder. "I did not take you for one who enjoys society, sir." Inwardly, she winced. It would not do to provoke the gentleman…at least, not until Jane's future was secure.

His responding smile caused her stomach to flutter. "No, Bingley is far more inclined to visit with neighbors and attend parties than I; yet I have found I do not object to the four-and-twenty families in and around Meryton." Elizabeth blinked. Had he just echoed her mother's own boast, spoken not so long ago in Netherfield's drawing room? Had he meant to reference it? To mock her? Or was it merely said without thought? His gaze held some deeper meaning, though she could not discern it.

"Have you read anything new lately?" The abrupt change of topic took her by surprise. "We are not in a ballroom, and so there is no impediment to the conversation."

Elizabeth gave a startled laugh, recalling her remark during their dance at the Netherfield ball. "I recently read some of Wordsworth's poems, sir."

"Yes, his words would certainly not qualify as poorly written; therefore, there is no danger of starving the first stirrings of love." He smiled, his blue eyes alight with mirth.

I think I see why he smiles so seldom. His features, already fine, became altogether striking when he smiled, rendering him devastatingly handsome. *Ladies would swoon at his feet when faced with such charm.* She also wondered how many of her words he recalled, for in so brief a time, he had alluded to two separate conversations.

"Wordsworth is, I confess, a favorite," Elizabeth replied. "His verses are soothing. I confess to some partiality for his poems on spring and nature. I recall one—*Lines Written in Early Spring*—"

"Yes, it is one of my sister's favorites." He drew a steady breath and began to recite:

> *Through primrose tufts, in that green bower,*
> *The periwinkle trailed its wreaths;*
> *And is my faith that every flower*
> *Enjoys the air it breathes.*

"Yes, those lines are very pretty," she replied, impressed by the ease of his recitation. His baritone was warm, and it washed over her like a summer breeze. "I myself adore *To the Daisy*." She took her turn, recalling the lines from her reading earlier that day:

> *With little here to do or see*
> *Of things that in the great world be,*
> *Daisy! again I talk to thee,*
> *For thou art worthy,*
> *Thou unassuming*
> *Common-place Of Nature, with that homely face...*

"Do you also read Coleridge or Smith? My library's poetry collection has grown considerably since Georgiana turned fourteen. She developed an avid interest, and, as a good brother should, I acquired as many volumes as I could so that we might study the differing styles together."

"You are an attentive brother, then?" Her interest in the conversation no longer felt forced or feigned. Mr. Wickham had claimed Miss Darcy to be proud—much like her brother. Yet now Elizabeth beheld a different side of him. Could she have also been misled about his sister? Or was she, perhaps, deceived by his new behavior?

"My sister is exceedingly shy. We are all the other has, having lost both our parents. My mother died when Georgiana was five, and our father when she was eleven. I have had the raising of her since I inherited. My cousin, Colonel Fitzwilliam, shares the guardianship. I am, I suppose, what one would call an attentive brother, though I do so from affection, not obligation." He paused, his gaze drifting toward Jane and Mr. Bingley. "Your sister reminds me greatly of my own. I almost did not see it."

She wondered at his meaning, but did not ask. Their conversation continued for some time until carriages were called to return guests to their homes.

Later, as she lay alone in her bed, Elizabeth reflected upon the evening and realized she had not enjoyed such agreeable discourse with a gentleman in quite some time.

Darcy

The journey back to Netherfield Park was not long. Darcy allowed Bingley to speak of the evening, content to listen and contemplate his own experience. Twice, he had overheard remarks made in reference to *himself*.

On both occasions, the subject had been his altered behavior, which was said to have changed overnight. In a sense, it had.

They speculated as to the cause, and, curiously enough, his altered demeanor was attributed, by both speakers, to the absence of Miss Bingley. The supposition amused him, and he could not deny the logic. Better still, it seemed the denizens of the neighborhood had resolved to give him a fair chance to prove himself. He did not intend to disappoint them.

He acknowledged that it was his own behavior that had most likely earned Elizabeth's firm dislike. If he could change—truly, and not superficially—then perhaps she might grow to like him. Her manner already appeared somewhat gentled. Their conversation that evening had been stimulating and agreeable. The usual challenging look he often saw in her eyes had given way to one of interest. Their discussion of poetry had reminded him of similar ones with Georgiana, though Elizabeth's insights were shaped by experience and perspective.

Still, something in her manner made him believe she did not yet fully trust him. She held back; her speech and bearing were more open with her friends and other neighbors. While she had moved around the room, she had appeared perfectly at ease, but by the window, when they conversed, he had observed a certain tenseness in her posture. Was it discomfort, or something else? Whatever it was, he wished it gone.

Though his original motives had begun as an attempt to alter *her* opinion, Darcy now desired improvement for his own sake. Men of his station were accustomed to looking down upon others. Such had been his behavior for many years. He now understood that he had long acted with selfish disdain for the feelings of those around him, and that the pride he had once considered justifiable had, in truth, been excessive. He would improve.

He had made every effort since his return to Hertfordshire. After a fortnight, the residents were only beginning to show him greater civility.

His last thought, as he drifted to sleep, brought him comfort. *If I can win their good opinion, then I can also win hers.*

Chapter Four

December 24, 1811
Haye Park
Darcy

IN THE DAYS LEADING up to Christmas Eve at Haye Park, Darcy saw Elizabeth almost daily. Bingley, an attentive suitor, called upon Miss Bennet whenever he was able. On occasion, business matters kept the gentlemen at Netherfield, but they called at Longbourn at least four times each week. Evenings were spent either in the calm of Netherfield's library or in company at one of the neighboring estates. Darcy soon came to know the four-and-twenty families very well, and he found himself pleased with the acquaintances both made and deepened.

Darcy noticed a difference in Elizabeth's manner toward him; she was still not entirely easy, yet no longer marked by resistance. Her arch glances and pert opinions remained, much to his relief, but the subtle antagonism she had once directed at him seemed to have vanished. Their conversations remained stimulating and lively—at least in his estimation.

The evening at Haye Park promised to be agreeable. Darcy had it directly from Mr. Long that there would be dancing and party games as part of the entertainment. While he had avoided such activities in the past, he longed to ask Elizabeth to stand up with him. Their dance at the Netherfield Ball had not unfolded at all how he had imagined, and he wished for more pleasant memories on which to dwell.

"I have never attended a soiree on Christmas Eve." Bingley strolled into the library where Darcy sat waiting for him. His cravat was tied in an elaborate knot, and his garnet pin caught the light from both fire and candle. "If it proves enjoyable, perhaps I shall make it a tradition in my own household." His attire was impeccable, more formal and carefully arranged than Darcy recalled ever seeing him wear. Darcy's own ensemble, fashioned by one of London's finest tailors, appeared subdued by comparison.

"With Miss Bennet, I presume?" he asked. "Tell me, Bingley, have you proposed to her yet? After every gathering, I half expect to hear you have done it, yet there is no word." His lips curved with dry amusement before he rose to pour a glass of port from the decanter.

"I am more certain of my path than ever, Darcy. She is an angel—truly! I intend to propose tonight if I can steal her away for a private word. Will you help me?" Bingley turned imploring eyes on him, and Darcy was quick to accede to his wish.

"Yes, of course. I dare say there will be ample opportunities throughout the evening."

Their carriage was soon ready, and both gentlemen prepared to depart. Darcy gave himself a final critical look in the mirror as he donned his coat and hat and nodded once, satisfied with his appearance. His valet had starched and folded his cravat in the Mathematical, a tight, structured and exacting knot. Symmetrical and stiff, it required proper starch to achieve correctly. The knot conveyed precision, intellect, and formality. He briefly wondered if he ought to have requested the Ballroom knot instead. That one was more pliant, tied looser and therefore ideal for dancing, with graceful folds and trailing ends, suggesting ease and charm. The Mathematical knot certainly suited his nature, but perhaps he should begin to appear better relaxed in company. He was no dandy to chase the fashions of the day, preferring practicality to ornament, but he took care that his attire reflected credit upon his name and station.

He longed to know what Elizabeth thought of him—whether her opinion had improved. How was one to discover if it was so? Could her friend, Miss Lucas, offer him some insight? To ask her outright would be most awkward, however, for he had but a slight acquaintance with her.

I need a Christmas miracle, he thought, rather dismally, as he climbed into the carriage. *Perhaps an opportunity will present itself this evening.*

The journey to Haye Park was brief, and soon Darcy and Bingley were ushered into the warmth of the drawing room. The Bennets had already arrived and were scattered about. Miss Bennet welcomed her suitor as he greeted her with an ebullient smile. Miss Mary, the middle sister, was seated at the pianoforte, playing tender arrangements of Christmas carols. The two youngest, Miss Kitty and Miss Lydia, were whispering in a corner with Miss Maria Lucas, erupting in frequent giggles as they typically did. Desperately, he scanned the company, but Elizabeth was nowhere to be seen.

Darcy's spirits dipped, but he resolved to make his rounds and greet the other guests. Surely, she would appear before long. He made his way through the room, offering polite greetings to everyone until he came upon Miss Lucas.

"Good evening," he said, nodding with civility. "How do you do, Miss Lucas?"

"Very well, sir," she replied. "My mother has, gratefully, ceased her talk of wedding preparations in favor of enjoying the evening. I may now take some pleasure in the festive atmosphere."

"Wedding preparations? Forgive me. I had not heard that congratulations were in order."

"Oh, I had quite forgotten that you and Mr. Bingley were still in London when it occurred. Mr. Collins proposed to me before returning to Kent, and I accepted." Miss Lucas beamed, her smile lending her ordinarily plain features a measure of warmth and animation.

Darcy thought back, recalling the awkward parson who had introduced himself at the Netherfield ball. Miss Lucas seemed far too intelligent for such a specimen, but who was he to protest?

"I wish you well," he said, rather than voice his thoughts. "My aunt is…very attentive to the needs of those she considers within her sphere of influence."

"Do you seek to warn me, sir?" Miss Lucas's shrewd observation took him by surprise.

"You surmise correctly," he admitted. "My aunt is officious and expects to be pleased by all who interact with her."

"Ah, I see." Miss Lucas pursed her lips. "As evidenced by Mr. Collins's character. Do not apologize, sir. I am well aware of my betrothed's deficiencies. I shall manage." Her eyes flicked away. "Though it is further proof of Elizabeth's presence of mind in refusing his offer. She would never bear the yoke of another's will."

"Miss Elizabeth—" he choked, "*refused* Mr. Collins? Refused what? Surely not an offer of marriage!"

The very notion of *his* Elizabeth marrying someone so ill-suited as Collins was abhorrent. Her intelligence, wit, and spirit would be quelled beneath Lady Catherine's strong opinions, and more intolerably still, by Collins's unthinking deference to them. Elizabeth could never hold respect for a husband who would so readily place another's judgment before his, nor her own.

He drew a steadying breath, reminding himself that she had refused to marry her cousin. No—it was the possibility that she might have married another that had momentarily crushed him. He turned his focus back to Miss Lucas as she went on.

"Yes, she did. My friend could not abide the idea of a marriage of convenience. She desires more from her future than a—let me see, how did she put it? Oh, yes, 'A cold, unfeeling union for security.' Elizabeth is quite the romantic." Miss Lucas's expression was all too knowing, and Darcy wondered what she suspected.

He cleared his throat. "I cannot disagree with her sentiments," he said slowly. "It speaks well of her fortitude to refuse her father's heir."

"But in doing so, Mr. Darcy, her family would have been left to face genteel poverty upon her father's death...if not for Mr. Bingley, that is." She hesitated. "*If* he proposes. Alas, she and Jane have never viewed marriage in practical terms. Both have vowed to marry only where love and affection are mutual." Miss Lucas quirked a brow at him, her gaze speculative. "Jane has found it. I cannot help but wonder if Elizabeth's good fortune in that regard is not far off."

She knows. Or at least she suspects. This was the opportunity he had been waiting for.

"If I may be bold," he said, measuredly, "will you tell me Miss Elizabeth's opinion of...*me*?"

He could feel the heat rise to his ears even as he had begun to speak the words. They were likely red. How fitting, for he was deeply embarrassed to be inquiring after the object of his affections.

Miss Lucas regarded him with a look of understanding. "I am afraid you have much to atone for in Elizabeth's eyes," she said sympathetically. "But I do not believe all is lost. She has spoken of you less sharply these last few weeks."

"Of what does she accuse me?" he asked. "I shall make amends." He clasped his hands behind his back, grateful for the relative privacy their position afforded.

"Your first offense occurred at the Meryton assembly. Your exact words were: 'She is tolerable, I suppose, but not handsome enough to tempt me.'"

Darcy groaned and closed his eyes in mortification. "I am grieved. My behavior was not above reproach. What else?"

"Your sins of pride and aloofness have largely been absolved." Miss Lucas gave him a small grin and, surprisingly, a wink. "However, the tales of a certain militia officer continue to cloud her opinion of you. Mr. Wickham did not hesitate to spread falsehoods once he knew you had quit the county. He stays away now not only because of your presence, but because he has begun to court Miss Mary King, a charming young lady who has recently inherited ten thousand pounds."

"No heiress is safe from him." Darcy glowered, though his expression lightened at once when he noted Elizabeth's entrance into the room. "Miss Lucas, I thank you for your candid replies. One last question: is there any hope for me?"

She nodded. "Remember, Elizabeth is a romantic. You are not far from earning her good opinion. She is a forgiving sort, provided she sees the change is genuine." With a curtsy, she withdrew, leaving Darcy to mull over their conversation.

Later, the company amused themselves with a parlor game called The Twelve Days of Christmas. It was a long poem, and points were awarded for those who could recite the full list of 'gifts' bestowed by the true love upon the grateful recipient. Should one falter, a forfeit was required.

Sir William presided over the game, and Miss Bennet, seated on a settee between Bingley and Elizabeth, soon took her turn attempting to recall each verse.

"Come now, Miss Bennet, surely you can recall the full list!" Sir William leaned forward, his eyes glinting with their usual good humor. "If you stumble, you must pay a forfeit."

Miss Bennet pursed her lips in thought, her cheeks warming as the assembled guests turned their attention upon her. Her shy nature revealed itself in the twisting of her fingers in her lap. A light touch on the arm from Bingley seemed to steady her.

"On the twelfth day of Christmas, my true love gave to me…" She hesitated, her cheeks reddening once more. "Ah—twelve Lords a-leaping?"

"Very good!" Lady Lucas called from her chair near the hearth. "And eleven?"

Miss Bennet wrinkled her nose. "Pipers?" she asked, a touch of desperation in her voice.

"Ten pipers piping, Miss Bennet!" Bingley laughed. "You have confused them with the drummers."

Laughter rippled through the drawing room, and Jane groaned. "Lizzy is much better at this game than I," she said, nudging her sister's shoulder. "Very well, what is my forfeit?"

"A dance with me, of course, when it is time." Bingley grinned as the musicians struck up a lively tune. "Unless you had rather compose a verse to mark your folly?"

She laughed merrily and shook her head. "Dancing is infinitely preferable to composing a verse. Oh, the things we endure for the sake of Christmas cheer."

Darcy took the seat beside Elizabeth as Miss Bennet and Bingley strolled toward the musicians. "Can you recall all the words to the poem?" His curiosity was plain. "Your sister's faith in you is very strong."

She glanced at him, her expression tinged with surprise, as though unaccustomed to such direct address. Darcy could not understand it—he had spoken with her often these past weeks, both in company and in private.

"I can recite the verses correctly," she replied with a slight incline of her head. "It is an easy poem to remember. Of more interest are the elaborate gifts the recipient receives from her lover. Why, he must have spent nearly one hundred pounds on his beloved! Such an exorbitant sum."

"How much is too much when a man wishes to demonstrate the depth of his regard to the woman he loves?" Darcy countered, his tone calm, though his gaze remained fixed upon her.

A flicker of skepticism appeared in her enchanting eyes. "Affection ought not to be measured by the price of a gift, sir. I would consider such displays superficial and insincere. Trinkets are no substitute for true understanding and attachment."

"But we do not know whether our mysterious suitor gave his true love only physical tokens," Darcy returned, the ghost of a smile on his lips. "Perhaps he took her to the museum on another occasion—or read her poetry beside the fire."

At that, Elizabeth laughed heartily, drawing the glance of a passing matron before she lowered her voice. "Touché, sir. We have but one record of his declarations of love, and you have filled the blanks in a most ingenious manner."

Darcy's smile widened, though he contained it. "Then let us suppose he offered her his time, his attentions, and his heart—and the turtle doves were merely added for good measure."

She angled herself toward him, the candlelight flickering across her features. "Would you have me believe that turtle doves are the language of the heart?"

"Only when given with sincerity."

A moment passed—silent, but expectant. Then he asked, lower still, "Would you object to an admirer expressing his sentiments through gifts?"

He knew the question ventured too near a confession—but for once, he did not care.

Elizabeth tilted her head, her eyes narrowing in thought. "If I were certain of this gentleman's regard—if he showed his admiration through kindness, respect, and genuine feeling—I should not object. Gifts, when accompanied by such attentions, may be charming. Without them, they are merely ornament."

Her answer warmed him, but he dared not reveal it. He gave a slight nod, unable to suppress the smile that curved at the corner of his mouth. "Then let us be assured that the gentleman in question will prove himself with something beyond ornament."

"Let us trust he will do so." Her eyes lingered on his, something subtle and curious dancing in their depths.

Darcy changed the subject, asking after her family's Christmas traditions. He listened with attentiveness as she described the Bennets' plans for the morrow. They, like the Darcys, exchanged gifts on Christmas Day. After a generous meal, the family passed the hours in quiet pursuits. It sounded...lovely.

As she spoke, the beginnings of an idea formed in Darcy's mind. He latched onto the thought, puzzling out its particulars while they conversed. When Mr. Long declared it was time for dancing, he was quick to ask Elizabeth to stand up with him. She did not refuse, but neither did she look as pleased with the notion as he had fancied she might. Their dance was a lively one, allowing little opportunity to exchange more than a few words. Afterward, he asked several other ladies to dance, conscious that one of her objections to him stemmed from the assembly where they first met.

When he and Bingley finally set off in the carriage, he sank gratefully into the squabs, brooding upon the idea that had taken root earlier. It had merit. Resolved, as soon as they arrived at Netherfield, he retired to his chamber to compose the notes he intended to send as part of his plan. With any luck, he could begin the very next day.

Chapter Five

December 25, 1811
Longbourn
Elizabeth

CHRISTMAS MORNING AT LONGBOURN usually began around nine o'clock. The youngest of the Bennet sisters were always the first to meander downstairs—Lydia with red and white ribbons woven into her hair, and Kitty drawing her favorite shawl tightly about her shoulders. Mary, Elizabeth, and Jane descended a little later, followed by their parents. After breakfast, it was their habit to spend a quiet morning together, each occupied with their own tasks or amusements.

Dinner that evening would consist of roast meats and fowl—typically beef, venison, and goose, followed by plum pudding filled with suet, dried fruits, spices, and brandy. Cook always served it with a rich sauce, setting the dessert alight for a dramatic flair. Both sweet and savory pies were also on offer, mince-pie being a family favorite. Cheeses, jellies, preserved fruits, nuts, and spiced wine or punch also graced the sideboard. According to custom, the servants were granted the day following Christmas, Boxing Day, to visit their families. Consequently, meals on that day comprised cold fare and simple bread and cheese.

Elizabeth awoke slowly that morning. She glanced toward the window, where the ice clinging to the panes promised snow upon the ground below. Her Aunt and Uncle Gardiner had arrived the night before and were already abed when the rest of the family had returned from Haye Park. A snowball fight, she thought, would be just the thing to entertain her young cousins.

Stretching luxuriously, Elizabeth rolled over and sat up in bed. She pulled back the covers and shivered slightly as the chill air enveloped her. The fire had burned down to coals, and she hastened to stir the embers into flame. Her long braid fell over her shoulder, and she pushed it aside lest it reach the now crackling blaze.

Holding out her hands, Elizabeth warmed herself for a moment. It was still early, barely seven o'clock, and she wondered what had woken her. She donned her dressing gown and moved to her favorite place in her chamber: a comfortable armchair near the hearth. As she settled herself, she noticed a wrapped parcel resting on the table beside it.

"That was not there last night," she murmured aloud.

With a shrug, she picked it up and examined the brown paper for any sign of the sender. She saw nothing other than her name written on the front in an elegant, masculine hand. She tugged at the twine and peeled back the paper. A velvet-covered jewel case lay within, and she stroked the smooth nap tenderly. As she opened the lid, a piece of paper tumbled into her lap.

A few lines were written on it in the same hand as the inscription on the outside.

> *On the first day of Christmas, a memory restored,*
> *A token once cherished, from a heart*

long ignored.
Your true love came softly, with hope to reclaim—
A locket he gave you, on a gold chain.

Inside the case lay a lovely gold locket. An oval diamond sat at its center, its edges encircled by red garnets. The gems were set in gold, and the locket itself measured more than an inch tall. It struck her that it might be a family heirloom, and Elizabeth gasped in delight as she traced the embedded jewels with reverent fingers.

Surely, this is not meant for me!

Elizabeth was incredulous as she opened the locket, scarcely trusting her own eyes. Inside, a lock of dark hair was curled in a ring and tied with a bit of white ribbon. It held no hint of who the sender might be. She snapped the case closed and slipped the chain around her neck. The pendant felt heavy against her chest, but somehow, the weight was comforting.

"Lizzy?" Her door opened, and Jane stepped inside.

Letting out a small squeak, Elizabeth startled and turned to face her sister. "Jane! You frightened me. Come in and shut the door—quickly!"

Jane did as she was bid and came to her sister's side. "What is that?" As expected, her first question concerned the mysterious gift.

"A gift…though I do not know who it is from." She explained what had happened in hushed tones, as though afraid her recitation might bring others to her bedchamber.

"Oh, how lovely! You have an admirer." Jane clapped her hands, excitement radiating from her in waves. "Could it be from Mr. Wickham?" she asked impulsively.

The hair in the locket was dark—just like the officer's. Yet Elizabeth immediately doubted it could be so. No one had seen the gentleman since Mr. Darcy's return to the neighborhood.

"I suppose we must wait and see if you receive another gift tomorrow. How very romantic for your admirer to recreate the Twelve Days of Christmas for you." Jane sat on the arm of the chair. "I have exciting news to share, too, Lizzy. Mr. Bingley proposed last night!"

"Jane! You sly thing, you did not say a word!" She swatted her sister playfully. "Tell me, was it terribly sweet and satisfyingly charming? When will he speak to Papa?"

"If you recall," Jane began, "last evening after the games, the furniture was moved for dancing. We danced a reel, and though my feet moved as they always do, my heart seemed quite untethered. Mr. Bingley—Charles—watched me with such fondness, as if I were the only one in the room."

"When the music ended, he asked if I might take the air with him. I knew it was snowing—it had begun sometime after supper—but I said yes. We walked into the garden behind the house. Everything was still, hushed under a fine mantle of white, and the snow was falling slowly, like lace drifting from the sky." Jane's expression grew dreamy, her gaze drifting far away.

"We did not stray far, pausing by the arbor beneath an old hawthorn tree, and for a moment, he said nothing. I could hear the snow settling on the leaves and feel his hand trembling slightly as he took mine. Then, in his dear, earnest manner, he asked me to marry him. I could not speak right away; my heart was too full. But when I nodded and he smiled, I felt as though the snow, the stars, the whole of the world had conspired to make that one moment perfect. It was a modest proposal, but in every way…it was mine."

"Be sure to record that in your journal, dear sister, for that is the most beautiful thing I have ever heard." Elizabeth sniffled. "Who knew your 'Charles' could be so very tender? I am extremely pleased for you, Jane. You will be very happy."

Her sister reached out and clasped her hand. "As for when he will speak with Papa, I believe he intends to approach him before we all dine this evening on the Christmas feast cook has prepared. He and Mr. Darcy are to attend, if you recall."

A small part of Elizabeth bristled at the prospect of once more enduring *that man's* company, though her displeasure had waned somewhat.

"Will you wear the locket to-day?" Jane asked. "It is very fine."

"I shall, though I mean to tuck it inside my gown. Can you imagine what Lydia will do if she sees it? I shall have to find a very good hiding place."

"It will look lovely with your cream gown, and the sheer gold muslin overskirt shall catch the light most charmingly." Jane jumped up and moved to the wardrobe, quickly finding the articles of clothing for which she searched. "Ah, here they are! Yes, these will do very nicely. We can weave a red ribbon into your hair, too."

She thought the ensemble Jane chose for her was better suited to evening wear, but she cheerfully accepted her sister's suggestions. Elizabeth then selected a moss green gown with cream embroidery for the day. She still wore the pendant, but it was tucked securely beneath the bodice of her gown. The chain was long enough that it would not slip into view unintentionally.

"It is a perfect gift," she murmured to Jane, who was about to return to her own chamber. "Who do you suppose left it in my room? I am certain that is what woke me so early."

"We shall have to be on alert so we can discover the identity of whomever left it." With that, Jane departed to dress for the day.

Darcy

Darcy stood before the mirror in his bedchamber, fastening the final button of a waistcoat he rarely wore. The deep gold fabric shimmered in the candlelight, its sheen catching the red embroidery that curled delicately along the edge of the lapels and framed the small brass buttons. It was festive, almost ostentatiously so, by his standards, and certainly not something he would have chosen for himself. But it had been a gift from Georgiana, her eyes full of apprehension when she had first presented it to him two Christmases past. He had thanked her warmly, expressing his affection with a gentle embrace. He had worn it only once before tucking it away, hidden deep within his wardrobe like some artifact too bright for daily life.

Tonight was…deliberate; like the waistcoat, he would no longer remain hidden.

He pulled the lapels taut and adjusted them slowly, brushing away invisible dust. The mirror reflected a man less austere than he normally appeared; still solemn, yes, but touched with something warmer. Christmas warmth, perhaps. Anticipation most likely. Tonight he would see Elizabeth again.

Elizabeth, who had unwittingly upended his ordered world and charmed him without design. Elizabeth, whose laughter danced on the air like sleigh bells. Elizabeth, who would, he hoped, wear his gift this evening.

The locket, a family heirloom once worn by his grandmother and then by his mother, was oval-shaped, etched with an elegant leaf motif, and inset with a diamond surrounded by garnets the color of pomegranate seeds. It was steeped in meaning, timeless in design. Like Elizabeth herself.

He had retrieved it from the safe at Darcy House just days before returning to Netherfield, having resolved, though not without some trepidation, that he would give it to her during the holiday season. The decision had not been made lightly. Nothing about her stirred frivolity in him. He had only needed the opportunity to present it, and fate—or Providence—had provided one. As he composed his new "Twelve Days of Christmas" poem, each verse a token, a gesture, a whisper of courtship, he determined that the locket must be the first gift. Not merely for its value or beauty, but for its meaning. It was an offering of legacy, of inclusion, of remembrance and promise. A lock of his hair, coiled and bound within, was a token of him she could carry next to her heart.

His fingers lingered at the cravat tied neatly beneath his chin. Was it too much? Did the gold fabric of his waistcoat suggest something too foppish? Would Elizabeth think he was trying too hard to impress? Would she even notice his efforts to please her? He sighed.

Brisby, ever-attentive and unruffled by his master's moments of doubt, stepped forward with unhurried assurance. "You are dressed to advantage, sir," he said, smoothing the sleeve of Darcy's coat.

"Thank you," Darcy replied, his gaze fixed still upon his reflection. "I begin to fear I resemble a gilded peacock," he added dryly, but Brisby only chuckled and handed him the coat.

"You will outshine the greenery and decorations at Longbourn," Brisby quipped.

Darcy allowed the corner of his mouth to twitch upward. "Let us pray not."

And yet he wished Elizabeth would notice—if not the waistcoat, then the sentiment behind the locket. He had written a short verse to accompany it, unsigned but unmistakably personal, delivered with the rest of the small gifts that had been dispatched in secrecy the night before. He imagined her reading it, her look intent, head tilted just slightly, her lips pursed in that way she did when she was puzzled—or perhaps when she was amused. Would she know? Would she guess?

Given her...uncertain feelings toward him, Darcy suspected she might be slow to connect the verses to their author. But that was well. He would have patience in his pursuit. The usual superficial flirtations of society had never held his attention, and any previous courtship he had considered had been perfunctory. But not this. Elizabeth was not a passing fancy. She was a flame that demanded steady tending.

He would woo her as best he could. Thoughtfully. Subtly. Honestly. Conversation would be his opening. He longed to engage her in one of their spirited discussions, to let their minds meet and twine and clash as they had before. And if fortune smiled upon him, perhaps that connection could deepen into something more intimate, more enduring.

"Mr. Bingley will be waiting in the library," Brisby said, stepping back after a final adjustment to Darcy's collar.

Darcy nodded and retrieved his gloves. As he paused at the door, he turned once more to Brisby. "Do not wait up. You have earned an evening's rest. I shall manage well enough on my own upon our return."

The valet blinked, surprised but grateful, and bowed low. "Thank you, sir. Happy Christmas."

Darcy stepped out into the hall, heart steadying with every step he took toward the evening ahead. Let the soiree begin. Let the music play. Let Elizabeth wear her garnet cross—and may she place the locket beside it, not merely for its beauty, but for what it represented.

A beginning.

Chapter Six

December 25, 1811
Longbourn
Darcy

THE JOURNEY TO LONGBOURN was a short one. Darcy knew every turn in the dark, every bump and rut in the road. Bingley, animated with excitement, had proposed to Miss Bennet the previous evening, and now rambled on about his intention to speak to Mr. Bennet before they would be called to dine. Darcy listened with only half an ear, his thoughts fretting over how Elizabeth might receive him.

Upon their arrival, they were shown into the drawing room. Darcy's gaze found Elizabeth at once. She sat beside Miss Bennet on the settee, the muted glow of gold muslin lending a festive air to her attire. She was breathtaking. He looked for the locket, but saw only the chain, and realized the jeweled piece lay concealed beneath the modest neckline of her gown. *Why is she hiding it?* A quick glance around the room offered the answer. Surely, she wished to avoid questions from the other guests. He did not recognize the fashionably dressed lady and gentleman who completed the party.

"Mr. Bingley, Mr. Darcy! Welcome!" cried Mrs. Bennet as she bustled forward.

"Good evening, ma'am," Bingley replied.

"Allow me to present my dear brother, Mr. Edward Gardiner of Gracechurch Street in London, and his wife, Mrs. Madeline Gardiner. Brother, Sister, this is Mr. Bingley and Mr. Darcy."

Darcy did not miss how Mrs. Bennet had named Bingley before him, in clear disregard of their respective ranks, but he did not mind. Her manner toward him had warmed of late, and he had no cause to complain.

"It is a pleasure," Bingley said. Darcy inclined his head in agreement.

"Mr. Darcy of Pemberley?" Mrs. Gardiner, inquired with polite interest. "I had the pleasure of knowing your parents when I resided in Lambton. You would have been quite young at the time, so I dare say you may not remember me. My father managed the haberdashery for some years, until my brother-in-law succeeded him."

"Thompson? He is your brother-in-law? I know him well. Pemberley makes every effort to procure goods from local proprietors and suppliers."

Mrs. Gardiner beamed. "Yes, my sister tells me so in her letters. It is a pleasure to meet you, sir."

After several minutes of polite conversation, the Gardiners moved away, and Darcy approached Elizabeth. She now stood near the window, watching the falling snow. Twinkling candlelight caught her features just so, illuminating the gentle curve of her cheek, the delicate arrangement of dark curls framing her features. The locket—a gift from him—remained hidden, but the glimmer of its chain at her neck had become, to him, a fragile sign of hope—no more, yet everything.

"Miss Elizabeth," he began, betraying none of the emotion that churned beneath the surface, "I trust your Christmas has been…enjoyable?"

Elizabeth came about to face him, her smile polite, yet touched with something else—something teasing, perhaps even intriguing. "Enjoyable, indeed," she replied. "And not without a few surprises."

Darcy, uncertain whether he had misread her tone, leaned in slightly. "Surprises? Might I inquire as to the nature of these wonders?"

She gave a slight shrug, a playful gleam in her eye. "Oh, nothing too out of the ordinary. Just the usual exchange of gifts, though some were rather…unexpected."

The words struck him with a sharpness he had not anticipated, and though his expression remained composed, his thoughts scattered. "And do you find such unexpected gifts…welcome?" He knew full well that he walked a precarious line, and he feared pressing her further, yet he had to know more.

Elizabeth's lips curved into a subtle smile, her eyes narrowing as though weighing the matter. "I do not mind." The playfulness in her manner did not falter. "Some gifts suit me better than others, and I dare say certain individuals do not know me at all."

The calm of his aspect gave way, his pulse quickening. Her words seemed to carry a double meaning, like a double-edged sword, and he could not help but feel the edge of it. Had his gift been unsuitable? Had it displeased her? Could she already suspect its source? But how could she know? Her words had pierced him with precision, as though designed to strike.

Does she not know how these words wound me? Could she begin to guess that I—discreetly, cautiously—have sought to please her, selecting each token with the wish that it might touch her heart.

Elizabeth went on, seemingly unaware of the turmoil she stirred within him. "Some believe that flattery and fine gestures suffice to make an impression. Yet they fail to grasp the value of true conversation. To engage with another…say, a lady, one must speak with sincerity, with some knowledge of her mind, her tastes and interests, and her character."

Elizabeth's words pressed against his conscience. He had offered her neither sincerity nor depth in their earliest acquaintance. In recent weeks, he had made an effort to change, but had it come too late?

Does she speak of me? The thought tightened his chest. His initial pride, his awkward silence, even his earnest yet clumsy attempts at civility—had all these served only to confirm her opinion of him? She did not believe him capable of proper conversation?

It was not lost on him that she addressed him directly, her words laced with the sting of a critique, even if she intended no such thing. But the sting of her insinuation sharpened his self-awareness all the same. *Have I failed her already?* He had allowed his insufferable pride, his discomfort, to cloud his every interaction with her. Had he only spoken with the honest care and attentiveness she desired, he might not be standing before her so uncertain, so exposed.

"True conversation…and knowledge of character," he repeated, almost to himself. "It is not something I have mastered, it seems."

Elizabeth met his gaze, her countenance unreadable for a moment. Then, after a pause, she spoke with a calmer air. "I think, Mr. Darcy, you would find it much easier to converse with others if you were willing to make the effort to know someone, rather than to impose your own expectations. I believe you are more than capable. Your efforts with my neighbors have not gone unnoticed." She smiled warmly, and the anxious tension in his chest eased.

"I shall take that to heart, Miss Elizabeth."

"Dinner is served, madam," Mr. Hill announced, stepping into the room and drawing the guests' attention to the door.

"Well, shall we go in?" cried Mrs. Bennet. "Cook has outdone herself, let me assure you! We have roast goose, mincemeat pies, plum pudding, and every delicacy you could wish for!"

"Christmas is Mama's favorite," Elizabeth murmured, still standing beside him.

"Is it? Do you share her sentiments?" he asked, his expression earnest as he regarded her with open curiosity.

"Yes," she replied. "'Tis truly the best part of the year." She did not continue, observing him with an expectant look he could not quite interpret. Her hand rose to the chain at her neck, fingers toying with it absently.

"May I have the honor of escorting you to dinner?" he asked, belatedly realizing he ought to have done so sooner.

"Thank you, sir." She slipped her arm through his, and Darcy could not help but feel this was precisely as it ought to be—forever.

Elizabeth

Her arch behavior seemed to discompose Mr. Darcy that evening. Elizabeth had observed him from the moment he had arrived with Mr. Bingley. His attire differed markedly from anything she had previously seen him wear, and she could not help but feel pleased by the change. His gold waistcoat bore red embroidery.—and to her surprise, she realized they were perfectly matched in their attire that evening. Even the gold chain and hidden locket complemented both ensembles.

Mr. Darcy had spoken kindly with the Gardiners, another point in his favor. In truth, she had expected him to look down his nose at her relations, as though they were dirt beneath his boots. Instead, he had smiled charmingly and conversed as though they were equals and friends.

If he continues this metamorphosis, I shall not be able to detest him any longer. She no longer disliked him, of that she was certain. But did she like him? That remained unclear. His manner had improved, and nearly every objection she had once held against him was resolved. He no longer appeared proud and above his company, and he spoke with greater ease than ever before.

But that does not excuse his treatment of Mr. Wickham. And he has never apologized to me. The last stung more than she cared to admit, even to herself.

And then he had approached her, and she had responded as she always had, and he had seemed wounded. Guilt pricked her conscience, and she resolved to behave civilly. When Mr. Darcy offered to lead her in to dine, she accepted with grace.

Mama had arranged the seating in her usual, predictable fashion. Jane and Mr. Bingley were placed on either side of Mr. Bennet; Kitty, Lydia, Mary, Mr. Darcy, and she herself occupied the middle of the table; her aunt and uncle Gardiner were situated to the left and right of the mistress's seat. As the highest-ranking gentleman present, Mr. Darcy ought to have been seated at her mother's right hand. That place, however, had gone to her uncle. Mrs. Bennet's deliberate breach in propriety was obvious, though Elizabeth could not bring herself to object—she did not mind having Mr. Darcy seated beside her in the least.

"I am sorry for my mother," Elizabeth felt compelled to say as they sat.

"I prefer this seat to the alternative." His eyes widened in sudden alarm. "That is to say, I am pleased I shall have the opportunity to speak with you. I meant no insult to your mother." He looked positively panicked, and Elizabeth chuckled.

"I take no offense, sir. My mother is difficult even in the best of situations. If I am a pleasant enough companion and you are satisfied, then I have no complaint and rescind my apologies for her behavior."

He smiled gratefully and helped her in serving the first course. Everything was done to perfection, and Elizabeth hummed in satisfaction as she partook. "Do you have a favorite dish for Christmas, Mr. Darcy?" she asked.

"Pemberley's cook makes excellent mince-pies," he replied. "Plum pudding is another favorite, and I have yet to taste one that surpasses Pemberley's recipe."

"Is that a challenge, sir?" Elizabeth affected a look of mock seriousness, hoping he did not mistake her light manner. "Well, you will have to tell me how Longbourn's dish compares! I will have you know, it is several generations old and has undergone many adjustments to make it what it is."

"I shall look forward to tasting it."

The rest of the meal was enjoyed in good cheer, until at last the plum pudding was brought out. Cook set it aflame, and the room erupted in applause. Servings were passed around the table, and once everyone had a plate before them, Mr. Bennet tapped his glass to gain their attention.

"Before we lose ourselves in Longbourn's greatest delight, I have an announcement. Mr. Bingley has asked for our Jane's hand in marriage and she has accepted. I have given my blessing to the happy couple. And so, I propose a toast to Mr. Bingley, my first son, and to my dearest Jane, my firstborn treasure. May you have many years of happiness together! And may the rest of us survive the wedding preparations with our sanity intact."

Everyone laughed and raised a glass, and Elizabeth saw a wistful look cross Mr. Darcy's features before he drank. He set his glass down and picked up his fork, turning to her with a cheeky grin.

"The test begins, Miss Elizabeth."

He took a generous forkful of pudding and chewed thoughtfully for a moment before his eyes widened. "Why, this is marvelous! I have never tasted anything so delightful!"

Elizabeth laughed, shaking her head as he took another bite. "I warned you, sir. You must ask Mama for the receipt."

"I shall do just that. Had I consumed too much wine, I might have called down the table. But alas, I am quite sober, and shall therefore wait until after the meal to compliment your mother and beg for her secret."

"She may refuse, sir. Fortunately for you, I have it recorded in my commonplace book and can make you a copy should she prove stubborn." Elizabeth had offered the receipt without thought, knowing full well her mother would not approve. Something within her desired Mr. Darcy's regard, and he granted her a warm, contented smile in return for her generous offer.

"I shall accept your aid, Miss Elizabeth. I thank you."

After dinner, they played parlor games. It was late when the gentlemen took their leave and departed for Netherfield. Jane and Elizabeth stood at the window, watching the carriage pull away just as snow began to fall once more. "Happy Christmas, Jane," she murmured, leaning her head on her sister's shoulder.

Chapter Seven

December 26, 1811
Longbourn
Elizabeth

ELIZABETH HAD RETIRED THE previous evening with an unshakable sense of delight blooming in her chest. The events of Christmas Day—the laughter, the warmth, the surprising poetry nestled among traditional festivities—had left her with a curious, pleasant flutter that lingered long after the candle had been snuffed.

Her fingers had lingered upon the delicate gold locket for a time before she had returned it to the velvet-covered jewel case, then carefully wrapped it in a square of linen, and placed it in a small wooden box on the uppermost shelf at the back of her wardrobe. There, it would be safe from prying eyes, from idle curiosity, and perhaps even from her own impulse to take it out repeatedly.

The accompanying verse—mysterious, clever, and undeniably charming—she had tucked into her journal, concealed beneath the lining of a drawer. She had read it thrice ere sleep claimed her, each time wondering anew the identity of its unknown author.

As the first pale streaks of dawn slipped through the frosted edges of her windowpane, Elizabeth stirred, her internal rhythm rousing her before the household began its bustle. The fire had been stoked while she slept, filling the room with a hearth-born warmth that contrasted pleasantly with the chill seeping through the glass. She stretched beneath the quilts, loath to leave the cocoon of comfort, yet her eyes had already fixed upon the small table beside her chair.

There, nestled atop the surface, lay another package.

Larger than the last, it too was wrapped in brown paper and tied with coarse twine, but something in its precise folds and symmetry bespoke particular care. A thrill of anticipation shot through her as she sat upright. She cast aside the blankets and stepped into her slippers with uncommon alacrity, reaching for her warm, quilted wrapper and drawing it over her night dress. Her pulse quickened with each step toward the parcel.

She seated herself next to the table, folding her legs and tucking them beneath her, then drew the parcel into her lap. The paper crackled as she untied the twine, lifting each fold with deliberate care, savoring the secrecy of it all. Who could be behind these mystery offerings? The locket alone had been too fine a gift to be given without purpose, and the accompanying verse had hinted at more to come. Had it been a jest? A mere whim?

No. This was deliberate.

A smile tugged at the corner of her mouth as she peeled away the final layer of wrapping. Whether the admirer was known or unknown, bold or bashful, she could not deny the delight his efforts had inspired. What would this day's gift bring? Inside the brown paper was a small box. She lifted the lid, and atop it lay a note:

> *On the second day of Christmas,*
> *With his beloved in view,*
> *Two silk gloves,*
> *Stitched delicate and true.*

Beneath the folded note lay a pair of white silk gloves—exquisite in every particular. Elizabeth gasped as she lifted them from the box, her fingers trailing along the delicately embroidered edges. The silk shimmered in the pale morning light, smooth as water beneath her touch, and the embroidery—fine gold thread forming an understated floral pattern—was wrought with the kind of skill only a true artisan could boast.

She slid one glove onto her hand with care, marveling at the manner in which it fit as though fashioned expressly for her. It embraced each finger perfectly, with no bunching or strain, and the wrist ended at precisely the right point below the sleeve of her wrapper. These were not gloves to be worn for running errands in Meryton or calling upon neighbors; no, they were meant for an assembly or a fine dinner—something elegant and festive. She could not possibly wear them on an ordinary day.

Her gaze returned to the note—another stanza, clever and well-composed, with a tone that danced between lightheartedness and tender regard. Whoever had written the verse owned a practiced hand and a romantic spirit.

She studied the gloves anew. "Three guineas at the least," she murmured. It was no exaggeration. Elizabeth knew quality when she beheld it, and these were of the highest. Such a sum placed them firmly beyond the reach of many, including, regrettably, Mr. Wickham. She liked him well enough, but she could not delude herself as to his financial constraints. And generous though he might be with his smiles and overt charm, he had never struck her as particularly extravagant in his affections.

A thoughtful crease marked her forehead as she considered which gentleman of her acquaintance might be her admirer. Generosity, poetic skill, refined taste, an eye for detail, and ample fortune; these were the marks of her mysterious suitor. Mr. Darcy flickered through her thoughts, like a shadow at the edge of her imagination. She dismissed the notion nearly at once.

"Mr. Darcy..." she whispered, incredulous. "He has not a romantic bone in his body...or does he?" She blinked, unsure whence the thought had come. His solemn demeanor hardly suggested secret passions, and yet...he had looked at her oddly the other day, had he not? But no—surely not. It must be someone else. Still, she smiled. *I shall have to be diligent in uncovering the answer.*

Her thoughts drifted to the conversation she had shared with Mr. Darcy some evenings past. Though love must rest not only on material offerings, she could not deny that a thoughtful token might increase one's admiration and regard.

A gentle knock at the door stirred her from her reverie, and Jane entered, fully dressed and ready for the day, an uncommon sight at such an early hour.

"You are up early." Elizabeth teased her, eyes alight with amusement. "Why, Jane, you are dressed as well! What has drawn you from your bed before your usual hour?"

Jane returned a knowing smile and perched herself upon the arm of Elizabeth's chair, just as she had the morning before. "Your secret suitor, of course," she said lightly. Her eyes sparkled with shared excitement as they fell to the open parcel in Elizabeth's lap. "You received another gift—what is it on this day?"

Without a word, Elizabeth handed her the gloves.

Jane caught her breath, her face alight with admiration as she examined them. "Oh, Lizzy! These are splendid. I have not seen such workmanship outside of London. The embroidery is exquisite. How is the fit?" She paused, and without waiting for her sister's reply, looked up, her voice hushed with awe. "Who can it be?"

Elizabeth laughed. "The fit is perfect, and I cannot say," she admitted with a sigh. "I truly have no answer, though I have puzzled over it until my head aches. All I have been able to deduce is that he must be a gentleman of means—and someone terribly romantic. That eliminates most of the gentlemen of our acquaintance."

Jane tilted her head thoughtfully. "Perhaps your admirer has hidden depths."

Elizabeth smiled wryly. "I suppose I ought to make an effort to see past outward appearances, as it seems my initial judgments are not always accurate."

"Then you have grown," Jane said with a proud smile.

"If you think it so, Jane, I shall take that as progress. I am learning, at least."

A momentary hush filled the room as both sisters reflected on the mystery before them. At last, Jane broke the silence. "As it is the servants' day, no one will be entertaining, and we shall spend it contentedly at home. Charles has promised to call, though. I expect he will bring Mr. Darcy with him."

Elizabeth shifted in her seat, her smile dimming slightly.

"I am sorry you are left to entertain his friend. I have been a dreadful sister, leaving you in his company for so long without reprieve."

She laughed, though there was a touch of hesitation. "He is not so bad as I once thought, Jane. Indeed, he improves upon further acquaintance. I do not know if I can absolve him of all his faults, but...he is not as objectionable as he once was."

Jane beamed. "Then I am glad. I never thought he was the villain you believed him to be. Perhaps he will further redeem himself."

Elizabeth pulled a face in reply, her nose wrinkling in playful skepticism. "I cannot see it. Nevertheless, you need not worry about my welfare. I can speak with Mr. Darcy without pain or discomfort. Feel free to give your betrothed all your attention."

Jane took her hand and gave it a squeeze. "Then I shall. But let us trust this day brings you clarity."

Elizabeth grinned. "Indeed. If nothing else, I am being most delightfully wooed."

Breakfast was simple fare, though sufficient to satisfy a household still buoyed by pleasures of the Christmas season. The kitchen servants had laid it out ere departing for their well-earned respite. Only necessary staff without family nearby remained for the household to ensure the family did not descend into chaos, and a groom was kept back at the stables to tend the horses and see to any arriving guests. Their free day would come on the morrow. Elizabeth was pleased they were granted the time at all—too many households treated their servants as little more than necessary furniture.

She and Jane entered the dining room together, the warmth of the fire spreading pleasantly through the space. The scents of toast, stewed apples, and tart preserves mingled with the faint, comforting aroma of cold slices of Christmas goose. Upon the sideboard lay a generous spread: hot rolls, slices of crusty toast, boiled eggs with bright yolks, cold meats artfully arranged, jewel-toned preserves, and tender apples spiced with cinnamon and cloves. Two large pots, one of tea, the other of hot chocolate, steamed gently nearby, offering their contents like old friends inviting conversation.

They selected their food in companionable silence before taking their seats. Elizabeth poured herself chocolate and inhaled the rich, sweet scent just as her father entered, his nose buried in a book.

"Good morning, Jane. Good morning, Lizzy," he said, without glancing up, as he moved to his place at the head of the table.

They greeted him in kind and began to eat, the clink of porcelain and silver a soothing accompaniment to the gentle crackle of the fire.

"When is your young man to arrive?" he asked dryly, eyes still fixed upon the page. "Did he not mention he would attend you this afternoon?"

Jane smiled, clearly unbothered by her father's habitual teasing. "Charles is to come at one o'clock. Have you something of which to discuss?"

Mr. Bennet shook his head. "No, but I expect he will bring Mr. Darcy. He promised me a game of chess when next he called at Longbourn. I have not had a worthy opponent in some time. I find myself eager to see whether we are evenly matched."

Elizabeth blinked. "Mr. Darcy? When did you speak with him?" She had not seen him approach her father the evening prior, though she had not observed him closely after dinner. Or had she?

Her father at last looked up, a trace of mischief in his eyes. "Just after the ladies withdrew he remained behind, and we had a pleasant exchange. He seems a sensible man, certainly well-read. We debated Locke and Hume, and were discussing crop rotation by the second glass of port."

Elizabeth set down her cup, her expression caught between amusement and disbelief. "You surprise me."

"I surprise myself," Mr. Bennet replied. "I begin to question whether the fae have replaced Mr. Darcy with one of their own, for he is not at all like the gentleman with whom we shared company in the autumn. That Darcy would scarce look at a lady but to observe a blemish."

Elizabeth's lips twitched. "It is peculiar," she agreed. "Charlotte believes it may be the absence of Mr. Bingley's sisters that has prompted the change. Without their constant whispering in his ear, perhaps he is now able to form opinions of his own."

Mr. Bennet gave a short laugh. "'Tis a sound conclusion. Miss Bingley scarcely let him from her sight. I imagine his time at Netherfield was intolerable, with her forever lurking about corners like a cat in search of cream." He shuddered and closed his book, laying it aside. "'Tis no wonder he was out of sorts. If Miss Bingley had shadowed me so closely, I should have turned sour long before he did."

"Papa!" Jane exclaimed.

"What? I speak as I find, dear daughter. She trailed after him like a ship dragging its anchor—heavy, clumsy, and impossible to ignore." He reached for his tea, then added with a pointed glance, "See that she does not do the same to your future servants, my dear, else they will be taking orders from the wrong mistress."

Elizabeth exchanged a glance with Jane, her amusement tempered by a flicker of agreement. Still, a part of her was unsettled. Mr. Darcy engaged in a chess match with her father? Debating philosophy? Discussing crop rotation of all things? Was he…attempting to endear himself to her family, or simply revealing that he was not so insufferable as she had long believed?

Jane watched her, amusement dancing in her eyes.

"I suppose," Elizabeth said slowly, "I must admit he is not so great a villain as I once painted him. I do not know that I can absolve him of all his faults, but he is…well, less objectionable than he was before."

Jane beamed, her satisfaction plain. "Then I am glad. I never thought him so dreadful as you believed."

Elizabeth pursed her lips and reached for a muffin. "We shall see. In any case, you need not worry for my welfare. I can speak with Mr. Darcy without pain or discomfort. You are free to devote all your attention to your betrothed, and I shall manage well enough."

Privately, however, she resolved to watch Mr. Darcy with additional scrutiny. If he had truly changed, she would be the first to perceive it—though she was not entirely certain she trusted herself to recognize what she might see.

Darcy

The gentlemen arrived at Longbourn promptly at one o'clock, their coats brushed free of snow and their boots freshly cleaned by the grooms. Though Darcy preserved his usual reserved countenance, a restrained eagerness stirred within him. It had been less than a day since he last beheld Elizabeth, yet he felt that a peculiar tension lingered—an anticipation at the prospect of seeing her again. Would she wear the locket? Or deem it too fine for such casual company?

The thought preoccupied him more than he cared to admit. His mother and grandmother had both worn the locket while mistress of Pemberley, unconstrained by time of day or formality, and he had selected it in part for its versatility. Elizabeth, however, was practical. She might consider it too conspicuous. He wanted to believe otherwise.

The gloves, of course, he did not expect to see. That particular gift was meant for the evening; it suited an elegant affair, a ball or concert perhaps.

She would not display them now, and so he must content himself with the knowledge that they were hers.

Darcy had orchestrated their delivery with care. Brisby had engaged a local lad from Meryton to carry the parcels—one entirely unknown to the staff at Longbourn. The boy, it turned out, had formed an attachment to one of the upstairs maids, and had persuaded her to assist him. Between the two of them, they had devised a reliable scheme. A shilling each per delivery was a princely sum to them, and Darcy had no doubt they would maintain the secrecy required for continued payment. Still, he remained ever mindful of discovery, and though he found the intrigue invigorating, he was not unburdened by it.

Upon entering the drawing room, his eyes found Elizabeth at once. She stood near the pianoforte, speaking with Mrs. Gardiner, and her smile—easy, bright—struck him with renewed force. His gaze, ever drawn to her, slipped to her throat. There, against her skin, lay the familiar garnet cross. Yet something else caught his notice—a second, finer chain nestled just beneath it, partly obscured by the modest neckline of her gown. She wore the locket.

Relief washed over him, mingled with something far warmer. She had deemed it worthy of wear—perhaps more than worthy. He observed how her fingers strayed to the chain now and again as she conversed, brushing it with unconscious familiarity. He longed to see the locket in full view—to admire how it rested against her skin, to witness her wearing it not as a trinket, but as a token of sentiment.

Darcy busied himself as best he could. He conversed with Mr. and Mrs. Gardiner, estimable people whose intelligence and manners would set them apart in nearly any company. He had come to admire them greatly over their short acquaintance, finding their gentle warmth a balm against the harsher tones of country society. Mr. Bennet, too, claimed his attention. They engaged in a lively game of chess before the fire, and to Darcy's surprise, the older gentleman proved a formidable opponent.

Darcy won by a narrow margin, but it was by no means an easy victory.

"I shall demand a rematch next time you come, sir," Mr. Bennet declared, a twinkle in his eye and the corner of his mouth twitching into a smirk. His tone was a curious mix of solemnity and teasing: a blend Darcy had come to recognize as the elder Bennet's particular form of approval.

"You have my word," Darcy replied with sincerity. "It has been some time since I was made to concentrate so thoroughly on a game. Thank you."

"Then there is chance of my victory yet!" Mr. Bennet chuckled, pleased with himself, and shuffled off to his study in search of a particular volume he claimed would *settle an argument with himself.*

With Mr. Bennet gone and the room's energy mellowing, Darcy allowed himself to wish for a moment with Elizabeth. He turned, meaning to seek her out, but she was gone. Miss Lucas had drawn her aside, it seemed, to discuss something domestic, and before she could return, Mrs. Bennet intercepted her to inquire after the household linens. When that matter was settled, the Gardiners had questions about a letter from London, and then Miss Kitty experienced a small mishap with her embroidery that required Elizabeth's patient hands.

Each time Darcy believed he might speak to her alone, another diversion arose.

It was maddening. He had imagined, foolishly, that their recent improvement in understanding might yield further opportunity for conversation. Instead, he was forced to admire her from afar, his expectations diminishing with each missed chance.

By the time he and Bingley made their farewells, Darcy's mood had darkened considerably. He masked it well, of course—his expression ever calm, his words measured—but inwardly, he simmered with frustration. Elizabeth had been gracious, kind, even attentive when they exchanged pleasantries; yet the moments were fleeting, the glances brief. He had offered her a piece of his family, of his heart, and though she wore it close, she did not yet know it had come from him, or that it carried the weight of his heart.

There will be another chance, he told himself as they stepped into the waiting carriage. He had not come this far to be disheartened by a single unremarkable afternoon.

And with little else to occupy his mind once they returned to Netherfield, he set to work composing the third day of Christmas for Elizabeth, determined that the next gift would speak louder than the last.

Chapter Eight

December 27, 1811
Longbourn
Elizabeth

ELIZABETH HAD BARELY SLEPT the night before, tossing and turning into the early hours. Throughout the evening, she had drifted about the room, speaking with her aunt and uncle, turning pages for Mary on the pianoforte, and singing carols with Jane and Mr. Bingley. Mr. Darcy had occupied himself with others, a fact that left her unaccountably frustrated. *Why do I care?* she mused, annoyed with herself. *He is nothing to me. He can* be *nothing to me.* Still, her gaze sought him often, and she observed his manner with a critical eye.

At every moment, she expected him to revert to the proud, haughty gentleman he had been in the autumn; yet instead, he continued to improve. Even Mrs. Bennet no longer sniffed in disdain whenever he entered the room. Gone was the distant, arrogant Mr. Darcy, and in his place stood an affable, gentlemanly—if reserved—man whom Elizabeth could almost admire. More and more, she found herself contemplating him, wondering if her conflicted feelings might ever be untangled into something comprehensible.

Mr. Bingley called often upon his betrothed, affording Elizabeth many opportunities to sketch Mr. Darcy's true character. Yet the question remained unanswered: which version of that unfathomable gentleman was his genuine self? *No matter,* she told herself as she stretched that morning, the conundrum the first conscious thought in her mind. *I shall continue my assessment and know the answer soon enough.*

Blinking sleepily, she repeated the same ritual she had followed each morning of late, reaching for her dressing gown and tying the sash at her waist. Elizabeth slipped her feet into a pair of slippers and shivered as she crept to her chair. There, upon the small table, lay the expected package. She untied the twine and removed the brown paper, tossing it into the fire. A familiar velvet box lay within. She opened it and found another scrap of paper, a single stanza written upon it.

> *On the third day of Christmas,*
> *Wisdom and beauty combine,*
> *Three pearl combs*
> *To grace thy locks so fine.*

Nestled within the box were three pearl combs. Two matched in size, suited for evenings out; the third was smaller, perfect for wear at home. The pearls were set in silver, each piece polished so finely that Elizabeth could see her reflection upon its surface. They were as lovely as the previous gifts, and she touched them reverently, wondering who could admire her so deeply.

It is certainly *not Mr. Wickham,* she stubbornly had to admit once more. To her surprise, she felt relief rather than disappointment. A sudden restlessness came over her, and she snapped the jewel box shut before rising to hide it in her wardrobe.

With the gift safely tucked away, she quickly dressed in a walking gown and donned her pelisse and gloves. Though she fetched her bonnet, she did not wear it; she only looped the ribbons around her fingers as she stepped out of the house toward the path that led to Oakham Mount. The day promised to be bitter, but she craved the clarity of mind that walking often afforded. Flattered as she was to be the object of such attentions, she disliked not knowing who attempted to woo her.

Pausing partway up the mount, she spoke aloud into the still morning. "There must be a reason for the secrecy." Leaning against a nearby tree, she folded her arms, her air thoughtful and intent. "Perhaps his family does not approve. Or maybe he has not the fortune to marry a woman with no dowry." That possibility she dismissed outright. Her admirer was evidently a man of consequence; the gifts he had bestowed thus far were not trifling.

Am I already acquainted *with the gentleman? What if he is* not *a gentleman, but a wealthy tradesman?* The idea struck her as absurd. She knew no wealthy tradesmen beyond her uncle and a handful of his associates. She recalled one Mr. Timmons, introduced to her last summer. A tall, reasonably attractive man of three-and-thirty, he had paid her some attention while she visited London with her relations. Yet her interest had been slight; indeed, she regarded him as an indifferent acquaintance and believed he felt much the same. Still, the timing now cast her assumptions into doubt. The first gift had arrived on the morning of the twenty-fifth, the day after the Gardiners' arrival. *Could Uncle have been entrusted with tokens of affection from one of his associates? Why would Mr. Timmons wait?* Elizabeth frowned. *Had he thought me too young last year and only now feels ready to pursue me?*

Still no closer to finding an answer, she pushed away from the tree and continued up the hill. It was far too cold to remain in one attitude for long. With long strides, she made her way to the summit, breathing heavily as the incline lessened and the ground leveled. Elizabeth crossed the small clearing atop the mount, observing animal tracks in the light dusting of snow and pacing to preserve her warmth.

The sound of an approaching horse disturbed her musings. When she lifted her gaze and caught sight of Mr. Darcy astride a large brown and white gelding at the edge of the clearing, she quickly donned her bonnet. The sunlight streamed across the open space, catching in the horse's glossy coat and the polished brass fittings of the bridle. Upon seeing her, Darcy dismounted with practiced ease and looped the reins around a low-hanging branch.

"Miss Elizabeth," he greeted, bowing his head with courtesy. His voice was warm, gentler than she expected, though she wondered whether the early hour lent her imagination too much sway. "How do you do this morning?" He tipped his hat, then added, "'Tis a lovely day, if a trifle cold. Beau needed a good gallop, and so I left the warmth of Netherfield to chase the frost across the fields."

"That is quite poetic, Mr. Darcy." Her eyes were bright with appreciation. She could admire a well-turned phrase, and he appeared unexpectedly fluent in them this morning. "I, too, was called by the morning air. Tell me, does your horse—Beau, is it?—wake with the dawn as I do, or must you rouse him from his stall to meet your sense of duty?"

He laughed; it was a low, rich sound that sent a pleasant thrill through her. "Beau is short for Beaudric. My sister saw the name carved upon a weathered stone in a country churchyard and declared it must be given to my next horse. One can hardly refuse an eight-year-old, particularly when she is so earnestly insistent." He glanced affectionately toward the animal. "Beau is a noble steed and an excellent companion; he is not as spirited as others I have ridden, but faithful and only mildly temperamental. He waits on me very patiently, I assure you."

Elizabeth nodded, her expression thoughtful. "He seems to be a fine specimen. We have only Nellie to ride, an old mare more content in the stable than under saddle. I dare say I can walk faster than she can canter. Thus, you discover the reason for my wandering the countryside with windblown hair and skirts weighted with six inches of Hertfordshire mud." She laughed lightly, recalling Miss Bingley's withering remarks on the subject.

Mr. Darcy's eyes caught the light, an odd glint in them that arrested her. At first, she believed he disapproved, and a spark of irritation stirred within her. But then she looked again, more carefully, and saw that the intensity in his gaze held no censure. Her cheeks warmed—no small matter on such a chill morning.

"I find a lady's eyes are brightened by frequent exercise," he murmured, stepping nearer. "There is nothing to be ashamed of. Your devotion to your sister is to be admired."

Elizabeth felt a strange flutter rise within her. The compliment, spoken with gentle sincerity, surprised her. "I thank you, sir, though I must confess I once believed your opinion to be quite the opposite. My arrival at Netherfield seemed…less than welcome to most of its occupants." She paused, uncertain whether her honesty had overstepped civility.

His expression changed, and she felt she could read it clearly—shame. The sight was unexpected. She had not imagined Mr. Darcy capable of such vulnerability.

"I believe I owe you a rather large apology." His eyes lowered to the ground as he nudged his boot across the snow, exposing the yellowed grass beneath. "From our very first meeting, I have not conducted myself as a gentleman ought. I insulted you grievously—without provocation. There is no excuse for my petulant, ignorant behavior. Though I have attempted some form of reparation since, I know I have not done enough."

Her mother had once proclaimed that a late apology was worth as little as a false one, but Elizabeth had never quite believed that. Sincerity was a currency of its own. And here stood Mr. Darcy, in all seriousness, offering his regret without defense or deflection.

"Thank you, sir. I admit I harbored…unflattering opinions of you after that night. But an earnest apology does much to repair the injury. Ought we to begin again—and go on as friends?" She smiled then—openly, warmly.

"Friends," he repeated, straightening a little, as though the word had settled something deep within him. "Yes, that is a good beginning."

He bowed, a deep, formal gesture as though they had only just been introduced. "Miss Elizabeth, my name is Fitzwilliam Darcy. How pleased I am to make your acquaintance."

She smothered a laugh, curtsying with equal grace. "The pleasure is mine, sir."

An awkward pause followed, and Elizabeth searched for a topic to carry them forward. The silence stretched, and then—too hastily—she spoke. "Is Miss Bingley's presence such a trial that it affects your behavior entirely?"

A look of surprise crossed his face, and then a low laugh escaped him. The sound warmed her more effectively than any winter cloak.

"It would be ungenerous of me to express the full scope of my thoughts regarding Miss Bingley. But yes, I confess her company at times tried my patience. Still, other factors weighed more heavily on my spirits during those first months."

He did not elaborate, and she chose not to press him.

"Well," she said at last, "I am glad your spirits have improved. My father has enjoyed your company greatly and wonders when you might next have the opportunity to call and play chess with him."

Darcy smiled, his mien gentling with remembrance. "I have not had so skilled a partner since my father's passing. I should be pleased to call on Mr. Bennet. Bingley and I are to dine at Lucas Lodge this evening; perhaps I might come on the morrow."

"We are to attend this evening as well." Elizabeth's thoughts drifted to the pearl combs hidden in her chamber. Would they suit the diamond and garnet locket? Perhaps she would wear one and not the other. "Sir William entertains more during Christmastide than at any other time of year. I expect he will host at least one more soiree before Twelfth Night."

The cold began to creep through her cloak and gloves, and Elizabeth rubbed her arms briskly. Her breath formed clouds before her lips.

"You are cold." Darcy stepped toward her, one hand half-lifted before he let it fall. "Come, allow me to assist you onto Beau. I shall escort you back to Longbourn."

"It is no matter, sir, though I thank you. The walk is short, and I shall be warm again once I am moving." She curtsied once more. "Until this evening, then."

"Yes. Yes, goodbye, Miss Elizabeth."

She had only taken a few paces before he called her name. She turned, glancing up at him with curious expectancy. He appeared torn between caution and courage, but ultimately, courage won.

"Sir?"

"If Sir William calls for dancing...may I be so bold as to claim your hand for a set?" The words tumbled over one another, as though they were restrained too long and now rushing forth unchecked.

His nervousness, so plainly seen despite his usual composure, only endeared him to her further.

"I accept, sir, and look forward to the honor with pleasure."

With a wave in farewell, she walked to the edge of the hill, and then down the path that led home, her steps brisk, her heart unexpectedly light. Though doubts and questions still lingered, she resolved to allow the answers to come as they may.

Darcy

Darcy watched Elizabeth depart, hopeful that this meeting had laid the path forward. She had forgiven him. The weight of her former disdain no longer pressed upon him; in its place lingered the faint glow of mutual understanding. He understood her better now—could read her expressions with far greater clarity. What once seemed cryptic or capricious now appeared deliberate, even artful. He could tell when she teased, when she mocked, when she was sincere, and when she was not. *She has forgiven me.*

It was no small thing. Her regard was not bestowed lightly, nor her forgiveness offered from mere politeness. That she had extended it at all meant she believed him capable of change—and he intended to prove her right. *Now,* he vowed in silence, *I will do everything in my power to become a man worthy of her love.*

He turned back toward the rise where Beaudric waited patiently, the bay gelding's breath visible in the crisp morning air. Darcy placed a gloved hand on the horse's neck, murmuring a gentle word of thanks before leading him to a nearby stump. He mounted with practiced ease, settling into the saddle as the sun climbed higher, gilding the hilltop in pale winter gold.

They descended the slope at a leisurely pace, the crunch of frost beneath the gelding's hooves the only sound aside from the gentle creak of leather and the occasional gust of wind that rustled the bare hedgerows. Darcy let the reins slacken slightly, allowing Beau to pick his way carefully across the uneven ground, while his own thoughts turned inward, as before.

Every word Elizabeth had spoken replayed in his mind—not merely the words themselves, but the warmth behind them, the spirited air she carried, the lilt in her voice when she challenged him with half a smile. She was no longer merely the lively country girl who had startled his notice at the Meryton assembly. He saw her now as the woman who held a mirror to his pride and made him better for it. Her laughter no longer stung; instead, it stirred something within him—something bright and undemanding—his unending desire for her regard.

At the base of the hill, he gave Beau the signal, and the horse surged forward into a gallop. The wind rushed past, tugging at his coat and loosening his thoughts. Sharp, clean air filled his lungs, and the pale sunlight caught in the frost, making the world shimmer around him. He leaned into the motion, exulting in the speed and freedom, as if the earth itself rejoiced with him.

Across the fields he rode, each hoofbeat echoing the rhythm of his heart. *She has forgiven me.* The phrase repeated with every stride, not as a question, but as a truth newly born.

He pictured many such rides—Elizabeth beside him, her cheeks flushed from the cold, her eyes alight with laughter. He imagined her at Pemberley, her presence lending grace to the great house with her wit and warmth. He saw her in every season—in spring among the blooming hedge rows, in summer's golden light, in autumn's quiet splendor, and even now, in winter, with its bare elegance and clear skies. Every vision of the future he conjured held her at the center.

For the first time in many months, Darcy allowed himself to believe. The distance between what he desired and what might yet come to pass no longer seemed insurmountable. Love, after all, was not declared and done; it was proven—patiently, earnestly—in quiet moments and steadfast acts.

And he would prove it, one day at a time.

Chapter Nine

December 27, 1811
Lucas Lodge
Darcy

Lucas Lodge was ablaze with candlelight, its windows glowing amber against the night. The snow fell light and slow, catching the glimmer of lanterns strung along the front steps and across the hedges. Inside, the sounds of laughter, music, and the clinking of glasses drifted from windows, left slightly open to provide relief from the warmth of the many bodies filling the manor house. The festivity of the season clung to every surface: garlands of evergreen adorned each doorway, holly berries glinted among polished silver, and the air held the faint scent of orange, clove, and evergreen.

Darcy disembarked with a murmur of thanks to the footman and adjusted the buttons of his coat. Beside him, Bingley straightened his cravat and bounced upon the balls of his feet like a schoolboy.

"It looks lively," said Bingley, his voice bright with anticipation. "Do you suppose there will be cards after dinner, or will the Lucases send us straight to the dance floor?"

"I can only surmise our host's plans from past experience," Darcy replied, brushing a snowflake from his shoulder. "Sir William favors dancing; we shall find out soon enough."

Though less elegant and certainly not as large as Netherfield, Lucas Lodge exuded warmth and welcome. As ever, Sir William spared no effort in impressing his guests. Dinner consisted of three abundant courses, filled with delicacies and delights, more than enough to please any guest. The table overflowed with roast goose, savory pies, vegetables, chestnuts, and puddings of every sort.

Conversation buzzed all around, but Darcy heard little of it. He sat far up the table from Elizabeth, across from her, yet frustratingly distant. As the highest-ranking gentleman in the room, he was seated at the right hand of their hostess. On his own right sat a widow whose name he could not recall. Resigned to having his nerves taxed throughout the meal, he responded politely when spoken to, but otherwise watched Elizabeth. Every glance, every smile she offered to others stirred in him a deep awareness of her. He knew the curve of her smile, the way her laughter warmed the surrounding space. And now, adorned with his mother's combs, she seemed impossibly near and yet forever out of reach.

After the gentlemen had enjoyed their port and cigars, they drifted into the drawing room. It had already been cleared for dancing, and a small ensemble tuned their instruments near the hearth. The polished floor reflected the chandelier's glow overhead, and cheerful conversation rose above the strains of a violinist preparing to play.

Darcy had no need to search; she stood just as he had imagined.

Elizabeth was near a window, her head inclined toward Charlotte Lucas as they conversed. She wore a gown of deep sapphire blue, its neckline and hem embroidered in a golden-hued thread that shimmered when she moved. Cream lace edged the fine fabric, and the whole of it suited her so perfectly he could scarce imagine her in any other attire at this moment. But it was not just the gown that held him fast—it was the cream-colored gloves, worked in gold thread, and the glint of pearl combs nestled in her dark curls.

The sight of those combs pierced him more deeply than he anticipated.

The memory surged forward, unbidden. He was a boy again—perhaps eight years old—tucked beneath the covers in Pemberley's nursery. His mother had come to bid him goodnight, her hair pinned up and the combs gleaming in the firelight. She had kissed his brow, her perfume sweet and familiar. He had asked where she was going, and she had replied, "To dance with your father, dearest. Do not grow up too quickly."

The combs had arrived just the day before, sent from Darcy House. Mrs. Hanson, his housekeeper, had seen they were cleaned and packed in velvet, and he had arranged for their delivery to Longbourn along with the next stanza.

On the third day of Christmas, he recited silently. She wore them tonight, and the gift from the second day as well. Bless his staff for their hasty fulfillment of his requests. Thankfully, they still had time to acquire the items needed for the remaining days of Christmas.

The combs and gloves suited Elizabeth better than he imagined. The silver gleamed against her chestnut curls; the pearls caught the firelight as she turned her head. His heart pounded with longing.

Darcy approached Elizabeth, coming to her side and smiling kindly at her and her companion. "Good evening, ladies," he said.

"Mr. Darcy," Elizabeth said, dropping a graceful curtsy. Her eyes sparkled, and a delicate flush rose in her cheeks as their eyes met.

"You are most welcome." He hardly heard Miss Lucas's greeting, so intent was his gaze on his love. Darcy did *not* miss the shrewd glance Miss

Lucas cast toward her friend before excusing herself with little more than that polite greeting.

"Miss Elizabeth." He bowed, his gaze lingering a moment longer than propriety allowed. "You look... quite fine this evening." She looked more than fine. Exquisite, magnificent, luminescent...those were the words that came to mind.

She seemed to divine his unspoken thoughts, and she regarded him with amused challenge. "Quite fine?" Her tone held a teasing lilt—light, not mocking.

Heavens, she is magnificent.

"Exceptionally so. Enchanting, if I am to be entirely honest," he murmured, his sonorous baritone low.

Her eyes danced. "I suppose the combs help," she said, angling her head just so, allowing the pearls to catch the firelight from a nearby candelabra. There was something almost expectant in her manner.

"They do," he replied truthfully. "The workmanship is exquisite. Were they fashioned in London?" He would play the simpleton, for he was not yet ready to confess he was the gentleman responsible for them.

"I am afraid I do not know," she answered, her smile dimming slightly. "They arrived just this morning. I cannot imagine who would wish to bestow such wonders upon *me*. I am no one."

Darcy remained silent, though he disagreed with her words most fervently.

"And to send them with only a brief note, without expectation of thanks... Can you think of anyone so kind? So self-sacrificing?" she asked lightly. Her eyes remained intently fixed upon his.

He swallowed hard and forced himself to hold her gaze. *Allow me to keep my secrets a little longer.* "I am certain such persons exist."

Her lips quirked. "Indeed. It is fortunate, is it not, to have such friends?" He could see the inquisitive light in her eyes—faint, yet true—and for that he felt grateful. Her dislike had so recently been banished; he dared not presume upon the change so soon and declare himself. He merely gave the barest nod, fearing more words might betray him.

A cheer rose from the younger ladies, and the musicians began a familiar air.

Elizabeth stood, and Darcy stepped forward, offering his hand.

"You did promise me a set, Miss Elizabeth," he said with a slight bow.

"I did," she replied, smiling. "And I am a woman of my word."

He led her to the center of the floor as couples took their places. The *Minuet de la Cour* filled the room, stately and refined, and they began. Even through the fine fabric of their gloves, the feel of her fingers sent a thrill through him.

They moved in slow, sweeping elegance, executing each step in perfect time. She was grace itself—pure perfection—and the air thickened with something unspoken. The other dancers blurred around them, their faces indistinct. For a moment, it seemed they alone occupied the room.

"You dance well, Mr. Darcy."

"I have had some practice."

She smiled. "How very surprising. Given the distaste you so often display for company, I should never have imagined it." She paused, and her playfulness gave way to something more earnest. "I confess I never thought to enjoy your company so much."

Now it was his turn to smile, his expression dear as he admired her beauty. "I am gratified to hear it, for I take great pleasure in *yours*."

They turned in the dance as the music swelled. She looked up at him.

"I have often wondered what made you so very...proud."

Again with her candor. Darcy could hardly complain; he had misunderstood her often enough. He frowned slightly as he considered her words. "Unrighteous pride is not the sentiment I would attribute to myself. I believe we spoke of vanity and pride when you stayed at Netherfield nursing your sister."

"Indeed. I recall the conversation clearly."

She spoke with a lightness that danced on the edge of mockery; he was certain a tease would follow.

"I remember you saying, 'Where there is a real superiority of mind, pride will always be under good regulation.'"

"Indeed. I do not believe you agreed with me." He waited, curious to hear her reply. She did not disappoint.

"I believe any pride, when used to place oneself above another, can never be considered in good regulation. Pride in one's accomplishments cannot be faulted; everyone deserves to be proud of themselves. But when that pride encourages feelings of superiority, the belief that someone is better than their neighbor simply by an accident of birth, greater fortune, or intelligence, then it turns into something twisted and unrecognizable. Then, we fall into a trap of our own making."

"'Pride goeth before the fall,'" Darcy recited.

"An excellent proverb," Elizabeth agreed. "Tell me, sir—if it is not pride, what would you call it?"

He considered. *Goodness, how she made him think!* "Perhaps...discomfort. Reserve. A failure to trust easily." All were true, though incomplete. "I have suffered with an abundance of pride in my life, but I never meant to fall into the proud behavior to which you refer. When one is born to privilege, as I was, it is exceedingly easy to become unbearably proud and insufferable."

She studied him for a moment. "Your description sounds very much like pride...dressed in finer clothes. I can, however, understand how one born into exalted circumstances might find their way down that path."

He grinned. "I have been well-accused."

She said nothing, but her lips parted slightly, and a blush touched her cheeks.

He continued. "There are few people in this world whose good opinion matters to me. Yours is...the most important of all." More than even his dear sister's. He silently entreated her to understand what his words conveyed. Though he would not yet claim responsibility for her gifts, he could tell her, in a way, how much she meant to him.

The music slowed.

Elizabeth swallowed. "You have changed, Mr. Darcy...from the gentleman I first met."

He looked at her intently. "I wish it to be so."

The final notes drifted into silence. The room erupted in applause, but Darcy and Elizabeth stood motionless for a breath longer. Then she curtsied, and he bowed low.

"Thank you for the dance, Mr. Darcy."

"The pleasure was mine, Miss Elizabeth."

She moved to rejoin her sisters but paused at the last moment.

"I would have the gentleman who sent the combs know how deeply they are appreciated."

Blast. Of course, she had no intention of surrendering her quest to discover his identity.

Darcy said nothing, still weighing his response as she walked away. He watched her weave through the crowd—laughing with Miss Bennet, nodding politely to Lady Lucas, her hair gleaming with silver and pearl. The combs sparkled in the candlelight, nestled like moonlight in her dark curls.

They suited her perfectly, just as he had imagined when he selected them for the twelve days and arranged their delivery. That she had worn them now, that she had chosen them for this particular evening, stirred something in him both tender and aching.

She belonged in that light, in that warmth, in that life. And he—Fitzwilliam Darcy of Pemberley—wanted, more than anything, to be part of it.

But desire did not bestow the right to possession. He had learned that lesson already. Still, the memory of their dance lingered with a sweetness that would not fade. The deliberate measure of the minuet, the feel of her hand in his, the careful grace of her movements—it was etched into him now. There had been something more than music in the way she had looked at him, something that made him believe he had not mistaken her sentiment. Her teasing words at supper, the smile she gave as she wondered aloud who could be so self-sacrificing as to procure such fine gifts—it had all felt like...an invitation.

Darcy danced with other ladies before the evening concluded, though none captured his attention as she had. Each set felt like an echo, a pale imitation of the moment he had shared with Elizabeth. Miss Mary made an adequate partner, though she seemed far more intent on extolling the merits of Handel's compositions than observing the steps themselves. Still, Darcy listened politely and even ventured a comment on the superiority of Corelli's concerti, which satisfied her.

He also stood up with Miss Lucas, who danced with the energy of one entirely in command of the social scene. Her confidence had grown with her engagement. The faster tempo of the English country dance left no room for conversation, but Miss Lucas's knowing glances spoke volumes. She missed nothing.

Bingley, for his part, had vanished into some corner with Miss Bennet. Their engagement, freshly announced, had turned them into the chief spectacle of the evening. Guests showered them with praise, exclamations, and half-teasing jests about future weddings and new carriages. Darcy did not begrudge them their brief escape. If anything, he admired their audacity.

When the pair returned, Miss Bennet's cheeks were flushed a cheerful pink, and there was a radiance of contentment about her that had not been there earlier in the evening. Bingley's smug grin told its own tale, and Darcy knew precisely which secluded corner they had sought. There was a kissing bough tucked between the drawing room and the music room, half-hidden behind a velvet curtain—perfect for a sweet holiday kiss.

And yet, it was not envy that stirred in Darcy. It was hope. Quiet, unfamiliar hope.

Elizabeth's company was in high demand. Sir William declared her the most admired young lady of the evening, and several gentlemen were eager to stand up with her. Her wit and charm made her the natural center of any circle she joined.

Darcy caught glimpses of her between sets—her laugh at something Sir William said, her delighted applause when Charlotte played a lively jig at the pianoforte, her gentle encouragement as she helped Miss Maria recover from a misstep. She was everywhere and nowhere at once, brisk as a bee.

He wished for more than a glimpse. He had, rather foolishly, intended to speak with her again—to engage in a discreet exchange that might edge them closer to understanding. But the evening wore on, and every attempt he made to cross the floor to her side was interrupted: by Lady Lucas, who insisted upon hearing how Christmas was celebrated at Pemberley, or by the vicar, or some well-meaning matron eager to remind him of his duty to the younger, unmarried ladies in attendance.

It was maddening. No one knew of his interest in Elizabeth but himself. The crowd was not conspiring to keep them apart. And yet, that was precisely how it seemed.

But still—she suspects. And she does not object.

The idea curled warm and possessive within him. Was that not the purpose of the combs? Of the gloves? The locket from the first day, and all the gifts yet to be given? Not to win her favor through material offerings, but to express, in the only way he knew how, the depth of his admiration—his respect. His love.

He could not speak it aloud, not without certainty that her heart was engaged. But these tokens were his silent language—a testament to all he felt but could not yet say.

As the night waned and couples departed in clusters of laughter and hooded capes, Darcy stood near the window, watching flakes drift past the frosted glass. His eyes sought Elizabeth once more. She stood beside Miss Bennet, wrapping a scarf about her shoulders, her countenance touched with gentle contentment.

A good evening. A happy one.

Mayhap when she later unpinned the combs from her hair and laid them on her dressing table, she would think of him. Not merely as the man who had once wronged her, but as the one who lingered at the edge of her world, longing for another dance, another word, another chance.

Perhaps soon, he would be brave enough to offer all three.

Chapter Ten

December 28, 1811
Longbourn
Elizabeth

THE PREVIOUS EVENING'S SNOWFALL had continued through the night, leaving a delicate veil of white across the landscape. Ice crystals wreathed the edges of her window, their fragile beauty casting shimmering patterns upon the glass. Elizabeth awoke to the gentle crackle of flames; the maid had coaxed the embers in the grate into a lively blaze, and the room was already warmer than on previous mornings.

Snug beneath the counterpane, her head nestled upon a soft down pillow, Elizabeth lingered, loath to stir. Sleep still clung to her senses, and she blinked drowsily as her dreams, sweet as they had been, slipped swiftly from her memory.

Then, sitting up with a sudden start, she glanced toward the fireplace and noticed a small parcel resting upon the table beside her chair. Eager curiosity stirred her fully awake. Casting aside the counterpane, she slid her feet into the waiting slippers, shrugged into her dressing gown, and drew the sash tight before crossing the room in quick steps to retrieve the package.

Lowering herself into her chair, Elizabeth gathered the parcel onto her lap. Her fingers trembled as she untied the twine and peeled away the paper. *How delightful a pleasure the opening of a present can be. Perhaps we ought to make it a tradition.*

Beneath the wrappings lay a length of satin, concealing a tender weight within. She unfolded the fabric carefully, snatching up the slip of paper that fluttered free before it could fall to the floor.

> *On the fourth day of Christmas,*
> *Wrapped in satin so rare,*
> *Four velvet ribbons*
> *To adorn thy hair.*

She began to lay the slip aside, only to notice writing upon the reverse. Curious, she turned it over and read two more lines.

> *These ribbons could never compare to the color of your lovely eyes. It is impossible to capture the exact shade, for never have I seen any so fine.*

The ribbons, in truth, were nearly to the exact hue of her eyes. She admired them instantly and resolved to tuck them safely away when not in use, lest Lydia discover them. They were far superior to anything to be had in Meryton, and her youngest sister, ever quick to covet, would be sorely tempted to claim them. Fortunately, the whirl of activities and invitations had thus far kept Lydia from noticing any of the small treasures Elizabeth had received.

She did not venture out that morning. Instead, she dressed in one of her warmest walking gowns, intending to walk into Meryton after breakfast. She wove one of the violet ribbons through her curls, pausing to admire her reflexion in the looking glass before descending the stairs. Jane looked up as she entered, her knowing gaze flicking to the ribbon in Elizabeth's hair before returning to her meal.

"Good morning, Lizzy." Mr. Bennet glanced up from his paper. "Did you sleep well?"

"I did, thank you." Elizabeth took a plate from the sideboard and began to serve herself. "I plan to walk into Meryton later. Jane, will you come with me?"

Jane shook her head. "Mama has decreed that I remain at home to help her plan my wedding." Her cheeks warmed, and a tender smile curved her lips, her whole countenance alight with a happiness that could not be mistaken. "We have not chosen a date, though our mother insists that a spring wedding is best." She pulled a face so uncharacteristic that Elizabeth could not help but laugh.

"Do you not agree with her, my dear?" Mr. Bennet turned his attention to Jane. "Your mother would like nothing better than to spend months planning a lavish wedding and wedding breakfast. Such extravagance will come at considerable expense to Longbourn's coffers. While I shall not deny you what is your due as my eldest, and the first of my daughters to marry, I would prefer not to be beggared by Mrs. Bennet's efforts."

Elizabeth and Jane exchanged an amused glance. Their father's sentiments were predictable; he would gladly leave the entire business to the ladies, provided it required little expense or trouble to himself. *At least he shows some awareness of my mother's talent* for *excess.*

"I have not yet spoken to Charles on the matter." Jane's soft-spoken reply drew Elizabeth from her musings. "I should prefer not to wait until spring...and I believe he will feel the same."

Mr. Bennet rustled his newspaper and said dryly, "Be so good as to inform me when you have fixed a date, my dear," effectively ending the conversation. His peace, however, would not last; knowing the others would soon be down, he left the table for his study.

"Is Mr. Bingley to call this afternoon?" Elizabeth asked, breaking a roll and spreading it with butter before taking a bite.

Jane replied with a ready nod. "He has some business to which he must attend, but I have invited him to spend the rest of the day at Longbourn." She beamed. "Oh, Lizzy, I am so very happy! He is everything a gentleman ought to be, and more. I cannot think of him without my heart swelling with joy. If only you could know such delight."

"Perhaps those pleasures will be mine in time," Elizabeth murmured, her fingers lifting to touch the ribbon in her hair.

Jane glanced at the ribbon. "Is that from your admirer? It is the fourth day, is it not?"

"Yes. I received four ribbons this morning, each in a slightly different shade of purple. The stanza spoke of satin and ribbons, but on the reverse side, he wrote that none could compare to the color of my eyes."

"'Tis very romantic." Jane smiled and stirred cream into her tea. "Do you have any notion who it may be? I cannot imagine Arnold Goulding or Joseph Long sending such thoughtful gifts."

"Those two? They have not a romantic sensibility to share between them! My admirer has more gallantry in his little finger than either of them has in his whole frame." *If it is either...*

Arnold Goulding and Joseph Long had been thorns in Elizabeth's side since childhood—ever resentful of a girl besting them and sulking dreadfully in the wake of every defeat. *I could never love either of them.*

"Perhaps it is Mr. Wickham?" Jane's innocent suggestion made Elizabeth's breath catch.

"I suspected him when the first package arrived," Elizabeth admitted, her words slow and deliberate as she sorted through her thoughts. "But the gifts are too fine—too costly for a man reliant upon a militia commission. Besides, I have heard he is courting Mary King, who has lately inherited ten thousand pounds."

"I am sorry." Jane reached over and pressed Elizabeth's hand. "I know you liked him."

Elizabeth frowned. "I did like him, but my heart was never engaged. He is charming and handsome, and had he shown me serious attention, perhaps I might have come to love him. His defection has had no effect on me; it proves I never regarded him as more than a passing acquaintance."

"I have yet to meet this Mr. Wickham." Aunt Gardiner's voice carried as she entered the breakfast room. "Will I have the pleasure before we depart for London?" The Gardiners were to return to town on the first of January. "From your letters, Lizzy, I understood that he and the officers are present at nearly every evening's entertainment, yet I do not recall having been introduced."

"He has not attended any gatherings we have frequented since the beginning of the month." Elizabeth realized the truth of this even as she spoke, and with a line of thought shadowing her forehead, she prodded her eggs and raised a bite to her lips.

"Well, then, let us hope circumstances allow us to make his acquaintance before we take our leave." Aunt Gardiner busied herself at the sideboard. "I am relieved to hear your heart remains untouched. Marriage to a penniless militia officer is hardly the romantic adventure Lydia and Kitty believe it to be."

"Pray, give me more credit than you grant my sisters," Elizabeth said with mock offense, though her easy smile robbed the words of any sharpness. "Though I liked him, I always knew a match was impossible. And now he courts Miss King, a local heiress. Poor men must have something to live on, I suppose."

"That is a mercenary point of view, or at least it casts Mr. Wickham in a mercenary light." Aunt Gardiner took her seat and spread butter over a slice of toast. "Did he admire this young lady before she inherited?"

Elizabeth's look grew uncertain. "I hardly know," she replied. "Miss King has not been well-favored in the past. She is a pretty girl, but her looks are not at all fashionable. Her red hair and freckles see to that."

"Then perhaps Mr. Wickham sees her only as a means to a comfortable future." Aunt Gardiner set the toast on her plate. "Poor dear; I should like to think she is aware."

Her appetite gone, Elizabeth pushed away from the table. Her aunt's words struck uncomfortably close to her own private misgivings she had entertained over the last few weeks. Once confident in her discernment, she now found herself questioning it. As her acquaintance with Mr. Darcy deepened, she recognized her earlier misjudgment—at least in part. Could it be that the amiable gentleman with whom she had danced last evening might also be capable of destroying a man's future? As she had confessed to Jane, she could not make them both good. Or could she?

Her steps were brisk as she walked towards Meryton. Elizabeth walked alone as she had on many occasions, grateful for the measure of freedom dwelling in the country afforded her. The snow that had fallen the night before was mostly melted, though white still lingered at the bases of leafless trees and shrubs. The ground was not overly muddy, but she was obliged to skirt puddles and damp patches. As the market town's main street came into view, she slowed her pace.

Red coats mingled with tradesmen and townsfolk, all going about their business and hurrying through their errands desirous of returning swiftly to the warmth within doors. Elizabeth entered the haberdashery, intent on finding a box in which to keep her admirer's gifts concealed. A sewing box might do, provided it was large enough to hold future tokens. For now, the items she did not wear were kept in a small wooden box hidden at the back of a wardrobe shelf—undiscovered by Lydia thus far, though there was always a first time.

After browsing the wares on display, the proprietress offered her assistance. Elizabeth explained what she sought, including her wish for a lock.

"You had better try the joiner's, Miss Elizabeth," the woman advised. "He has a greater stock than I and may even install a lock for you."

Thanking her, Elizabeth departed, walking the short distance to the joiner's shop. There, Mr. Jens presented a plain wooden box with a lock for five shillings, complete with a shallow tray that concealed the contents beneath when in place. It was perfect. Elizabeth thanked him and made the purchase, wincing as she parted with so much of her pin money.

The box, wrapped in paper and tucked within the spacious basket she carried, was heavy but manageable. She had just stepped out of the shop when she collided with a figure in red. He caught her shoulders to steady her, keeping his hands there until he was certain she would not stumble.

"Miss Elizabeth! What a pleasant surprise. Why, it has been weeks since we were last in company." Mr. Wickham smiled broadly, his dark hair neatly styled and his uniform pristine. "May I walk with you?"

She grinned. "Good day, sir. Yes, I would be glad of the escort. I am bound for Longbourn."

His smile faltered. "I...that is, I cannot walk so far, for I am to call upon Miss King." His smile turned apologetic. "You understand, do you not? I am in circumstances that require some attention to fortune when choosing a wife. Miss King is well-dowered..." He trailed off, his gaze roaming her features before fixing upon the satin peeking from beneath her bonnet. "Your ribbon is lovely," he murmured, lifting a hand to where it touched her cheek. "It matches the color of your eyes."

Elizabeth's pulse quickened. Could it be him? Was this some subtle farewell? *Do not be foolish,* reason chided. *Why would he heap such attentions upon you while attempting to woo another?* He had admitted as much—that Miss King's dowry was his incentive. Upon further reflection, she noted an anxious sort of feeling in her chest rather than the familiar excitement reserved for her admirer.

Could Mr. Wickham have been my admirer if Mr. Darcy had not ruined his prospects?

The old resentment stirred, and Elizabeth felt anger brewing anew. How readily she had forgotten Mr. Darcy's hauteur when first he came to Hertfordshire.

"I thank you," she whispered. "I must be going."

Stepping aside, she hurried away, eager to free herself from the tangle of her opposing sentiments. She no longer disliked Mr. Darcy, but Mr. Wickham's sudden presence rekindled old doubts. Could the gentleman she had begun to respect heartlessly cast off a friend his father had loved as a godson? Such duplicity, if true, was not to be excused.

How is one to understand another's true motives? she wondered as she strode away, leaving Mr. Wickham standing before the joiner's, his polished smile fading with each step she took. The basket on her arm thumped lightly against her hip as she walked, though she scarcely felt its weight.

With frustration tightening in her gut, Elizabeth quickened her pace, turning her steps toward Oakham Mount. The little hill called to her, a place of solitude and open sky where her thoughts might unravel in quiet nature. The path she chose was the longer route to Longbourn, a full two miles, but the exertion would be welcome. By the time she returned home, she might better understand the unrest stirring within her.

As her boots crunched over frost-laced leaves, she allowed the steady rhythm of her walk to guide her thoughts. The contradictions between the two men loomed large.

Mr. Wickham had, in their earliest acquaintance, spoken of his nemesis without restraint. He had described him as proud, unfeeling, and unjust; yet the gentleman she had since begun to know did not align with that telling, leaving her in a state of confusion more acute than before.

By all appearances, Mr. Wickham was the epitome of warmth and affability. He conversed with ease, charmed effortlessly, and wore his likability as though it were a well-tailored coat. He had offered ready explanations, painted himself the injured party with an admirable command of sympathy, and delivered subtle criticisms of his former friend with just enough reluctance to give them an air of truth.

Mr. Darcy, on the other hand, had been quite the opposite at their first meeting. Reserved to the point of incivility and seemingly disdainful of the society in which he found himself, he had scarcely appeared to tolerate the company of others. His pride had struck her as bordering upon insolence.

Of late, however, his manner had become less severe. His attentions had grown more deliberate, more personal. Though still not a man inclined to easy banter, he now looked at her—*truly* looked—and spoke with a thoughtful gentleness that gave her pause. What of his civility as they danced at Lucas Lodge, his careful praise of her wit and spirit? Surely, such a man could not be wholly bad.

Could both gentlemen be in the right? Or were both hiding truths to suit their ends?

Yet had she not, until now, accepted Mr. Wickham's account without question? She had never heard Mr. Darcy's version of events; all she possessed was the charming lieutenant's tale, colored as it must be by his own resentments. And Mr. Darcy, when given the opportunity during their dance at the Netherfield ball, had chosen silence. Whether through pride or reserve, he had left her in ignorance, and that silence unsettled her much as Wickham's words.

Was it not possible that even scoundrels could wear good manners when it served them? Or that the proud might extend courtesy when it aligned with their personal affections?

She paused at a bend in the path, tilting her face to the gray winter sky. The sun, weak and pale, offered little warmth, but the brisk wind cleared her mind somewhat. Still, there remained a storm within—a tumult of impressions and recollections vying for precedence.

Elizabeth had always prided herself on her discernment. She trusted her ability to read people, to see through pretense. And yet here she was, uncertain whom to believe, uncertain who had spoken falsehood and who had been wronged. One man she had liked at once; another she had dismissed with scorn. Now she began to doubt not only her first impressions, but her own judgment.

Her pride stung at the thought.

She pressed on, boots slick with half-melted frost. The hedgerows stood bare, the trees stark and brittle against the dimming sky. Nature, at least, was honest in its severity. It did not pretend to be what it was not.

As Oakham Mount came into view, Elizabeth allowed herself a sigh of relief. She would reach the summit, sit awhile, and attempt to sift truth from affection, logic from emotion. Mr. Wickham's easy charm, Mr. Darcy's awkward attentions—both were layered with complexities she had not anticipated.

She would not allow herself to be deceived—not by appearances, not by manners, not even by her own wounded pride.

Chapter Eleven

December 28, 1811
Oakham Mount
Darcy

Darcy was restless. Bingley was otherwise engaged that morning, catching up on matters long neglected in his distraction with Miss Bennet. His solicitor had ridden from London and, before departing, would draw up the marriage articles for Mr. Bennet's approval and signature.

Fortunate fool, Darcy thought, though without malice. He felt genuine happiness for his friend, but envy still pricked at him. His emotions ate at him; he longed to offer his heart, his hand, and every worldly possession to Elizabeth. Each day strengthened his confidence; she had grown more receptive, he felt certain of it. But he was already four days into his secret scheme, and he would not stop now.

As much ground as I have gained, I still have far to go before she may feel the same for me.

He would continue sending tokens of his regard, hoping she would not resent him for stepping beyond the dictates of propriety and risking her reputation. Secret admirers abounded in town. If matters reached their natural conclusion—the conclusion he longed for—all would be well in the end.

Unwilling to stay within doors another moment, Darcy ordered his horse saddled and readied. He reached for his coat and gloves, set his hat firmly upon his head, and strode across the lawn toward the stables. The grass lay damp where the morning frost had melted, and though the chill had yet to dry the ground, he kept to the graveled paths to avoid the worst of the mud. Even so, the ride would leave his boots and clothes spattered.

His horse waited, stamping impatiently. He gave a gentle cluck, murmuring reassurance, then mounted in one smooth motion. With a flick of the reins, he urged Beaudric forward, holding back until they cleared Netherfield's gatehouse. Then, leaning low, he pressed his heels into the horse's sides and sent it into a full gallop.

The cold air bit his cheeks, though he scarcely felt it. From his earliest years, the freedom of riding had been unmatched by any other pleasure. The rush of the wind past his face, the exhilaration of clearing a high fence, the scenery blurring as he raced forward—no other experience compared. In the saddle, he felt as though he could conquer anything.

Darcy slowed Beau as they neared Oakham Mount, guiding him toward the summit. They climbed at a measured pace, and soon his thoughts drifted to the fourth gift he had left for Elizabeth. He pictured her with the opened parcel, her fingers brushing over the lengths of velvet ribbon, each shade chosen with care to echo the rare violet hue of her eyes. A careless remark made to Miss Bingley weeks past had inspired the offering for the fourth day of Christmas. He had, in an unguarded moment, admitted his admiration for Miss Elizabeth's fine eyes. Miss Bingley had taken great offense and, in response, had teased him mercilessly ever since. Though her barbs had tried his patience, he had met the lady's jibes with silence.

Elizabeth's eyes were, indeed, remarkable. Most often they held the rich depth of amethyst, but in certain lights, and when she wore particular colors, one could see hints of indigo or even silvery lavender within their depths. A delicate ring of paler violet surrounded the pupils, reflecting an uncommon luminosity. When she laughed, those eyes danced with light; when she delivered an arch comment, touched with saucy sweetness, they gleamed with dangerous brilliance. He could lose himself in their depths and never wish to be found.

A sharp whinny from his horse drew his attention, and he looked up. As though conjured by his thoughts, there stood Elizabeth. Her back was to him, but at the sound, she turned. Reining in his horse, Darcy dismounted with practiced ease and tethered Beau to a convenient tree.

"Good day, Miss Elizabeth," he greeted her, stepping to her side with a bow. Something in the way she curtsied, graceful but cool, put him on his guard. Those eyes, usually so beguiling, carried a flicker of warning, perhaps even ire. Which, he could not yet tell. "How do you do?" he finished, the words landing with an awkwardness he despised.

"I am well, sir," she answered steadily, though a thread of tension belied her words. Elizabeth gestured toward the basket resting on a stump a little way distant. "I walked this way after visiting Meryton."

"Did you find the village pleasant?" The moment the words left him, Darcy regretted them; any man with sense could see that something troubled her.

"No, in fact, I did not." Then, as if weighing her words, she fell silent.

Darcy waited, patient but uneasy, until she angled to face him, her eyes—those striking violet depths—bright with restrained emotion. He watched as his love struggled for words for a moment before she began.

"I do not understand you, Mr. Darcy. You can be...amiable—kind, even. And yet..." She drew a steadying breath. "I have heard another account of you—a story—one that sketches you as a man of cold pride and deliberate cruelty. If that tale is true, then you are the reason an old friend of yours is now forced to marry where his heart does not lie. I wish to believe that cannot be so, but how am I to reconcile the portrait he painted of you with the image I have lately begun to sketch in my own mind?"

A muscle tightened in his jaw, and he clenched until his teeth ached. *Of course, she still defends Wickham,* he thought bitterly, all the pleasant thoughts from his ride vanishing and leaving an uneasy weight in his stomach. His feelings, his past with the blackguard, were his own. Why must he explain himself? *Because she does not deserve to be misled.*

For a moment, silence stretched between them. He had sworn never to speak of it—well...at least not most of it—not to anyone. His cousin, Colonel Richard Fitzwilliam knew some of the particulars, but Darcy could trust him not to reveal his darkest secrets. He forced himself to answer with calm.

"There are two sides to every story, Miss Elizabeth," he said woodenly.

"Are there? Then pray, allow me to hear yours. I know I have no right to ask, yet I would rather judge with the whole of the truth than half of it." She still stood facing him, arms akimbo, but her stare was no longer hostile.

"I tried to warn you at the ball, madam. That man is a reprobate. A swindler."

"But what proof have you to offer?"

"And what proof did he offer you?"

She flushed, no longer able to meet his gaze. "None. When he related his tale of you, he offered no proof either." She sighed. "You must know, sir, that to me you have been...perplexing. At times proud, at times—lately—something else entirely. He, at least, has seemed constant in his civility."

Color flared along his cheekbones. "He tried to elope with my sister." The words came out raw, stripped of restraint.

Elizabeth stared, stunned. "Surely not," she breathed, hushed and uncertain.

He exhaled shakily, running a hand through his hair before sinking onto a fallen log. "Allow me to tell you everything, and then you may judge me as you think proper."

She nodded, her features unreadable, and he began.

"George Wickham is the son of my father's former steward, a good and loyal man. He and my father had been friends long before he and his small family came to Pemberley when I was but two years old. Old Wickham was dedicated to his work and willing to entertain a young, curious boy such as I. He and his wife had one child, a babe in arms when they arrived. He shared a name with my father—an odd coincidence—and the steward asked my father to stand as godfather. George and I grew up together. With no brothers or sisters and few companions but my cousin, Richard, I looked upon him almost as a brother. My father, in particular, cared deeply for him."

Darcy paused in reflection and continued. "Mrs. Wickham was an elegant woman—the daughter of a gentleman who had been forced to marry beneath her after her father squandered her dowry. Accustomed to the comforts of a more prosperous life, she chafed under the constraints of a steward's income. Rather than embracing economy, she spent frivolously and with little thought to consequence. More than once, George and I sat beneath the parlor window of the steward's cottage, listening to her rail against the unfairness of her situation—how she had been reduced to living in the shadow of Pemberley, when, as she claimed, her true place was within its walls."

Darcy rubbed a hand over his eyes. "She never forgave her lot and made certain her son heard her every complaint. By the time she passed, she had planted in him a sense of grievance and poisoned everything. My father pitied him, perhaps too much, and when George went with me first to Eton, then to Cambridge, my father indulged him. At school, I noticed the first stirrings of discontent, and soon he fell in with bullies and troublemakers. At Cambridge, Wickham turned to gambling...and other vices I would not mention to a lady; matters that would have seen him sent down, had my family's name not shielded him."

When Darcy looked up to meet her gaze, Elizabeth appeared stricken.

"Do you mean to say that your father had no notion of his godson's true character?"

A sardonic curl touched his mouth. "I tried to tell him once. He dismissed it as jealousy and refused to hear another word. In time, I resolved to distance myself from Wickham. When I completed my studies at Cambridge, I began to assume some of the responsibilities at Pemberley. My sister was so young when our mother died and with her loss, Georgiana clung to me for comfort. And then...father died, too—so suddenly." His voice caught, roughened by the memory, and he paused, choking back tears. *Do not cry. I will not cry.*

The rest was difficult, but Darcy pressed on. "Then came the reading of the will. George arrived at Pemberley with every expectation of being treated as a second son. My father left him one thousand pounds, and the promise of the living at Kympton when it should fall vacant. It was not enough. His look, one of disgust, of entitlement, I shall never forget."

"He told me of the living. He claimed that when it fell vacant, you denied him."

Darcy let out a low, humorless laugh. "Denied? Yes, of course I did! But he neglected to tell you that within weeks of my father's death, he wrote to me, declaring his resolution never to take orders. In lieu of the preferment, I paid him three thousand pounds—four thousand in total, including the thousand already bequeathed him. I can produce the papers, if you wish.

Were he a better man, possessing habits fit for a clergyman, I would have honored my father's wishes in an instant. But he had other plans. He took the money, went to London under the guise of studying law, and within three years it was gone."

"Four thousand pounds? That is…that is a considerable sum. He could live very well on the interest with some economy. And yet he is now in the militia. What did he do with it?"

"I know not. When I denied him the living, he swore revenge. I thought the matter ended there and all contact between us severed, but I was mistaken. Last summer, he intruded on my notice in the worst possible fashion. I returned from a brief journey to find that, in my absence, he had been courting my sister in secret—with the collusion of her companion."

Elizabeth paled. "Miss Darcy…"

"Georgiana was but fifteen. She believed herself in love. She trusted him. When I returned earlier than expected, she confessed everything. I turned the companion out of the house at once and made it clear to Wickham that he would never again cross our threshold. He left, but only after lashing out at Georgiana most abominably. The dear girl has yet to fully recover her spirits."

Elizabeth closed her eyes. Darcy could see he had shocked her. When she spoke again, her tone seemed remorseful.

"And then you encountered him here and have borne his slander in silence."

"I saw no benefit in exposing him. My sister's suffering is not public discussion, nor is my family's honor."

"I can only admire your forbearance. I do not believe I could be silent in the face of such…treachery."

Darcy looked at the ground, elbows on his knees. When her feet appeared in his line of vision, he looked up.

Sheepishly, with contrition in her eyes, she whispered, "I believe it is me who owes you a rather large apology. I have misjudged you. Indeed, it is worse than that—I trusted a man I barely knew and judged you without the benefit of your account. That was badly done of me, Mr. Darcy, and I am sincerely sorry."

Darcy rose, taking her hand before he quite realized what he was about. "No apology is needed, Miss Elizabeth, but I accept it with gratitude. My behavior gave you little reason to think well of me when we first met." It was then that he noticed the ribbon in her hair, a glimmer of violet against the dark strands, barely visible under her bonnet. He could not look away, and the words he might have spoken died on his lips.

"It is lovely, is it not?" She smiled coyly and reached up to touch the adornment where it slipped free from her bonnet. "Shall I tell you a secret, Mr. Darcy? You are a friend, and friends share such things, after all."

"Of course. The words stumbled from him. *She wishes to confide in me! Surely, that is a very good sign.*

"I have a secret admirer." Her eyes brightened with a spark of mischief. *Oh, what joy to see her smile once more.*

"I have received no fewer than four gifts from this mysterious gentleman—or so I must assume, given the nature of the tokens. I search earnestly for some clue, some hint of his identity, yet I cannot arrive at any conclusion."

Darcy allowed himself the ghost of a smile. There was no speculation, no suspicion in her gaze as he had observed the other evening. *I stand here before her, and she cannot imagine her admirer might be me.* The thought amused him even as it stung. Did she dismiss the notion because she deemed him incapable of such affection? Or did she still think him too above the daughter of a country squire?

"Shall I help you discover his identity?" he asked, before he thought better of it.

"Could you?" She sounded doubtful.

"Gentlemen speak of many things when there are no ladies present." He stumbled a little over his words as he attempted to conjure up a reason why he might be of use.

"Is that what you speak of when we ladies withdraw after dinner for the drawing room?" She laughed. "And I thought you shared snuff and drank port whilst you spoke of your conquests and hunting exploits."

He chuckled. "Well...that is not the *only* thing of which we speak. Sometimes we discuss pugilism or the war... And sometimes we speak of ladies." He waggled his brows—something very out of character, but it elicited another laugh, and so he did not mind.

"Is that so? Tell me, sir, how often do you speak of ladies? Am I to believe your words are...complimentary." She stepped closer. Darcy mimicked her movements until they were almost touching. He tilted his head down a little. She was so close, so tempting. Elizabeth's eyes widened, and she licked her lips. Her gaze drifted to his mouth. A loud crack sounded somewhere nearby, and they both jumped before taking a few steps back. The extra distance helped Darcy clear his head, and he tried to make light of her last comment.

"Oh yes, the discussion is usually very complimentary." He tugged on his coat sleeves, unable to look at her. His heart raced, and he longed to gather her in his arms and kiss her passionately.

"Usually?" she repeated, skeptical. "Very well. I shall have to be satisfied with that." Elizabeth rubbed her hands together. "Well, I had best return to Longbourn. Good day, sir. I expect we will see you tomorrow?"

"Indeed, or whenever Bingley chooses to call." He bowed. "Goodbye, Miss Elizabeth." He watched as she gathered her basket and set off down the hill. He did not look away until she was out of sight.

Chapter Twelve

December 29, 1811
Longbourn
Elizabeth

As she had on every other morning, Elizabeth went at once to the table beside her chair to retrieve the day's gift. This time, a long, slender parcel awaited her and was done up in the usual brown paper and twine. She opened it to find a note with two lines written for the fifth day laid atop a long wooden box.

>*On the fifth day of Christmas,*
>*I penned thee a line,*
>*And presented five quills,*
>*Gilded and fine.*

Inside were five handsome quills, their feathers plucked from either a swan or a goose; Elizabeth could not be certain which of the two. At the bottom of the box lay an elegant pen knife, perfectly suited for trimming and sharpening nibs. Nestled on top of the quills was another note.

Forgive me for purloining another's words instead of penning my own. Perhaps this verse will not starve your affection as one of my own might.

The words struck a familiar chord, though she could not recall the conversation to which they alluded. But where was the poem mentioned? Elizabeth rifled through the box until she found it—another paper, folded and tucked beneath the quills. She opened it cautiously and began to read, instantly recognizing *She Walks in Beauty*[1] by Lord Byron. Though she knew the poem by heart, she read it through, aware that her mysterious admirer had chosen it because he thought of *her* in this light.

> *She walks in beauty, like the night*
> *Of cloudless climes and starry skies;*
> *And all that's best of dark and bright*
> *Meet in her aspect and her eyes;*
> *Thus mellowed to that tender light*
> *Which heaven to gaudy day denies.*
>
> *One shade the more, one ray the less,*
> *Had half impaired the nameless grace*
> *Which waves in every raven tress,*
> *Or softly lightens o'er her face;*
> *Where thoughts serenely sweet express,*
> *How pure, how dear their dwelling-place.*
>
> *And on that cheek, and o'er that brow,*
> *So soft, so calm, yet eloquent,*

The smiles that win, the tints that glow,
But tell of days in goodness spent,
A mind at peace with all below,
A heart whose love is innocent!

"How very wonderful!" She pressed a hand to her chest, heart racing as she considered who might have presented her with such a thoughtful gift. Carefully, she gathered the quills and penknife and placed them in her writing case, where they would be safe, for Lydia would never have cause to look there for treasures she might pilfer. The other gifts had been moved into the wooden chest she had purchased from the joiner the previous day. Into it Elizabeth now set the poem and the accompanying notes, adding the new stanza to those from earlier days.

Her thoughts still dwelt on her secret admirer as she readied herself for the morning. The diamond locket joined the cross at her neck, though she tucked it beneath her gown as she had before. How fervently she hoped the time would soon come when she might wear it openly.

Charlotte Lucas called later that afternoon, bringing tidings. "Mr. Collins will return to Hertfordshire just after Twelfth Night," she said, settling beside Elizabeth on the settee. Jane joined them, smoothing her gown as she glanced to the window. Their friend observed her distraction. "Is Mr. Bingley to call?" she asked archly, her countenance bright with merriment as she looked at the besotted Miss Bennet.

Jane blushed, but smiled with delight. "Yes, he gave me his most faithful promise. I believe he intends to present the first draft of the marriage articles to my father."

"I am very happy for you," Charlotte returned warmly. "He is wealthy, amiable, and handsome—quite perfect for you. We all knew he could not long resist your beauty and charm. A man might travel to the ends of the earth and not meet another with such a union of elegance, beauty, and poise. And you have a good heart, which is of even greater value."

Elizabeth laughed. "Though I will not protest your praise of my sister, I must question its design. Pray, Charlotte, have you some great favor to ask?"

"Why should I not compliment Jane?" Charlotte batted her lashes in mock innocence. "In truth, I came to inquire whether Mr. Collins might be welcomed back at Longbourn before the wedding. My mother insists it is not proper for a gentleman to stay in the same house as his betrothed. He might stay at the inn in Meryton, but I doubt he would receive the suggestion with equanimity."

"And Mr. Collins did not write to Mr. Bennet because…" Elizabeth allowed her words to trail off, awaiting explanation.

Charlotte shook her head. "You know your father is not the most reliable correspondent. Mr. Collins may write with the request only to have it go unanswered. By presenting it in person, I can reply to him myself with the arrangements, and so relieve all parties of uneasiness."

"We shall consult with my father." Elizabeth fiddled with the chain of her locket as she had done many times. They were alone in the sitting room, her habitual fidgeting soon drew the trinket forth from beneath her gown.

"That is very pretty, Eliza," Charlotte observed at once. "A present from Christmas?"

Elizabeth felt the color rise in her cheeks. "Yes." Her brief reply caused her friend to fix her with a questioning look. "Have a look." She leaned forward, offering Charlotte a clearer view.

After examining it carefully, admiring the workmanship and the lock of hair concealed within, Charlotte asked Elizabeth who had given it to her.

"I do not know," came her reply. She quickly explained how the packages had appeared each morning since Christmas Day. "They are always in my chamber before I rise, and each gift has been elaborate and costly. I have endeavored to discover who the giver is, but I have not succeeded. All the single gentlemen of our acquaintance are either not wealthy enough to afford such expensive presents, or are unlikely."

"Are you certain your admirer is a *single* gentleman?" Charlotte's question silenced Elizabeth, who gaped in astonishment.

"How could it be anyone else? Can you imagine? A married man bestowing such gifts upon a young lady, the daughter of a gentleman? It is absurd!" The locket suddenly felt heavy against her throat, and she tucked it hastily back into her gown.

"Is it so impossible?" Charlotte's penetrating look held Elizabeth's gaze. "The man clearly does not wish to be identified, but to admire you from afar."

Jane disagreed. "Secret admirers are not so rare. Do you not recall the gentleman from London who sent me a poem when I was fifteen? I never learned his name. I think whoever it is favors Elizabeth but fears she may not return his regard. He is attempting to woo her before he declares himself. I suspect it is someone with whom we are very familiar."

"And yet, Elizabeth has no notion who it may be?" Charlotte regarded her keenly. "I did not say it cannot be a single gentleman, but perhaps your sister ought not dismiss the possibility that her admirer is someone unable to court her openly."

Elizabeth could not frame a reply and hurried to turn the conversation. "I thought it might be a militiaman," she said in some desperation. "Many will eventually come into an inheritance of some kind."

"And you fancied it was your favorite, Mr. Wickham?" Charlotte asked with a sly smile. "I am sorry to disappoint you, Eliza, but he is courting Miss King."

"Oh! No, I never entertained such a thing. I admit I considered it possible, but now..." She hesitated, uncertain how much she ought to reveal. "I have it on good authority that Mr. Wickham is not the wounded, wronged gentleman he would have us believe. He is a libertine, a reprobate, a gambler, and a seducer." Her arms folded as she frowned. "Moreover, he lied to us regarding the living and Mr. Darcy's actions."

"Those are grave accusations," Charlotte cautioned. "And you have evidence to support them?"

"Beyond the testimony of an honorable gentleman—which, I must remind you, is the very evidence Mr. Wickham gave—no. But my source can produce documents to support his account. Can Wickham? I think not." She swiftly related to Charlotte and Jane what she had learned of his character, omitting only the matter of Miss Darcy.

"Mr. Darcy told you all of this?" Charlotte appeared...almost self-satisfied. "I knew he liked you, Eliza. He would not speak so freely otherwise. Have you considered it might be he who sends you tokens of *his* affection?"

Elizabeth was already shaking her head. "No, it cannot be so. We only just agreed to be friends." Yet, something within urged her to reconsider each exchange they had shared. *Perhaps Charlotte's words hold some truth.* She would have to reflect upon it later. "The more pressing question is, how can we allow that scoundrel to remain among us? Surely, he has not changed his ways."

"He might," Jane said thoughtfully. "What if he joined the militia to establish himself anew?"

Charlotte laughed derisively. "Had that been his intention, I suspect he would have joined the regulars. I shall speak with my father—no details, I assure you, but he will know how to act. Though he may seem nonsensical at times, he will take seriously any threat to our community." She rose. "I must be going. Mama needs my help with the rest of my wedding clothes. Elizabeth, will you accompany me to speak with your father for a moment?"

After Charlotte secured Mr. Bennet's agreement that Mr. Collins might lodge at Longbourn, she departed.

"Your mother will be furious, but we can tolerate him here for several days," Mr. Bennet mused. "Besides, we owe Miss Lucas a kindness for removing him from Longbourn for the last days of his earlier visit." He chuckled and waved his daughter away.

When Elizabeth returned to the sitting room, she found Jane no longer alone. Mr. Bingley and Mr. Darcy were there, together with Mrs. Bennet.

"Lydia and Kitty have walked into Meryton to call on Mrs. Forster. She is the colonel's wife, have you met her? Of course you have. She is as lively as my Lydia, though not as pretty, I fear. Her skin is too sallow, and her hair will not hold a curl. Poor dear. Still, she is fortunate indeed to have married such a handsome and suitable man. If only Colonel Forster had not been engaged before coming to Meryton!" Mrs. Bennet lamented. "I am certain he would have fallen in love with Lydia instead."

Elizabeth inwardly groaned as her mother's monologue wandered from Mrs. Forster's appearance to Lydia's supposed charms and Colonel Forster's imagined regrets. Mrs. Bennet's high, carrying voice monopolized the conversation, leaving Jane to smile demurely and Mr. Bingley to nod in bewildered agreement.

With practiced subtlety, Elizabeth slipped into the vacant seat beside Mr. Darcy, grateful for the reprieve. She let one fingertip tap lightly against the table between them, marking him as the object of her coming jest, her grin quick and knowing. "I trust you recognize your fortune in not receiving my mama's attentions. She reserves those exclusively for her future son-in-law."

Mr. Darcy laughed, a genuine sound that warmed her more than she expected. "I prefer to remain unnoticed," he confided, his tone low and confidential. "I know she looks on me more kindly than she once did, and I am grateful, yet she directs her attention elsewhere with untroubled ease. Society has always been a trial, and I much prefer my present obscurity to being smothered with conversation and eager young ladies."

He shifted almost imperceptibly, their shoulders nearly touching. Elizabeth's breath caught—not enough to raise alarm, but enough to feel. Though she could not quite admit that Charlotte's conjecture might have merit and prove correct, she could not deny the thrill of his nearness, nor the warmth it stirred.

"Has your admirer sent another token of esteem?" he asked, his tone still low, as though sharing a secret.

"Indeed," Elizabeth said, lowering her own voice to match. She leaned closer, sharing the intimacy. "This morning I received five gilded quills. They are finer than any items of a similar nature I have ever owned, and I am eager to put them to use."

"Marvelous," he said with an approving nod. "You seem pleased, so I must suppose you are a diligent correspondent. Is it so?" he whispered.

"It is," she replied, unable to suppress her smile. "I shall pen a letter to my aunt as soon as they depart Longbourn." She hesitated, then carefully withdrew the locket from beneath her fichu and held it toward him, glancing at her mother to ensure she remained occupied with her conversation. "This is the locket of which I told you."

Mr. Darcy examined the delicate item, turning it with care between his fingers. It caught the candlelight, casting a warm glint upon the gold. "A fine piece," he said in a subdued tone, and she thought she saw the tips of his ears redden. He cleared his throat and returned the locket. "Are the Gardiners still here?" he asked, his manner a trifle awkward. "I do not believe I heard when they were to depart for London."

"My aunt and uncle will remain until New Year's Day. They will accompany us to Haye Park this evening. Will you and Mr. Bingley be in attendance?" She lifted a hopeful glance to him, fully aware of how much her sister would enjoy the evening if her betrothed were present—and how much she herself was beginning to anticipate Mr. Darcy's company.

"We will." His reply was immediate and reassuring. "In fact, I intend to win every game played. Tell me, which do you most enjoy?"

"Oh, I prefer bullet pudding or charades. Both grant me ample entertainment, especially when the company is clever. There is another—The Minister's Cat—which always sets the company laughing. I enjoyed it at Lucas Lodge and anticipate it might be played again."[2]

"Ah, the alphabet game." He smiled in recollection. "The minister's cat is an amiable cat…an obstinate cat…a winsome cat. 'Tis all in the timing and wit, is it not?"

Elizabeth laughed. "Precisely! And the best part is when someone forgets their word, or repeats one that has already been said. Kitty often insists the cat is 'dainty,' no matter the letter."

Darcy leaned a fraction nearer, his voice touched with warmth. "Then I must prepare an uncommon string of adjectives. Perhaps I may surprise you with my vocabulary."

"I look forward to it, sir," Elizabeth replied with a light curtsy from her seat, her eyes bright. "But be warned—I am quite competitive."

"As am I." His expression grew amused, then he regarded her intently. "I believe this evening shall be most diverting."

Their conversation continued until tea. When the tray was brought in, Mrs. Bennet busied herself with the serving, leaving Jane and Mr. Bingley to enjoy uninterrupted discourse. Before long, the gentlemen rose to take their leave. Elizabeth felt a pang of regret at Mr. Darcy's parting and wished fervently they had had more time to converse. *Well, at least I shall see him tonight.*

---

1. She Walks in Beauty was published in 1814. I took creative license for this story.

2.

Chapter Thirteen

December 29, 1811
Haye Park
Darcy

As he adjusted the folds of his cravat for the third time, Darcy caught his reflection in the looking glass and shook his head. No amount of starch or symmetry could still the tumult pressing at his heart. He was not nervous—at least, not in the manner others suffered nerves. He was expectant, restless with expectation and dread in equal measure. The evening at Haye Park might prove like any other social call, filled with polite laughter and predictable amusements—or it might mark the beginning of something altogether different.

Would Elizabeth wear the locket openly this evening? Perhaps she had already set the quills to use; he thought it likely. It was not in his nature to bestow tokens lightly, yet the thought of her fingers clasping the chain, her ink-stained hands guiding one of the gilded pens he had chosen, stirred something deeply possessive within him. She wore his gifts as though they belonged to her, as though they had long waited for her alone. If all went well—if she returned his affections—she would one day bear his name. *Mrs. Fitzwilliam Darcy.* The very notion made him draw a steady breath and let it out slowly.

And yet...

It was a novel thing to feel uncertain. He had never known doubt in such matters, not truly. For most of his adult life, the world had yielded to him. He had inherited both a name of consequence and a fortune to match, and he had been taught to expect deference in all respects, especially in marriage. Ladies swooned, mothers schemed, and chaperones pressed their daughters into his path with near-comic frequency. Their admiration had long since become background noise—insistent, predictable, and wearisome.

But Elizabeth...she had unsettled everything. She met his gaze with open challenge, measured his words, and found them wanting. She had wounded his pride, sharpened his wit, and—without intending it—captured his heart. Ambition and greed held no sway with her. Indeed, he feared she might sooner marry a poor curate, if affection and respect were present, than accept a man simply because he possessed ten thousand a year. For that very reason, he wanted her, needed her, all the more. And he could not simply *offer* her a life of wealth and consequence.

He had to be worthy of her.

Bingley's familiar voice called from the library, drawing him from his thoughts. The gentlemen had formed a habit of sharing a glass of port before their evening excursions, a last comfort before venturing into the cold carriage.

Darcy joined him by the fire, noting the heat rising from the bricks at their feet and the thick lap rugs draped across their knees. Still, their breath misted the air, a stark reminder of the winter beyond the panes.

"Evening soirees are far more agreeable in June," Bingley muttered, tugging the rug higher. "There is something unnatural in dressing for company when one's fingers are stiff from cold."

Darcy gave a low grunt of amusement. "I believe you say this whenever the temperature falls below forty degrees."

"And yet it remains true. We have been out nearly every night since returning. Far more than we ever are in town. Is it always this lively in the country?"

"I suspect not. Perhaps the local families are eager to take advantage of our presence."

Bingley laughed. "Perhaps *someone* is hoping to take advantage of *your* presence. Not that you would notice. You remain impervious as ever."

Darcy gave no reply. Bingley knew him well, but not well enough to guess how very *vulnerable* he felt in Elizabeth Bennet's company. Not yet, at least. In time, perhaps, he might tell his friend everything.

"I do enjoy these evenings, but I suspect you would prefer to remain here with a book."

Darcy's gaze lingered on the firelight dancing across the floorboards. "Normally, yes."

He felt Bingley watching him—curious, probing—but offered no further explanation. He would not speak her name, not here, not yet. Too much was at stake, and he could not bear the thought of hearing it bandied on another's lips until he knew it belonged to him.

The carriage drew up before Haye Park's wide front steps. Light streamed through the windows, warm and inviting, as though beckoning them inward. Music and laughter echoed from the drawing room, underscored by the measured rise and fall of conversation. Darcy paused before entering, breathing in the cold, sharp air and pressing down the fervent wish that threatened to overwhelm him.

Had she arrived? Was she thinking of him? Did she wear the locket? He could not say. But as he crossed the threshold into the fire-lit hall, he knew with certainty that he would trade every estate he owned—Pemberley included—for a single smile from Elizabeth Bennet.

She stood near the fireplace, speaking to a pair of gentlemen, the flickering light playing over her features. Miss Lucas stood beside her, adding the occasional comment, but it was Elizabeth who animated the circle, her eyes alive with intelligence and humor. Darcy lingered in the hall longer than propriety required, content for a moment simply to observe her. She laughed at something one of the men said, and the sound sent a thrill coursing through his frame.

One of the gentlemen was Mr. Arthur Willis—married, respectable, and dull. Darcy recalled the name from one of Mrs. Bennet's early boasts when she had spoken of the "four-and-twenty families" as evidence of Meryton's consequence. Mr. Willis's wife stood a few paces away among the matrons, gesturing animatedly as she spoke, her look reminding Darcy of Mrs. Bennet when she discoursed on lace.

At length, Elizabeth and Miss Lucas curtsied and politely excused themselves. Elizabeth faced the company, and a gentleness stole over her countenance as her gaze swept the room and landed on him. Her eyes lingered. Something passed between them—subtle, yet powerful. Darcy offered a small, tender smile, one reserved for her alone, willing his feelings to be read in that single glance.

She murmured something to Miss Lucas and then crossed the room with unhurried grace, every step purposeful. He admired the poise she bore, not derived from fortune or high connections, but from confidence and character.

"Good evening, sir," she said, pausing before him. Her fingers toyed with the gloves she wore—*his* gloves, sent days earlier with only a stanza and without his usual note, left to speak for itself and trusting she would understand. In her hair, pearl combs gleamed, catching the candlelight like moonlight on water. About her throat hung a fine gold chain and the diamond locket he had wrapped with his own hands. She wore his gifts openly, each one a silent acknowledgement of his regard.

"Good evening to you, Miss Elizabeth. I scarcely recall seeing you look so lovely."

And she did. The cream gown she wore was simple, yet elegant, its lines drawing the eye to her light and pleasing figure. Her cheeks were flushed from the warmth of the fire—or perhaps laughter—and her eyes shone with such brightness that his heart quickened.

Grasping at conversation, he recalled Bingley's remark and seized upon it. "Is Hertfordshire always so…eventful during the festive season?"

She laughed, the sound on him like sunlight through leaves. "Yes, it is, sir," she said, leaning in a she set a gloved hand upon his arm, a casual gesture, but one that made his pulse leap. "The four-and-twenty families in the area have made a kind of rivalry of it. Those whose houses can accommodate a crowd vie for the most splendid assembly. It is no formal contest, not officially, but everyone understands it as such. Nearly every evening in December is thus spoken for."

He regarded her with amused indulgence. "How *very* entertaining." He privately thought the custom absurd, but it pleased her, and that was enough. "I believe I have gone out more this winter than in many years past."

"Are you so unsociable, sir?" she teased, withdrawing her hand from his arm, as if belatedly aware it had lingered there. "I thought you had amended your ways."

"I have, which is why my words hold. My time in Hertfordshire has altered me, I assure you."

He held her gaze as he spoke, willing her to hear the words he left unsaid—that *she* alone had wrought the change. That every moment in her company had schooled him in humility, growth, and love. Before she could reply, a voice broke the silence between them.

"Lizzy! Come, it is time to play!" Lydia's shrill summons cut through the hum of conversation as she bounded toward them, bright-eyed and breathless. "Oh, and Mr. Darcy, you must come too! We are playing *The Minister's Cat*! You simply must—it is new to me, and I have never played it!"

Elizabeth gave him an apologetic glance as Lydia seized her arm with all the force of sisterly enthusiasm. "You need not, of course."

"I would be delighted," Darcy replied gently, surprising even himself with the readiness of his answer.

"Indeed?" One side of her mouth curved in a half-smile that dared him to prove it.

"Most assuredly, madam. Though I have never played the game, I should imagine it will not prove too difficult to follow."

"I should not have thought children's games would tempt you."

"They never have," he admitted, "but I suspect they may…in certain company."

"You mean to say you expect me to guide you?"

"I should count myself fortunate if you did," he returned, lowering his voice so she alone could hear. "Though I warn you, I learn quickly."

"Then prepare yourself. I do not surrender easily."

"Nor do I," he said, allowing the faintest smile, "but perhaps I may be persuaded—once—if the victory is yours."

Her cheeks tinged with color as a gentle laugh escaped her and gave him a look that was part amusement, part admiration. "Very well. We shall see, Mr. Darcy. Let us see how you rise to the challenge. I should not like you to forfeit so soon."

This time, he threw Elizabeth an apologetic look as her sister returned to tug him away. Darcy followed Miss Lydia into the drawing room, wondering whether any other gentlemen present could claim such delight at the prospect of playing a child's game—solely for the chance to sit beside a certain lady.

He suspected not.

The laughter in Haye Park's drawing room rang like cheerful bells as the group gathered into a circle, cushions scattered on the floor and chairs pulled close. A roaring fire blazed in the hearth, and half-eaten ginger biscuits and spiced cake lay neglected on side tables.

"The Minister's Cat!" Lydia cried gleefully, bouncing in place. "We must play. It has been too long since we enjoyed such a merry party present for parlor games." She darted forward, weaving through chairs and card tables like a child set loose in a confectioner's shop. "Kitty! Mary!" she called, arms flung wide. "We are playing the Minister's Cat! Everyone must join!"

"Indeed," Elizabeth said, beaming. "Kitty, will you explain the rules?"

"Of course," her sister replied, already giggling. "We must describe the cat with an adjective beginning with the letter given. Any mistake, hesitation, or repetition, and you are out!"

Darcy, all pretended sobriety, composed himself with exaggerated solemnity. "A game of vocabulary and precision? I shall do my utmost to refrain from humiliating myself."

Elizabeth's lips curved. "I dare say you will manage it, sir."

The game began with A.

"The minister's cat is an *amiable* cat," Jane offered sweetly.

"The minister's cat is an *arrogant* cat," declared Sanderson, puffing out his chest.

"The minister's cat is an *abominable* cat," Elizabeth pronounced with mock severity, earning a chuckle from Captain Denny.

"The minister's cat is an *ambidextrous* cat," Darcy said smoothly, allowing the corners of his mouth to lift. Elizabeth's answering glance suggested she had noticed.

Round followed round, and players began to falter as the letters advanced. Miss Lydia lost at C by calling the cat both *cheerful* and *charming*—Miss Kitty had already used both. She pouted, then scampered off to the side with Denny in tow. John Lucas was undone at F, describing the cat as "fantastic" after Arnold Goulding had already said the same, which earned groans and laughter. Goulding himself stumbled on H, blinking furiously before blurting, "The minister's cat is a…a…heavenly cat!"—but he had already lost the rhythm.

Miss Kitty managed to reach J before dissolving into helpless giggles, forgetting her word entirely.

"Out, dear sister," Miss Mary said primly. "The minister's cat is a *judicious* cat."

Sanderson fared better, glancing often toward Mary with a smile that seemed to please her and brought a deep blush to her cheeks. She even missed a beat once, though no one called her out. At P, however, Sanderson faltered.

"The minister's cat is a…a…*pleasant* cat," he said with confidence.

"Used already," cried Bingley, clapping his hands. "By me, good sir, at the very start of P!"

Sanderson groaned theatrically but settled near Mary's chair without protest. "Miss Bennet," he said with a mock bow, "you are my champion now."

Miss Mary ducked her head, a pleased smile tugging at her mouth as she resumed with the letter Q.

Darcy leaned nearer towards Elizabeth. "Do you suppose his admiration is idle or intentional?"

Elizabeth tilted her head, her eyes still fixed on the pair. "I cannot say. But Mary seems...receptive." Her countenance darkened. "If he toys with my sister's heart..." She broke off, the warning clear without completion.

"Indeed," Darcy murmured. "Such sport would be intolerable."

At the letter U, Miss Mary faltered. "The minister's cat is *ubiquitous*—no, *untimely*—no, *unified*—"

"You are out. Mary!" Miss Kitty cried, gleefully striking an invisible bell.

Miss Mary flushed and rose, a touch breathless, while Sanderson immediately offered his arm. They withdrew together, and a low murmur passed through the room.

"That leaves three," said Bingley, rubbing his hands together. "Shall we raise the stakes? A friendly wager?"

"What do you propose?" asked Jane, half amused.

"A plate of mince pies from the sideboard to the victor, and the honor of being declared the cleverest in the room." He glanced about. "But beware—Darcy is known for his absurdly long words. Four syllables or more whenever possible. He will likely trounce us all!"

"I cannot help it if the vocabulary is at hand," Darcy returned with dry amusement. "One uses the words one knows."

"You must not let him intimidate you, Miss Elizabeth," Bingley teased. "You have the nimblest mind among us."

The three advanced swiftly—V, W, X. Elizabeth triumphed with *xebec*, and Darcy countered with *xiphoid*. Bingley, however, sputtered helplessly at Y.

"The minister's cat is a...a yellow cat?"

"Out!" Elizabeth and Darcy chorused.

The room erupted in laughter, and applause rang out.

"And now," said Bingley, grinning, "the final round. Will it be Miss Elizabeth Bennet or Mr. Fitzwilliam Darcy who reigns supreme?"

"Z is upon us," Miss Lydia whispered loudly, with every intention of being heard. She had reappeared with a rather flushed Captain Denny a few moments before.

"The minister's cat is a *zealous* cat," Darcy began.

Elizabeth did not blink. "The minister's cat is a *zany* cat."

Darcy's lips quirked. "The minister's cat is a *zodiacal* cat."

"The minister's cat," Elizabeth said with relish, "is a *zetetic* cat."

A beat. Darcy opened his mouth, closed it, and bowed his head.

"I concede. Z has defeated me."

Applause rang out around them.

Elizabeth's eyes danced with triumph. "Even four-syllable words may meet their match, sir."

Darcy extended his hand to help her rise. "You have earned your mince-pies. But I shall demand a rematch—perhaps on the morrow—over bullet pudding."

She placed her hand in his, her fingers lingering—light, gloved, but unmistakably lingering—as she replied, "I accept."

The brief pressure stole his breath. Victory was hers, but the touch was his undoing.

Chapter Fourteen

December 30, 1811
Longbourn
Elizabeth

> *On the sixth day of Christmas,*
> *In crystal so clear,*
> *Six vials of scent*
> *From London procured.*

ELIZABETH SAT ALONE IN her bedchamber, the pale light of morning slanting in through the frosted panes. A fire burned in the grate, casting a mellow glow upon the worn carpet and the rosewood dressing table, where a velvet-lined box had been set with reverent care. The sapphire-blue case gleamed, its brass clasps polished bright. She reached for it, unable to resist the temptation to see within.

Lifting the lid, she drew in her breath.

Six elegant glass vials nestled against midnight velvet. Each was a small work of art: the glass delicately etched, the contents luminous—some pale as morning dew, others tinged with gold or blush-pink as a winter sunrise.

Around each neck was tied a tiny scroll of fine paper, upon which words had been written in a precise, unmistakable hand.

She read them, her heart fluttering at the meaning behind each one:

Rose Water — for the first evening we danced.

Who? She had danced with many men since her come out. Rose water was a favorite, and surely she had shared more than one first dance whilst wearing it.

Lavender Water — for my devotion to you.

Her heart skipped a beat. This was a vow, tender and unsought, yet offered freely. Lavender, the flower of constancy, long grown in the hedgerows of Longbourn, had never seemed more dear. *What a romantic sentiment!*

Eau de Cologne — fidelity in love.

Whoever he was, he offered not mere affection, but loyalty. One need not betray another's body to show unfaithfulness. Her parents were the proof enough of that.

Violet Water — you have taught me humility.

This puzzled her. To whom had she taught humility? Could it be John Lucas? Elizabeth had certainly humbled him often enough in childhood.

And as heir to Lucas Lodge, he might, on occasion, afford to spend so lavishly.

Orange Blossom Water — for purity and eternal love.

This was her favorite. The floral scent most often linked with brides and with promise. Elizabeth's breath caught. *Surely, this means my admirer wishes to marry me.* Yet if so, Charlotte's suppositions of a married gentleman must be false. *Not necessarily. The man might long to marry you yet be hindered.* How vexing!

Bergamot Essence — happiness and, it is hoped, success.

That final note made her smile. Ever practical, ever guarded—this was hope wrapped in citrus, bright and sharp. She drew out the stopper and held it beneath her nose. The fresh scent lifted her spirits. *This may become my new favorite scent.*

Each vial proved a revelation, each fragrance more luxurious than the last. The name *Floris of London* adorned the interior of the box in gilded script—a name she recognized even in the country. That her admirer had gone to such effort...such expense...

The perfumery on Jermyn Street had stood for nearly a century, its patrons the discerning few—the royal family, foreign dignitaries, duchesses and marchionesses. And now...her. She was but a gentleman's daughter, with little fortune or consequence. Yet this gift bespoke that he saw her as worthy of every indulgence.

She lifted the rose water, drew out the stopper, and dabbed a few drops upon her wrists. The fragrance bloomed at once—lush, heady, far more refined than the distillations made in Longbourn's still room. She raised her hands, eyes half-closed. This was a scent to linger long after the moment had fled.

A sigh, slow and sweet, escaped her. It was too much. It was everything.

She replaced the stopper with care and pressed her fingers to the ribboned note one last time. Then, closing the lid and securing the clasps, she rose and carried the case to her wardrobe. The box of scents were too large to fit within the box she purchased. So she placed it behind the folded shawls and lace-edged handkerchiefs, near where she kept the box containing her other gifts. There they rested at the back of the wardrobe, in the same secret place where she kept the locket, the pearl combs, and the letters she read by candlelight when the household slept.

Her hand lingered upon it, a tender caress sealing her unspoken gratitude and the fragile hope that blossomed in her breast.

Her admirer had gifted her more than scent. He had given her memory, meaning, and promise—and she treasured them all.

The breakfast table at Longbourn was already well laden when Elizabeth descended the stairs. A warming tray of boiled eggs and ham sat near the hearth, while a silver rack held neatly stacked slices of toast, browned before the kitchen fire. Mrs. Hill had set out blackberry preserves, cold meats, and a fresh loaf of bread, its crust still crackling from the bakehouse. Jane, as usual, had risen early and poured the tea.

"Good morning, dearest," Jane said, her smile serene and knowing as she offered Elizabeth a cup.

"Thank you," Elizabeth slid into her seat and reached for the toast. "How cheerful everything appears this morning!"

"Mama has not yet come downstairs. Neither Kitty nor Lydia. Mary left but a moment ago—she claimed some matter of business she must attend." Jane buttered a scone and took a bite.

Elizabeth laughed, slicing a boiled egg. "Could it concern Mr. Sanderson? He paid her a great deal of attention last evening. I trust he is not trifling with our sister's heart, for I shall be forced to defend Mary if he has."

Jane's eyes kindled with amusement. "Yes, I saw the looks they exchanged. Do you know his situation? Most officers are not in a position to take a wife unless they have some additional income."

"No, I know little of him. Lydia may be able to tell me, but I hesitate to ask. She would wonder at my curiosity, and I would not have Mary feel uneasy. She so rarely receives such attention."

"Yes, that is prudent." Jane paused, then continued, keeping her tone light but not unaffected. "I wonder whether Charles might call. He mentioned the possibility last evening."

Elizabeth glanced sidelong at her sister. "He will. You are betrothed, after all. If he can stay away, I shall be astonished. Nothing short of urgent business could keep him from your side. And if not to-day, then on the morrow."

Jane's eyes brightened. "Yes, you are correct. Oh, Lizzy, I am so happy! But what of Mr. Darcy? Do you suppose he will accompany him? Would that please you?"

Elizabeth stared at her sister, aghast, as she stirred a spoonful of sugar into her tea. "Why, Jane, what are you implying? He may or he may not—what can it signify to me? He often attends his friend." She lifted the locket chain and turned it between her fingers. The locket remained hidden in her bodice. Jane observed the motion, her features touched with gentle curiosity.

"Have you considered he might be your mysterious admirer?" she asked, feigning innocence.

"I have scarcely taken the time to entertain *any* name." The admission came in a whisper, though she felt no shame in it. "I confess, I have speculated and possibly eliminated gentlemen, yet I have not dared give my admirer a name. But Mr. Darcy? He could not be the one, could he? The gifts began before we made amends and began afresh."

"I always said he liked you more than you believed. Do not dismiss him."

Jane's words echoed in Elizabeth's mind. The notion seemed impossible. Mr. Darcy had not been in her reckoning at all. *Could it be?* The thought sent a flutter through her stomach. She felt no distaste, as once she might have done.

They finished the meal in companionable ease, the clink of cutlery the only sound. Afterward, the sisters withdrew to the front parlor, each to her chosen pursuit—Jane with a bit of fine needlework, Elizabeth with a book she had long wished to finish but had too often laid aside of late.

An hour passed, and Elizabeth was absorbed in the pages of *Evelina* when a familiar knock drew her attention. Mrs. Hill entered with a curtsy. "Miss Lucas to see you."

Charlotte came in briskly, her cheeks pink from the cold and countenance troubled despite her composed manner.

"Charlotte!" Jane rose with a welcoming smile. "Come warm yourself."

"I will not stay long," Charlotte said, drawing off her gloves, "but I thought I ought to tell you what has come to light."

Elizabeth set aside her book. "You look as though you bring troubling news."

"I do. It concerns Mr. Wickham."

Jane laid her needlework down, frowning.

Charlotte continued, lowering her voice. "After our conversation the other day, I went to my father. He listened with gratitude and began making inquiries. Since then, he has heard a number of disturbing accounts. It seems Wickham has run up debts throughout Meryton—and at every shop imaginable. Nothing has been paid. Worse, there are whispers of impropriety with several shopkeepers' daughters."

Elizabeth's stomach turned, though she could not claim surprise. After what Mr. Darcy had revealed, it was only to be expected that the reprobate would persist in his dissolute ways.

"Poor Miss King," Jane whispered. "Do you think she knows?"

"I doubt it. My father has written to Mr. King, her uncle and guardian; he is in Liverpool at present. They have been acquainted these twenty years. He believes the man ought to know." Charlotte straightened. "It is only right to protect young ladies from Wickham's dreadful conduct. And Miss King does not deserve to have her life bound to such a man."

"That was wisely done, Charlotte." To think Miss Darcy had almost been resigned to that fate. But Charlotte had not finished her account.

"He has also spoken with several local shopkeepers, urging them not to extend Wickham any further credit. Maria has been forbidden to be alone with any soldier and may not go to town without one of us to attend her."

Jane gasped. "How dreadful. But Lizzy, what of Longbourn? What shall we do?"

Charlotte looked to Elizabeth with concern. "Yes. What *will* you do?"

Elizabeth exhaled, her hands clasped tightly in her lap. "You know my father. He will laugh at me, say I imagine things, or accuse me of meddling. He has never taken his daughters seriously."

Jane's lips pressed together in thought.

"We shall have to find another way," Elizabeth considered. "I must protect our younger sisters, even if Papa will not act."

Her thoughts strayed to Mr. Darcy—his steady manner, his sense of responsibility. *He would not dismiss my concerns. If anyone can help, it is he. But shall I ask him? Could I? And why has he done nothing until now? Why has this dreadful man been allowed to go on ruining lives?*

Charlotte stood. "I am sorry to be the bearer of such tidings. It is better to know."

"Yes, I agree." Elizabeth and Jane both rose with their friend. "Thank you for coming."

"I will call again soon," Charlotte said, adjusting her bonnet. "Let us hope something can be done."

Elizabeth walked her to the door and watched as Charlotte made her way down the path. The day had grown colder, clouds thickening overhead. Turning back into the house, Elizabeth felt the weight of responsibility settle heavy upon her shoulders—and, somewhere in her heart, a firm resolve to speak to Mr. Darcy after all.

The rest of the morning passed without incident—though in a household such as Longbourn's, "without incident" rarely meant quiet. The only true excitement came from a pitched quarrel between Kitty and Lydia over a bonnet. Kitty had purchased a new one with her pin money and spent two evenings remaking it with ribbons and clever pleats. In her eyes, it was a triumph of fashion. Lydia, of course, snatched it off the hat stand at first sight and declared it hers by right of being the younger and, in her opinion, the more charming sister.

Kitty shrieked like a wounded cat and chased Lydia through the upstairs passage. Their cries echoed down the stairwell until their mother's voice rang out.

"Oh, do stop making such a racket!" Mrs. Bennet called from the parlor. "You will wake the dead, and no man ever admired a shrieking woman. Lydia, if you want the bonnet, wear it. Kitty, you ought to be proud your handiwork is admired."

"Proud?" Kitty retorted, stomping into the room with her cheeks aflame. "You never let me keep anything for myself!"

In retaliation, she seized Lydia's favorite pelisse and shawl and boldly paraded them about the house as if they were her own. Lydia, unused to being crossed, wept with fury and threatened to tear Kitty's bonnet to pieces. Yet, as always, the pair reached a peaceable truce: each surrendered the stolen goods in exchange for a hasty pact to share their hair pomade and a new number of *La Belle Assemblée*.

At the first sound of raised voices, Mr. Bennet had retreated to his study and locked the door, not to emerge until harmony had returned—or tea was served. A man who delighted in irony but abhorred noise, he remained resolutely hidden. Mrs. Bennet, on the other hand, reveled in the commotion. With her shawl drawn snug about her shoulders, she presided in the parlor, surrounded by her daughters, sipping tea and peering out the window between pronouncements.

"I have tea and cakes ready to be served," she announced, her voice swelling with importance. "Does Mr. Bingley like cake, Jane?"

"He does," Jane replied, shy yet happy. Her needle moved with practiced skill, though she paused to smile. "Charles has a sweet tooth—he told me so only last evening."

"How very amusing!" Mrs. Bennet tittered. "One could never guess it. His figure is fine, tall, and slim. A man with money and no stomach—what a rare find!"

Elizabeth glanced up from her stitching and rolled her eyes. Trust Mama to utter such a thing aloud. Jane's cheeks flushed with color, but she looked genuinely pleased, nonetheless. Their mother was incorrigible, yet her words did not sting. Not when Jane's happiness was assured.

"Does he have a favorite?" Elizabeth asked with a sly grin, eager to draw her sister out.

Jane looked up, her face brightening. "He says he likes lemon. Lemon creams, lemon cakes, lemon syllabub—anything with that sharp-sweet taste."

Mrs. Bennet clasped her hands together. "Then I shall have cook make her best lemon loaf this very afternoon! I must always please my future son!"

Elizabeth laughed under her breath. Only several weeks earlier, none of them had dared hope Mr. Bingley would return to Netherfield—let alone propose. His absence had been a source of heartbreak, especially for Jane, whose suffering had drawn Elizabeth's deepest sympathy. Now all was altered. The proposal had been made and accepted, the marriage articles signed and sealed under Mr. Gardiner's careful eye. The settlement was generous, and, more importantly, Jane would be happy.

Still, Elizabeth could not help wondering whether Miss Bingley and Mrs. Hurst had been informed. She doubted it. Mr. Bingley's sisters had never approved of Jane, for all her beauty and sweetness, and their politeness toward her dear sister had been mere pretense. They had plainly wished to guide their brother toward a bride of greater fortune or consequence. Should they learn what had transpired, they would descend upon

Netherfield like carrion crows. *Better they remain away. Everyone is happier without their schemes and interference.*

Jane, too kind to utter such sentiments aloud, simply bent over her needlework, her contentment reflected in every tranquil movement.

Elizabeth glanced about the cozy parlor. Beyond the windows, the winter sun glimmered upon the frosted lawn. Within, the fire burned bright, filling the room with cheer. For all the squabbles, for all her mother's absurdities, the house felt warmer than it had in many weeks.

She looked at Jane and mused, *At least one of us has found happiness without complication.*

But her thoughts strayed—inevitably—to Mr. Darcy.

Chapter Fifteen

December 30, 1811
Longbourn
Darcy

THE PARLOR AT LONGBOURN was abuzz with conversation when Darcy and his friend were announced. Bingley, ever amiable, began a lively discourse with Miss Bennet, while Darcy's eyes sought only one lady. Elizabeth sat near the window, her profile touched by the pale winter sun streaming through the glass. Her curls were gathered with unstudied elegance, and as he drew near, a familiar fragrance teased his senses—rose water, delicate and elusive.

He wondered whether she liked it. The perfumer on Jermyn Street had prepared the selection at his express request. The box was fashioned to suit, the sort rarely offered save by special order. Though Elizabeth did not yet suspect him as the author of the gifts, he thought she might include him in her speculations as she puzzled over her secret admirer's identity. Breathing the fragrance that lingered between them, a profound satisfaction stirred within him.

Their eyes met, and she smiled. "You are very welcome this morning, Mr. Darcy. Was the journey from Netherfield pleasant?" She touched the empty place beside her on the settee, and he joined her, angling his body so he could face her.

"Thank you, Miss Elizabeth." He inclined his head, his voice lower than usual, his eyes steady upon hers, as though daring her to suspect what he alone knew. "You look remarkably well today. The ride was cold yet bracing. I dare say Bingley was eager to see your sister." He glanced toward Miss Bennet, who conversed with her betrothed while Mrs. Bennet fussed around them. The ease between the pair amidst the bustle of the drawing room struck Darcy afresh; they were plainly made for one another.

He turned back to Elizabeth. She tilted her head, a glimmer of mischief alight in her eyes. "Jane was scarcely less eager. She is very well this morning. Good health and a warm hearth are all one can wish for in winter." She hesitated, biting her lip as she often did.

"I have a confession. I told my friend, Charlotte Lucas, of Mr. Wickham—without revealing particulars concerning your sister. In turn, Charlotte told her father just enough to prompt inquiries. She came to call upon us yesterday with news. It appears he has run up debts with every tradesman and engaged in…dissolute practices."

Darcy's surprise was evident. "Indeed?" It was more than he himself had done, and he had long known the scoundrel for what he was.

Elizabeth nodded. "His manner and borrowed charm misled several shopkeepers, it seems. The more I learn of Mr. Wickham, the more I see how greatly I erred in judgment. I once thought myself an excellent judge of character." She shook her head with a weary breath. "Sir William has cautioned the merchants. It rests with them now to heed or disregard his counsel."

Darcy's gaze hardened, and he turned aside before answering. "I sometimes wonder whether I failed him by not acting sooner. Perhaps it was guilt—or misplaced loyalty. My father cherished hopes for him. Perhaps I would not admit Wickham was beyond redemption."

"Would your father be content with what he has become?" Her question, so rational, cut him at once.

"No," he said at last, the word heavy with conviction. "He would be grieved." For had his father foreseen the lies, deceit, and debauchery Wickham would embrace, he would have exerted every power to prevent such ruin. Darcy had done little beyond settling debts and issuing threats.

The others were engaged elsewhere, leaving them to their privacy. Their conversation was of a delicate nature and not one meant for curious ears. Darcy fell silent, brooding for a moment before he chose to speak.

"I shall do something," he added with resolve. It was long past time for him to act; long past time to bring Wickham's mischief to an end. How many lives had he despoiled? How many daughters had he left with broken hearts and tarnished prospects? How many tradesmen had gone unpaid, their households burdened for Wickham's selfish indulgence? Darcy knew there were likely many of his debts he had not been able to trace.

Elizabeth regarded him, eyes steady. "As I said, Sir William has already warned the shopkeepers, but I am certain there is more you could do. He must not be allowed to injure anyone further."

"I shall see it done," Darcy replied. He meant it with his whole heart. Wickham's days of deceit were numbered. Only one question remained—how was he to accomplish it?

The conversation soon shifted, Elizabeth apparently satisfied with his vow. She asked after Georgiana, and Darcy's lips quirked.

"She has written to say she is disappointed I cannot visit until February. My uncle and aunt Matlock will be in town then and have requested my presence. She has lately taken up painting in oils." Georgiana had enclosed a small canvas with her last letter.

"Oils?" Elizabeth leaned forward, intrigued. "That is ambitious. Has she a good hand for it?"

"She does. Though she still prefers watercolors, she has begun to experiment with landscapes. She sent me a small view of Pemberley painted from memory. It was remarkably accurate." Even now, it rested on the table beside his bed, where he might look upon it often.

Elizabeth's smile deepened. "She must have a very thoughtful brother who encourages her talents." Her eyes shone with good humor. There was no hint of teasing, and Darcy believed her in earnest.

His heart leapt at the compliment, though he betrayed no outward sign. "She is a sensitive soul, and I am proud of her." The undertones of Georgiana's letter reassured him that she was healing. Once Wickham was checked, she might mend still further. He found himself speaking without calculation—an uncommon state for him, but one he welcomed in Elizabeth's presence.

"When I was nine," he began, casting her a sidelong glance, "I attempted to impress my cousins by leaping from one mossy stone to another across the pond at Pemberley."

Elizabeth looked at him keenly, clearly intrigued. "Did you succeed?"

"I made it halfway. Then I misjudged and fell straight in. It was early spring. The water was...bracing."

She laughed, a rich and unguarded sound. "You? Mr. Darcy, the paragon of composure, drenched to the bone?"

He allowed himself a rueful smile. "My mother stood on the bank with a handkerchief pressed to her mouth, trying not to laugh. She said, 'I warned you, Fitzwilliam! What will your father say?'"

Elizabeth grinned. "What *did* he say?"

"That I ought to be thankful I had not broken my neck and that next time I should swim in a proper lake instead of leaping about like a frog before an audience."

Amusement danced in Elizabeth's eyes. "'Tis rather comforting to imagine you as a mischievous boy."

"Not mischievous—" His look turned mock-solemn—"merely...ambitious."

She smiled at him. "In that case, I ought to confess my own folly."

"I would be most interested to hear it."

"When I was nine, I insisted on helping Hill carry the wash to the drying green. I loaded the wheelbarrow far higher than I could manage. Halfway down the path, it tipped—wet sheets everywhere, straight into the mud. Mama declared I had undone a week's labor in one grand gesture."

Darcy's laugh was low and genuine. "I cannot imagine you idle, even in mischief."

"It was not idleness, sir, but zeal—a good Z word by the bye—most unfortunately misapplied."

His smile deepened. "Zeal, yes, but joined with industry, it makes a formidable combination. I trust you have long since mastered the art of balance."

"I should ask you the same, sir," she teased. "But some would say otherwise."

For a time they sat in contented silence, the memory of childish misadventures warming the air between them.

"I think," Darcy said at last, "those are the moments that shape us most. Not the times we succeed, but the times we fall into the pond or overturn the wheelbarrow and learn that we are not infallible."

Elizabeth's look grew reflective. "And that there is always someone—be it mother, father, or footman—whose presence steadies us if we falter, and whose hand helps us find our way back."

He inclined his head. "Quite right, Miss Elizabeth." Never had he felt so understood.

Soon after, the call drew to its natural end, and the gentlemen took their leave. Without, as the winter wind bit through his coat, Darcy paused beneath the skeletal trees lining the road to Netherfield and considered all Elizabeth had said. Her judgment had sharpened, her compassion deepened—and he had failed both her and himself by allowing Wickham's misconduct to go unchecked for so long.

Back at Netherfield, he took up his pen. By lamplight he wrote swiftly, the ink scarcely dry before he set it aside. The letter was brief, direct, and spare in its wording.

Wickham,

Meet me at the glen at the base of Oakham Mount at four o'clock. There is a matter we must settle. Come, or be sought out.

F.D.

Darcy sealed the letter and gave it to Brisby.

"Please see this delivered into Wickham's own hand at the militia barracks...and without delay."

"Yes, sir. At once," his man replied and departed for Meryton.

He did not expect Wickham to come. But if he did, their reckoning would begin.

The wind rustled through the bare limbs of the trees as Darcy stood alone at the edge of the glen, the winter air cutting through his great coat. His horse was tethered nearby, stamping at the cold ground and snorting his breaths into the chill. The stillness with the sound of approaching steps—light at first, then deliberate, even defiant. Wickham emerged from the shadows, his features thunderous.

"I should have known it was you," he spat. "No one else could have turned Meryton against me so quickly."

Wickham had ever been careful to present himself the gentleman—his attire usually arranged with studied precision, his manner calculated to charm. Yet on this day the façade was cracked. His uniform was clean, but it was evident he had dressed in haste, the fastenings misaligned so that it hung crooked upon his frame.

Darcy did not move. "I asked you here that we might speak plainly. I have as little desire for your company as you do for mine." He brushed at an invisible speck upon his sleeve, his hands sheathed in leather gloves. Nothing provoked Wickham more than the show of indifference.

"Plainly?" Wickham gave a bitter laugh. "You mean to justify yourself? Do not feign civility, Darcy. You warned the shopkeepers. Now my debts are called in, I can no longer purchase on credit, and my fellow soldiers, facing the same restrictions, lay the blame at my feet. Once more, you have made me an outcast."

Darcy's voice remained calm, measured. "Your present state is of your own making. Had you proven yourself worthy, I would have granted the living. Instead, you cursed me and then sought to abscond with my sister."

Wickham's jaw tightened. "I was owed that living. Your father promised—" He advanced a step, rage darkening his features.

"My father trusted you," Darcy cut in, his gaze hard. He did not flinch. "But trust is not blind. Your conduct broke every claim you had to his good opinion, and to mine."

"You sanctimonious—" Wickham came nearer, fists clenched. "You think yourself superior because you hide behind duty and pride. You know nothing of what it is to have no portion, no prospects."

Darcy's tone grew colder. "You had every advantage—a generous patron, an education, opportunity. Portion and prospects. Bah! You squandered them on gambling, dissipation, and vice. Do you comprehend what one of my tenants would give for the interest on four thousand pounds? One hundred sixty a year, man!"

The silence stretched between them. Wickham's breath rose white in the frosty air. He offered no reply, though for a moment Darcy thought he discerned regret upon his countenance; or perhaps it was only self-pity.

"I came here," Darcy said at last, "to give you a choice. Leave England and begin anew elsewhere, far removed from those you have deceived. Or remain and face the consequences. Debtors' prison is not merciful, George."

Wickham's expression flickered—anger, calculation, and for an instant, fear. "I shall escape Meryton before the collectors come to call," he seethed.

"I will not see another innocent suffer from your schemes," Darcy pressed. "Not my sister, nor anyone in Meryton. You forget, I hold enough of your debts to see you confined for the rest of your miserable existence."

At this, Wickham paled. "You would not dare," he choked, his eyes bulging. "Your father—he would disapprove! What would he say, were you to send his favorite into that filthy den? I should die there, Darcy!"

"My father would be ashamed of the man you have become." Darcy's reply carried the weight of sorrow. "I thought the world of you when we were boys. I believed we should stand side by side for life. You might have applied your learning and managed Pemberley when your father died. Our own children might have grown together."

Wickham's laugh rang hollow. "I would not want a child of mine, especially a son, to suffer the humiliation of living beneath the shadow of Pemberley's heir," he spat. "Second best, always less. Never good enough."

"You were more than equal, George. My father would not have sponsored your education otherwise. But you looked ever at what you lacked, rather than what you had."

"That is easily said by one born to everything!" Wickham's voice rose, startling a bird from the hedge. "Blast it all, Darcy. Can you not see? One day, something will strike you from your high horse, and then you will know why men turn to dishonorable means."

If only he knew. Elizabeth had already done so. She had humbled him as none other, and he had not grown less honorable for it, but more. Why could Wickham not see that path? Darcy stepped forward then, his words low and firm. "You have three days. Choose."

He turned to go, but Wickham called after him.

"You know I must accept. I need no three days."

Darcy faced his former friend once more. "Very well. I shall write a draft. My man will see you to London. He will give you enough to begin anew. Go where you please, but if you ever return, I shall call in every debt I own and see you locked away forever. Am I understood?"

"Yes, *master*," Wickham sneered. "As the great man commands."

"Careful, Wickham." A mirthless smile crossed his face. "Debtor's prison is still an option. At least then I should know exactly where you are."

Wickham blanched, swallowing hard. He said nothing.

"Be at the Netherfield gatehouse at dawn." Darcy turned his back on Wickham for the last time that day and went to his horse. *If all goes as planned, Wickham will be gone by tomorrow.*

Chapter Sixteen

December 31, 1811
Netherfield Park
Darcy

A LIVERIED FOOTMAN FROM Darcy House had arrived at Netherfield the evening before bearing the seventh gift of Christmas. Though Darcy had wrestled with indecision over the selection, a sincere conversation with the Gardiners a few days earlier had offered inspiration. Their warm praise for the fine wares of Gardiner's Emporium—their pride in quality and uniqueness—had settled his mind. The seventh gift would come from the very heart of her family. Something beautiful, practical, feminine—and personal.

Darcy had penned a note to his steward with careful instructions, detailing precisely what he wished to be procured and how it was to be prepared. The task was not lightly entrusted. He had selected each piece by description, size, and material, requesting that all be wrapped individually in fine cotton squares—items useful in themselves, yet chosen to display forethought.

The footman, Jameson, tall and broad with the air of a seasoned soldier, had delivered the package to Darcy with solemn efficiency. His greater purpose, however, had not merely been to carry a parcel to the Gardiner household, but to stand ready for another mission: to escort George Wickham to London and, ultimately, out of England. Darcy had not forgotten his vow—to Elizabeth and to himself—that he would put an end to Wickham's threats and misdeeds.

Later that night, in the solitude of his guest chamber at Netherfield, Darcy sat at the writing desk with the delicate fans spread before him, inspecting each one with painstaking care. They were exquisite—crafted of varied materials, painted and gilded with refinement. All were perfect for a lady of wit and grace, suitable for assemblies or evenings at the theatre.

He took especial care with the final wrapping, securing the parcel himself and enclosing the seventh stanza of his Twelve Days arrangement in his own hand. The thought of her discovering them filled him with a boyish eagerness. Though he would not witness her delight, the knowledge that she would find joy in it was reward enough.

When prepared, the gift was entrusted to his valet, who would see it placed in the proper hands at first light.

But dawn brought with it a far graver duty.

He rose early, foregoing breakfast, and donned his great coat before the rest of the house had stirred. The morning brought little change in the weather; the air remained raw, the frost lying as heavy as it had all week. He strode to the gatehouse where Jameson waited, arms folded, his posture that of a man braced for unpleasant work.

"He will come?" Jameson asked, eyes still on the road.

Darcy gave a single nod. "He will. Wickham never neglects opportunity; not when it promises money."

They waited in silence as the first tendrils of light crept over the distant hedgerows, catching on the bare branches and turning them to lace against the morning sky. Every hedge and tree seemed cloaked in the glitter of cold fire.

At length, a figure appeared in the lane, sauntering with an ease wholly at odds with his precarious circumstances.

"Good morning, Darcy," Wickham called, his voice too bright, too forced. His gaze flicked from the waiting carriage to Jameson. "I see I am to be chaperoned. How thoughtful."

Darcy did not answer the pleasantry. "Jameson will accompany you. He will see you aboard a vessel bound for the Americas. The funds I have arranged will be delivered at the docks. My man will leave once the ship has cleared the harbor."

"And if I refuse?" Wickham smirk was half-hearted.

"Then you will be escorted to Marshalsea, where you may enjoy the comforts of your own making."

Wickham's features twisted, amusement and bitterness mingled. "Still so cold, Fitz. All business, as ever. Not even a farewell handshake for an old friend?"

"My offer is rescinded in ten seconds if you are not in that carriage." Darcy's words fell like granite, immovable.

"Very well, very well." With a careless flourish, Wickham mounted the steps. "You always did lack a sense of humor."

Jameson followed, shutting the door behind them. The carriage lurched forward.

From within came a muffled remark—Wickham's final barb: "Give my compliments to Georgiana."

A *thud*, followed by a faint *oof*, reached Darcy's ears. A grim smile tugged at his mouth. He had instructed Jameson that Wickham's taunts were not to be indulged. It appeared his man had dealt with the provocation in earnest.

The carriage rolled down the frozen path, wheels crunching against the rime. Darcy let out a breath he had not known he held. It was finished. Wickham was gone.

For so long, the blackguard had coiled a noose around his and Georgiana's lives—deceit, manipulations, debts—and now he had ensnared the people of Meryton as well. At last Wickham was gone, and none of them would be bound by him again. In removing his foe from their lives, he had acted as honor demanded, as justice required. And above all, as love compelled.

He turned back toward Netherfield. The wind swept across his cheeks and lifted the fur collar of his coat. They were safe now. And on the morrow would come the eighth day. When she opened it, would she begin to suspect? Would she smile? The notion warmed him more than the wan morning light.

December 31, 1811
Elizabeth

> *On the seventh day of Christmas,*
> *With a flourish so grand,*
> *Seven painted fans*
> *From a faraway land.*

The morning began much as others had of late, with frost upon the panes and the same still, wintry cold. Yet for Elizabeth there was a brightness in it, for she woke with the happy expectation of another gift. Already dressed in a simple gown, she was fastening her sash when Jane entered her bedchamber, eager to hand over the latest delivery.

"Another parcel has arrived for you, Lizzy." Jane held up a box in the now-familiar style, wrapped in brown paper and tied with string. She came to her sister's side and dropped it into Elizabeth's lap and clapped her hands once.

"I am very excited to see what lies within. How are you not bursting with curiosity?"

Elizabeth laughed. "Oh, but I am, dearest, I assure you."

Jane sighed, a fleeting bit of envy mingling with her smile, yet her eyes shone with genuine happiness for her sister. "It is very romantic. How carefully your admirer woos you."

"Goodness, Jane, is Mr. Bingley such a poor lover that you must live vicariously through me?" Elizabeth's playfulness made her sister laugh.

"No, Charles is not lacking; but 'tis exciting to witness what new treasure this mysterious gentleman presents. Now hurry and open it!"

Elizabeth pulled the string, her heart fluttering more than she cared to admit. "Seven swans a-swimming?" she guessed, her voice laced with dry humor.

Jane laughed as she leaned closer. "I suspect this suitor has something more fashionable in mind. Open it!"

With unsteady fingers, Elizabeth folded back the paper. Within, laid upon tissue and wrapped in neat cotton squares, were seven exquisite fans—each one more beautiful than the last.

Elizabeth sat stunned, a hand rising to her mouth. "Oh..."

Each fan was unique, though clearly part of a set. One was made of black lacquered wood, its surface edged with delicate gold filigree, French in design. Another was ivory, with the silk panels embroidered and painted with pastoral scenes. A third boasted rich navy silk stitched with silver stars, the thread catching in the morning light. The fourth was bamboo and paper, hand-painted with cranes and lotus blossoms, surely imported from Asia. Another bore Spanish boldness, red lace over bone sticks, vivid and flirtatious. The sixth was simple yet refined: white silk mounted on mother-of-pearl sticks, embroidered with pale pink roses. The last, Elizabeth's favorite, was pale green silk with gold leaf detail, bordered in the faintest blush of rose.

"They are breathtaking," Jane whispered in awe. "And see—each one is wrapped in a cotton square—handkerchiefs, perhaps? 'Tis two gifts in one."

Elizabeth lifted one of the squares. It was supple, finely woven, the edges neatly hemmed and ready for embroidery. "How lovely," she murmured, stroking the weave. "What shall I place in the corner?" If only she knew her generous admirer's name—she would work his initials on at least one.

Jane peered over her shoulder. "Whoever he is, he knows you well." She looked at her sister with a curious tilt of her head. "Have you no suspicions, Lizzy?"

Elizabeth returned the fans and cloths back to the box and folded the paper once more, as though preserving the mystery might quiet her tumult within. "I have entertained many notions. But no—I cannot say who is behind these gifts."

That was not wholly true. She had begun to wonder—no, to hope—that it might be Mr. Darcy. Each time he called with Mr. Bingley, her heart faltered and her stomach fluttered with anticipation. She looked forward to their walks, hoping he would offer his arm.

More than that, his name arose in her thoughts, unbidden. Of late, his presence at Longbourn had been marked by civility and accompanied by a most attentive manner. Where once she despised him, now she longed for his conversation. He spoke with greater ease, asked after her reading, her opinions, and her memories. In his eyes she discerned a warmth she had not seen before—or perhaps had not allowed herself to see.

In truth, she had long since dismissed the prejudice she once held against him. The tales of his pride and interference had lost their edge in the face of his recent kindnesses. His steadiness, his patience—even with her most trying relations—had not gone unnoticed.

She thought of what she had heard from him of his tender care for his sister, of the sincerity with which he confessed his faults. He had told her, with more feeling than she had credited him, that he had been raised to think meanly of others; she knew he was striving to do better.

No, she would not name him, not even to Jane. It was folly to attach such meaning to anonymous gifts. And yet...the fans were too elegant, too carefully chosen, to be the work of common taste or means.

She faced her sister, diverting the subject. "I am only glad you have found someone to love. Mr. Bingley is an excellent man, and your happiness brings me joy beyond measure."

Jane's smile widened. "And what of your own happiness, Lizzy? Do you not think yourself worthy of such gifts?"

Elizabeth flushed and turned aside. "I think...I think I am still learning of what I am worthy."

Later that morning, the parlor was unusually still. The three younger Bennets had gone to Meryton in search of a diversion. Their peace was shattered when Lydia burst in like a storm wind, her voice loud enough to make even Jane start and drop her embroidery. Kitty followed close behind, protesting that *she* ought to be the one to tell the news.

"Wickham has left the regiment!" Lydia declared, wide-eyed and breathless. She raised her voice over Kitty's complaints. "He has gone! Disappeared! And poor Miss King—she is in tears."

"What?" Mrs. Bennet nearly spilled her tea. "What do you mean, gone?" She set her work aside and gave her full attention to her youngest child. "Tell me everything."

"Her uncle arrived from Liverpool," Lydia said, throwing herself into the nearest chair in high dudgeon. "The gossips say he heard some unsavory tale of Wickham and told freckled Mary she could not marry such a man—as if any of it were true! He carried her straight back to Liverpool with him saying there would be no match. And Wickham? He vanished—*before* the Kings even knew he had gone."

Mary stood in the doorway, cheeks warm. "It is shameful to abandon one's post in a time of war." Elizabeth pressed her lips together to hide a smile.

Their mother seemed to agree. "Quite shameful," Mrs. Bennet huffed. "And after we were so good to him! To leave the militia so suddenly! Who will protect Meryton now?"

Lydia rolled her eyes. "There are others enough to do that. The officers are searching for him. But 'tis a scandal, that is what it is. He was the handsomest of all the officers. I am certain I shall die without him."

Mary's color deepened as she looked down. "Not all redcoats are dishonorable," she murmured. Elizabeth guessed her sister's mind was with Mr. Sanderson, who had lately returned her dropped prayer book with gallantry and continued to call. They seemed to be getting on well.

Elizabeth held her peace, though her mind was in turmoil. Mr. Wickham gone? What could it mean? Was it linked to what Sir William had uncovered about his debts in Meryton? The shopkeepers had begun to whisper, and Mr. King had lost no time in removing his niece.

Could Mr. Darcy have had a hand in the lieutenant's sudden disappearance? Her chest tightened. Had he acted upon what she told him? She recalled their conversation in the drawing room but a day earlier—his stricken look, as though guilt or his late father's memory pressed upon him. She had not believed he would not stir himself to intervene in his former friend's affairs. Yet it seemed he had already fulfilled that vow. Once more, she had misjudged him.

Elizabeth's thoughts returned to the fans, now hidden with the other tokens of affection she had received. Seven days. Seven thoughtful gifts. Seven moments of wonder, confusion—and hope. She could not name her admirer. But with growing certainty, she knew who she wished him to be.

Later that evening, Elizabeth sat at her writing desk intending to write in her journal, one of the gifted quills in hand, but no words came. The candle beside her guttered low, throwing wavering shadows across the page, while the paper remained untouched. The day had left her unsettled, not with alarm, but with a restless mingling of thought and emotion that would not be stilled.

Her eyes drifted toward the wardrobe. Almost without thought, she rose to retrieve one of the gifts. Her fingers closed around the ivory fan—the one adorned with a pastoral scene painted with such delicate strokes that the tiny shepherdess beneath the tree seemed to move in the candlelight. Elizabeth carried it back to her desk and unfolded it, the whisper of silk on polished sticks soothing her mind.

The fan, with its tranquil scene, set her to picturing Pemberley as she had heard it described—broad landscapes, ordered and serene, echoing a world of taste and stately grace. Such a house, she mused, must surely reflect the character of its master—controlled, elegant, and deeply thoughtful.

She held the fan close to her face and let her fancy wander. She saw herself at an assembly, standing amidst a glittering throng, catching Mr. Darcy's eye across the room. Would he notice the fan in her hand and know it as his gift, if indeed it came from him? Would he allow the barest hint of a smile? He looked so handsome when he smiled.

The notion made her blush. She snapped the fan closed, the warmth rising in her cheeks not unwelcome. She had not sought his attention—not at first. Now, with each passing day, her feelings shifted like the tide, slow but inexorable.

If it was Mr. Darcy—if he truly stood behind the twelve days of Christmas—what then? Could such careful tokens be a silent courtship, a way of proving not only his affection, but his constancy and depth?

Her thoughts were a blend of wonder and trepidation. She had long prided herself on her discernment, her wit, her independence. Yet as she reflected on all her suppositions regarding him—his pride, his arrogance, his cruelty—it was with a sense of humility that bordered on awe.

She had been mistaken. Not merely in him, but in herself. She had let first impressions, wounded pride, and the words of a charming deceiver sway her judgment. But now...now she saw more plainly. In the steadiness of Mr. Darcy's manner, in his efforts to make amends, in the quiet strength with which he bore himself even among her family, she saw a man deserving of her esteem, perhaps even of her affection.

She smiled to herself, her heart warming against the chill. She could not be certain of the sender. No name, no confession, no signature betrayed him. But her heart whispered a name nonetheless—not with assurance, but with yearning.

Elizabeth turned her eyes back to the sheet of paper before her. It remained blank, though her mind was crowded—with questions, with possibilities, and with desires newly awakened. She dipped her quill, but still she did not write. Instead, she leaned back, looking through the window, where stars pricked the winter sky and the moon laid silver across the fields.

Seven gifts had come. Each more personal than the last. And with each, her defenses had fallen, like leaves fading in autumn.

One truth was clear now: her heart was no longer indifferent. And perhaps the finest gift would not be the seventh nor the eighth, but the last. For that gift might hold more than a token—it might bring her the answer. And just maybe, it might bring him.

Chapter Seventeen

January 1, 1812
Longbourn
Elizabeth

THE PARCEL AWAITING ELIZABETH that morning was heavier than any she had yet received. She paused as she lifted it, her arms straining beneath the weight, curiosity piqued. As always, a neat billet awaited her, the elegant hand she now knew so well, lay atop the brown wrapping as before:

> *On the eighth day of Christmas,*
> *With words soft and sweet,*
> *Eight books of poetry,*
> *Bound in gold leaf.*

Her eyes widened. With careful fingers, she untied the twine and peeled back the paper. Within lay a breathtaking collection—eight volumes of poetry, each bound in rich, supple leather, the titles gilded upon the spines, every one adorned with a ribbon marker of a different hue. A delighted gasp escaped her as she traced her fingers along the golden script with a reverent touch.

She read each title aloud, almost as if invoking them.

"*Lyrical Ballads* by Wordsworth and Coleridge... *The Works of Alexander Pope*... *The Poetical Works of Thomas Gray*... *Poems in Two Volumes* by Wordsworth—how generous!... *The Task* by Cowper... *The Seasons* by James Thomson... *The Works of John Milton*... and—oh!—*Poems* by Charlotte Smith."

Within each cover, she discovered a bookplate, delicately secured, blank save for a flourish that seemed to beckon her to inscribe her name. Her hand trembled as she opened the last volume and turned to a familiar piece.

She released a long breath. "Beautiful," she murmured, overcome not merely by the verse but by the thoughtfulness of the gift. Surely, only one who knew her heart could have chosen such titles, and bound so exquisitely that they were works of art in themselves.

Jane entered, halting mid-step at the sight of books arrayed across Elizabeth's lap. She pressed a hand to her mouth, astonishment written plain upon her features.

"Good heavens, Lizzy. These must have cost a small fortune." She moved forward, bending to examine them more closely. "They are bound like presentation copies. I should think the set might fetch five or even ten guineas; they must be very dear indeed." She lifted one and smoothed a hand across the leather, admiration plain in her manner.

Elizabeth gave a breathless laugh. "Whoever sent them must know me well indeed, Jane. This is my dearest gift by far—and one Lydia will never contrive to pilfer. I may display them openly...unlike the rest."

Their shared laughter lingered as Elizabeth bore each volume to her modest bookcase beneath the window. There, nestled among well-thumbed essays, novels, and books of travel, the new treasures found their place. She stepped back to regard the transformation. Her little library had never looked so elegant.

"Now, let me help you dress," Jane offered kindly.

Elizabeth allowed herself to be fussed over, stepping into her long-sleeved morning gown of sprigged muslin. She drew a warm shawl about her shoulders, its cream fringe trailing, while Jane arranged her hair into a neat chignon.

While Jane worked, Elizabeth's thoughts wandered—to a pair of proud eyes, to the warmth of a hand at Lucas Lodge, to the reverence with which he had once spoken of poetry. Mr. Darcy—no, Darcy—for the man who had written such verses and chosen such thoughtful gifts could hardly be the same proud gentleman she once dismissed. This was the name her heart had begun to whisper.

"Did you hear me, Lizzy? You are woolgathering," Jane teased, smiling as she fastened the final pin.

Elizabeth started from her reverie. "I beg your pardon—what did you say?" Heat touched her cheeks. *Stop this folly. You do not even know if it is him.*

"I asked if you thought the gentlemen would call. It is the first day of the new year." Jane stepped back to admire her work.

Elizabeth looked to the window, the frost at its edges giving way to beads of melting dew. "I cannot say," she replied truthfully. "But…I think I should like it if they did."

The breakfast table at Longbourn was in its usual state of morning commotion. Lydia and Kitty were engaged in a spirited debate on the relative merits of the officers quartered in Meryton. They bickered at the end of the table, scarcely attending to their breakfast.

"Colonel Forster is far more handsome," Kitty declared, spreading jam upon her scone.

"He may be handsome," Lydia retorted, "but he is also *married*. Besides, Lieutenant Pratt has five hundred a year and the bluest eyes I have ever seen. And he danced with me twice." She released a sigh, her gaze dreamy as she absentmindedly forked a bite of egg.

Mary, who had been silently stirring her tea, lifted her eyes. "I dare say such trifles are not the best measure of a gentleman's character or suitability—"

"Oh, do not speak of suitability, Mary," Lydia broke in with a scoff. "Just because Sanderson has shown you the smallest notice does not mean we wish to hear your opinions on love or courtship. You are such a dull, colorless creature!"

Kitty giggled into her teacup. "Yes, it is not as if you are an authority now."

"Kitty, Lydia," Jane interposed gently, "that is unkind. Everyone deserves to be heard, regardless of *your* opinions." Ever the peacemaker, Jane's tones did not rise above their usual calm measure. She buttered a muffin and added preserves, pausing only to lift her eyes in gentle reproof at her younger sisters.

Mr. Bennet glanced up from his plate, amusement glinting in his eyes. "I begin to suspect I am breakfasting with a gaggle of geese, all honking over one another without pause." He laughed at his own joke before folding his newspaper and rising. "If you will excuse me, I find the morning news may be enjoyed in a quieter corner than this menagerie."

As he quitted the room, Mrs. Bennet, seated at the opposite end of the table, called after him, "Mr. Bennet! I intend to have Mr. Bingley and Mr. Darcy dine with us this evening."

From the hall came his indifferent reply. "Invite the whole county, my dear, so long as the meal is as delicious as ever."

After breakfast, the family repaired to the drawing room. Elizabeth excused herself and ascended to her chamber, where she retrieved *Lyrical Ballads* from its new place in her bookcase. The navy leather cover gleamed in the morning light, its gilded edges and title shimmering with subtle splendor. A crimson ribbon slipped from between its pages like a whisper of hidden ardour, and she lingered a moment, stroking its silken end.

Book in hand, she hastened to the drawing room, where her sisters and mother were occupied with their customary pursuits, from embroidery to the trimming of bonnets. Drawing her shawl close about her shoulders, Elizabeth seated herself by the window and opened the volume where it chanced to fall to a poem she had read before. But the lines seemed altered, as though a shift within her heart allowed the words to strike deeper root.

"Lizzy?"

She looked up to see Mary standing before her, curiosity evident.

"That book—I have never seen it in your keeping. I do not recall it from Papa's library." Mary's manner was even, though her eyes behind the spectacles were wide.

Elizabeth's cheeks warmed. "No," she answered too quickly. "You have not." She closed the book with deliberate care, tucking the ribbon within, then clasped it to her breast.

Mary's lips pressed together, her dissatisfaction plain. Before Elizabeth could frame a plausible explanation, Hill appeared and announced, "Mr. Bingley and Mr. Darcy, ma'am."

Elizabeth rose as the gentlemen entered. Mr. Bingley's gaze flew at once to Jane, his countenance bright with unstudied affection. Darcy's eyes, however, sought Elizabeth, and he advanced toward her with deliberate grace. She was struck afresh by the distinction of his figure—tall and broad-shouldered, with hair of deep brown touched by the natural curl where it brushed his collar. Upon his finger gleamed a heavy gold signet ring, one she marveled she had not noticed before.

Presently, he stood before her. "It gladdens me to find you well, Miss Elizabeth."

She still clutched the book of poems. "Indeed, I am quite well, thank you. I have been reflecting on the nature of misjudgment."

His gaze sharpened. "Have you?"

She allowed a small smile. "Yes. For instance, my sister Mary. I once thought her overly solemn, pedantic even. Yet of late she seems transformed." Elizabeth turned slightly, her eyes falling upon Mary.

Darcy followed her glance. Mary had gone to sit near the pianoforte, her posture easier, her features touched with something almost tender.

"There is a gentleness in her now," Elizabeth continued. "She smiles more freely. She listens before she speaks. 'Tis...remarkable." Truly, Mary had never looked better. Even her attire was altered; instead of drab gowns, she wore delicate colors, likely long neglected in the back of her closet.

"Love," Darcy observed, the word falling from his lips with unguarded warmth, "can have that effect on a person."

The remark startled her, and Elizabeth tilted her head. "You believe her in love?" She herself believed it, though if Mr. Sanderson simply trifled with Mary's heart, he was unworthy indeed. *I pray for Mary's sake he is not such a man.*

"I do. I have become more observant of late," he added sheepishly with a rueful smile.

Elizabeth studied him closely. There was something beneath his words, something withheld. He was not merely reflecting on Mary. *Could he be reflecting* on *himself?* His manner had altered so greatly since November. Perhaps he had examined his behavior and found it wanting.

She felt the weight of his gaze; the silence between them charged with a meaning neither was ready to reveal. "Speaking of love," she ventured, "Miss King has not been so fortunate in that regard. Wickham is gone." In expectation, she willed him to answer.

"Yes, I had something to do with it," he admitted without hesitation. "I offered him an opportunity he could not refuse. I pray he finds contentment in his new life."

Before she could make a reply, Mrs. Bennet's voice rang from across the room, shattering the spell. "Gentlemen! You must return for dinner this evening! I insist!"

Mr. Bingley laughed and turned toward the door. "It would be our pleasure, Mrs. Bennet."

Darcy looked away from Elizabeth, inclining his head towards her mother. "We are at your service, madam."

Elizabeth clutched her book to her breast once more and allowed herself an unspoken thought. *He is watching. And he sees me now.* Something within her longed to reach for his hand, but she resisted. *It is him. It must be.* The idea that her admirer could be anyone else was intolerable. *But does Darcy know me so well?* She could not be certain.

The gentlemen departed after tea with a promise to return for dinner that evening. Mrs. Bennet's praises of Mr. Bingley flowed unrestrained—indeed, they pursued him, and Mr. Darcy as well, out the very door of Longbourn, trailing after them like overexcited hounds in full cry. Her volume and zeal were such that Elizabeth felt certain the gentlemen heard her acclamations well into the lane.

Elizabeth remained at the parlor window, feigning interest in the waning light, but in truth she inwardly recoiled from the memory of her mother's exclamations and her sisters' poorly concealed giggles. Mortification washed over her in waves. Never had she been so acutely aware of her family's failings. Not even at the Netherfield ball, when Lydia had danced too freely and her mother had proclaimed Jane's prospects so openly, had she felt such humiliation.

When the gentlemen's carriage vanished from view, Elizabeth pled fatigue and withdrew upstairs. Once within the sanctuary of her bedchamber, she sank into the window seat, her shawl draped loosely about her shoulders, and stared out at the wintry garden below. Her thoughts ran in restless circles.

Why did her mother's behavior wound her so keenly? It was nothing new. She had grown accustomed to it. And yet…it mattered now as it had never done before. She did not need long to find the reason.

Her feelings for Darcy—once denied, then scorned, and at last reluctantly acknowledged—had taken root. And now those roots twisted with unease. *What must he think of us? Of me?*

With a determined shake of her head, she strove to cast the thought aside. It was foolish to dwell on it. She could not be certain of Darcy's affections; he had not declared them. And yet, she could not help but hope.

The creak of her door roused from her reverie. Mary entered, crossed her arms and lifted her chin with purpose. "I am ready, Elizabeth," she said with arch precision, and perched plump on the edge of the bed.

Elizabeth blinked. "Pardon?"

"I am ready to hear your explanation for possessing the book you were reading before the callers arrived—*Lyrical Ballads,* was it? I did not recognize the binding. Meryton's bookseller would never stock such a fine volume. Did Uncle Gardiner bring it from Town?"

Elizabeth felt the heat rise in her cheeks. "No," she admitted slowly.

Mary's air turned inquisitive. "Then from whence did it come?"

Elizabeth sighed and gestured with the book. "Very well. But you must promise not to tell Lydia. Or Kitty. Or Mama."

Mary inclined her head solemnly. "You have my word."

Thus compelled, Elizabeth unfolded the tale: the first unexpected gift with its accompanying verse, then each new token in turn, culminating in that morning's treasure trove of poetry. Mary's countenance shifted as the story progressed—from suspicion to surprise, from doubt to dawning wonder.

"And there has been no hint of the sender?" Mary asked, voice hushed.

Elizabeth shook her head.

"It is highly improper," Mary muttered, frowning. "A gentleman ought not to send a lady anonymous gifts—it borders on scandal."

"I know," Elizabeth groaned, throwing up her hands. "Believe me, I have argued the matter with myself for days. Yet secret admirers are not unheard of."

Marry's disapproval remained. "What if it should prove someone unsuitable? A married man, as Charlotte suggested?"

Elizabeth held up a hand. "Then, as Papa says, *'a girl likes to be crossed in love now and then. It is something to think of, and gives her a sort of distinction among her companions.'* I have chosen to no longer torment myself. If the man reveals himself, and if his intentions are honorable, he already holds some part of my esteem—he has gone to great effort, and each gift has been thoughtful and personal."

Mary pursed her lips but offered no further censure on the matter. At length, her eyes fell to her hands resting on her lap. "Do you think Mr. Sanderson truly admires me? I know I am not the prettiest Bennet sister, nor the most clever."

Elizabeth left her place at the window and sat beside her sister, slipping an arm gently around her shoulders. "If he is playing with your heart, Mary, I shall march to Meryton and tell the whole regiment of his misdeeds." Mary managed a small smile. "But in truth, I believe he does admire you. I have never seen you glow as you do when he speaks to you."

Mary's smile broadened, and the reserve she usually carried seemed to lift. "Thank you," she whispered.

"Now," Mary said briskly, rising with renewed purpose, "let us choose something for you to wear for supper. We must find a gown that best becomes your trinkets and baubles."

Elizabeth laughed, light and genuine. "Yes, by all means—let us dazzle."

Together they moved to the closet, the easy companionship of sisters blossoming in the aftermath of secrets shared and worries eased.

Chapter Eighteen

January 1, 1812
Longbourn
Darcy

BINGLEY CHATTERED ENTHUSIASTICALLY AS the carriage rolled toward Longbourn. Darcy listened with but half an ear, his mind dwelling upon Elizabeth and what her reaction to the eighth gift had been that morning.

"You may cavil at Mrs. Bennet all you like, Darcy, but you must allow that she sets a fine table. I can scarce wait. Meat pies, pastries, rolls, preserves, pheasant, duck, goose, venison—I have never quitted her table unsatisfied."

"What?" Darcy looked across the carriage toward his friend. "Forgive me. I was not attending."

Bingley laughed. "And here I thought your silence as proof of disdain."

"I have endeavored to behave better these last weeks." He shifted in his seat. "Mrs. Bennet has grown kinder toward me—surely you have marked it."

"Indeed, I have. I meant no offense. The neighborhood takes pleasure in our company, and I have no cause to repine. Pray, forgive my jest."

"Think nothing of it. I must also agree with you. Mrs. Bennet lays a fine table. She would rank among London's most notable hostesses, had she the means. Indeed, the fare at Longbourn rivals my Aunt Catherine's." His aunt's dishes, in truth, often left Darcy ill, their richness lying heavily upon the stomach. In contrast, Mrs. Bennet saw to it that her guests departed gratified rather than burdened.

The carriage drew up, and Bingley sprang out. Darcy descended at a more deliberate pace. The shadows of late afternoon had long since melted into darkness.

In a moment, the gentlemen were announced. As they entered the drawing room, fire and candlelight created shifting patterns across the floor. From beyond came the clatter of dinner preparations, yet here there reigned only the rustle of pages and the murmur of low conversation.

The two youngest Bennets shared a settee, whispering together over fashion plates, unheeding of the gentlemen's arrival. Miss Mary sat at the pianoforte playing a sonata, while Sanderson dutifully turned the leaves.

Bingley went directly to Miss Bennet, who rose to receive him with warmth, smiling as he placed a gallant kiss upon her hand. Darcy scanned the room until his eyes rested on the lady he most longed to see.

Elizabeth, who had yet to look up, sat near the window, where the glow of candles lent auburn fire to the darker shades of her curls. Her hands held a volume Darcy recognized as *Lyrical Ballads*. Her fingers traced the fine paper, her whole manner intent, as if savoring each word by touch alone, her lips parted in silent contemplation. The shawl about her shoulders slipped as she turned a page, the fringe brushing her wrist in a delicate fall.

He remained at a distance, hesitant to intrude upon her contemplations. He had come to Longbourn intent on speaking with her, on strengthening whatever sentiments she might have begun to feel for him, on inspiring in her a tenderness to equal his own—to love him as he loved her.

Something in the hushed intimacy of the scene held him still. The very air seemed alive with unspoken feeling, and his heart quickened as he yearned to remain within its spell. At length, he made his way to her.

"Good evening, Miss Elizabeth."

She raised her eyes from the book with a smile of gentle surprise.

"Mr. Darcy! I was so engaged with the page that I could not lift my eyes sooner."

"I beg your pardon. I did not wish to intrude. You appeared...absorbed." His heart thundered as she gestured to the chair next to hers, inviting him to sit.

"I was." Elizabeth held up the book. "Absorbed, that is. Wordsworth has a way of drawing one in. He writes as though nature itself were a companion—as though emotion and landscape are one."

Darcy nodded, moving his chair nearer. "Wordsworth," he repeated, tasting the name upon his tongue. "I have read him, though not in recent months." He recognized the volume as one that he had included among the gifts. "A handsome copy—finer than the one I have in my library at Pemberley." It was true; the one he owned had grown worn from frequent reading.

"Do you enjoy poetry, Mr. Darcy? I have lately become rather fond of it."

A low chuckle escaped him. "I recall your opinion once being quite the reverse." The corners of his mouth curved as he studied her, waiting for recognition. He was not disappointed as he noted the recollection in her eyes.

Elizabeth laughed outright. "'I wondered who first discovered the efficacy of poetry in driving away love!' Yes, I remember it well."

Darcy assumed a veneer of hauteur. "'I have been used to consider poetry as the food of love.' Imagine my mortification when I turned to

Shakespeare that evening, only to discover the line referred to music, not verse."

"Yes, I knew it then." Her mirth continued as she leaned forward, quoting herself. "*'Of a fine, stout, healthy love, poetry may feed and nourish. Everything nourishes what is strong already. But if it be only a slight, thin sort of inclination, I am convinced that one good sonnet will starve it entirely.'*" She sobered. "I have since learned that a well-wrought stanza may hold the power to persuade to love."

She looked at him expectantly, and Darcy swallowed hard, torn between longing to reveal himself, and fearing her reply. Would she welcome the truth of his heart? All seemed to encourage him, yet still he faltered. At last, he spoke.

"There is power in its economy—a world conveyed in but a few lines." He silently willed her to take his meaning—that he was her secret admirer, though he shrank from full avowal. To ease the moment, he gave her a wry smile. "I confess I am not always equal to discerning the intent of the great poets. My own attempts fall far short."

Elizabeth regarded him, a knowing glint in her eyes, then released a soft laugh. "That is the beauty of poetry. It speaks differently to each reader, and sometimes differently at each reading." Her hands caressed the book with reverence. "I am very grateful I am in possession of so many such treasures."

She set the book upon the side table, her fingers still lingering over the binding before letting it rest. Darcy marked the motion, inexplicably struck by it—the tenderness she bestowed on something others might call ordinary. *Not ordinary,* he thought. *She sees the gift for what it is.*

"Have you a favorite poet?" she asked, turning her attention wholly to him.

He hesitated. "I once believed it to be Milton. The grandeur, the command of language...it appealed to my youth. But of late, I find myself drawn to gentler voices."

Elizabeth tilted her head. "Gentler voices?"

He met her eyes. "Those who speak less of heroics and more of understanding...of the soul in quiet places." Darcy waited, his heart suspended. for her reply.

Elizabeth

Elizabeth felt a flutter in her chest. She had not expected such an answer. "Then Wordsworth may suit you after all."

Darcy leaned nearer, the space between them narrowing until she could scarcely draw breath. The tilt of her head brought her so close she might have felt his warmth upon her cheek, and a shiver passed through her at the thought of what a kiss might be. When he drew back, disappointment pricked, though she told herself it was folly.

"And you, Miss Elizabeth? Have you a favorite?" His reply was steady, though the faintest catch betrayed itself as he withdrew.

"It changes with the seasons, I think. Her smile warmed. "Yet I often return to Cowper. There is a sincerity in his melancholy that does not weigh one down. And Charlotte Smith—her verses are like confidences whispered in the dark."

Milton, Cowper, Charlotte Smith, Wordsworth... She ticked the names silently. Four of the eight from that morning's gift. *'Tis him. It must be him. Then why does he not yet speak?*

Darcy's look carried a warmth she had not observed in him before. "On occasion, I take pleasure in Pope. But *you* read poetry as if it were a tongue learned from birth. That is enviable." He paused. "My sister inclines towards Gray, Thomson, and Coleridge. I wish she may come to comprehend them as you do. "

A light laugh escaped her. "Perhaps I only feign understanding, and the verses are too kind to betray me. As for Miss Darcy, she is still young. Her comprehension will deepen with time."

Darcy's eyes strayed to the book resting on the side table. "You appeared lost in thought when I entered."

Elizabeth dropped her gaze to the cover. "There was a passage that struck me." She leafed through the volume, then held it out. "Here: *One impulse from a vernal wood may teach you more of man...* There is tenderness in the notion that nature may guide us when society and words fall short." Had she not learned more of Darcy amidst fields and gardens than in all the drawing rooms of Meryton?

He regarded her in stillness, his countenance grave. "I envy those who find clarity in verse. I often perplex myself with over-fine distinctions where all ought to be plain."

"You make it sound as though verse conspires against you. How is that so?"

"In conversation, particularly. I do not always say what I mean. Or rather, I say it poorly—too direct, or too guarded—and the sense is lost. Writing has always been preferable. It grants time to weigh each phrase, to consider what may be implied. I am no poet, but I can frame a fair letter."

"Is that why you turn to poetry? Because another has already found the words?" The thought explained much—his reserve, the hauteur she once mistook for pride, the effort he must have made of late to appear more open.

A flicker of surprise, then gratitude, crossed his countenance. "Yes. Precisely."

She returned a small smile, hoping it conveyed gentleness and understanding, and...dare she consider it—*love*. "I think many feel that way, Mr. Darcy. Even those who speak readily. There is safety in poetry; it does not intrude."

He gave a low laugh, touched with boyishness. "Indeed." His hand stirred against his knee, as though some impulse urged it forward. A sudden desire that he might take hers rose within her, and she felt her heart beat all the faster for it.

She held still, willing her heart to calm. "I sometimes wonder if that is why some look to books of poetry—lest they crush what has scarcely begun to grow. Yet they need not. If a sentiment is genuine, it will flourish. Depth of feeling can be shown without words."

The remark settled between them like snow—silent, but undeniable. She thought she discerned understanding in his eyes. *I care for you,* she longed to say, but the first avowal must be his. *What if I mistake the matter? What if I am mistaken altogether, and it is not him?*

"Yes. New feeling is fragile. One word spoken too soon—or too carelessly—and it may be lost."

Elizabeth kept her eyes upon him, searching. "But silence may also destroy." *Please understand me!*

He nodded, his features gentling. "A more cunning destroyer, perhaps."

They lingered in that quiet communion until footsteps sounded from the hall—Mrs. Bennet's shrill fussing announced her approach, and the company looked expectantly on as the matriarch bustled in.

Elizabeth glanced toward the door. "It seems supper is nearly ready."

Darcy inclined his head. "I believe you are correct."

She rose, slipping the book into a workbasket beneath her chair. "Just in case," she murmured. Lydia could be unpredictable.

They moved together toward the door. There was no grand declaration, no dramatic transformation—yet something shifted. A thread spun between them—slender, silken—holding promise of what might bloom if nurtured.

And for once, neither sought words. The silence was enough.

Darcy

Darcy stood at the window of his bedchamber at Netherfield. The waning gibbous moon shed a pale, silvery light upon the landscape, where snow dusted the hedgerows and softened their outline. Within, however, his thoughts churned with anything but serenity.

Elizabeth knew.

She had not said so outright, but there had been a flicker in her eyes when they spoke of poetry that evening. The volume of *Lyrical Ballads* was one of the eight leather-bound books of poetry, he had chosen with care, each marked with his favorite verses. She had let her fingers trace the gilded title, smiling in a way he now recognized as genuine pleasure. Then she raised her eyes to his, and in that instant something passed between them—recognition, or understanding, perhaps.

She suspects at the very least. And she does not appear averse.

That thought alone unmoored him. In darker moments, he had feared her recoil—feared that she would laugh, or shrink from the affection revealed in his gifts. Instead, she had received each token, and now with what he dared to believe was curiosity; even gratitude.

He turned from the window and paced the room like a man beset. Four days remained—four carefully chosen offerings still to come. Four more chances to tell her what his heart longed to utter openly. Yet with so little time left, he found himself caught in a paradox.

Should he tell her now?

Part of him—impetuous, yearning—longed to do so, to lay all before her and hear his name spoken without reserve. Had he not already revealed enough? Had she not, in her manner, responded?

But the other part, the one schooled in caution and honor, held him back. From the outset he had meant to remain unnamed until the twelfth day. Not as some idle amusement, but as a true gift: a way to approach her not as Fitzwilliam Darcy of Pemberley, but as a man who admired her, who saw her, and sought to prove that she was valued beyond measure.

He had guarded every word in her presence. And now she suspected, yet did not turn away. That was progress; it was more than he had once dared believe possible.

Would he risk unsettling the balance?

Darcy pressed a hand through his hair. No, he would not hasten what had taken such care to cultivate. The final four days were not mere formality. They were a chance to deepen their understanding, to move from admiration to affection, from wonder to warmth.

But the last day...it must be different. A culmination not only of gifts, but of feeling. She deserved more than trinkets and riddles. She deserved the truth.

He would wait. He would see the twelve days through. But on the twelfth—yes, then—he would speak. And he would hope—pray—that what he had begun in secret might find its rightful answer in her heart.

Darcy glanced once more through the glass. Snow had begun to fall once more, a steady veil descending. Four days. He could endure four days.

After all, he had waited a lifetime for someone like her.

Chapter Nineteen

January 2, 1812
Longbourn
Elizabeth

ELIZABETH WOKE WITH A start, her breath catching as the last threads of a dream clung like morning mist. Her eyes opened to the pale dawn glimmering at the casement, yet she wished with every fiber of her being to slip beneath the coverlet and return to that strange, tender vision. In the dream, Darcy had confessed his love, a truth spoken with a gentleness and certainty she had never dared expect. He was the secret admirer who had sent the gifts, those mysterious tokens of regard that had charmed her for more than a week past.

The memory of his words, deep and unwavering, lingered as she reluctantly put aside the warmth of her bed. "It was I," he had said, "who admired you from afar."

A blush rose even in the solitude of her chamber. She wished the dream were real, yet feared it was but her heart's yearning at play. Still, the tender promise glimmered like a secret light in the early gloom.

Her attention shifted to the small table near the window, where the previous gifts had appeared overnight—delicate, thoughtful, and extravagant in their several ways. There, among the remnants of the last, stood another parcel, larger than any before: an elaborate bandbox tied with silk ribbons that gleamed in the morning light.

"Surely he did not gift me nine hats!" she murmured, a wry smile tugging at her lips as she swung her legs to the floor. The boards were chill against her bare feet, but she paid it no mind. Curiosity and wonder carried her forward.

She crossed the room and lifted the lid with careful fingers, revealing a stack of finely folded fabrics. A neatly penned note lay within—the next stanza of the mysterious rhyme:

On the ninth day of Christmas,
Through streets lined with frost,
Nine shawls to soften
The chill winter tossed.

(Woven of silk,
From a Bond Street display,
To warm gentle shoulders
In fine winter gray.)

Her thoughts strayed to Darcy's claim the previous evening that he was no poet. The rhyme's cadence might halt in places, yet her heart was all the warmer for it. *"Not the best verse,"* she allowed, *though I do not care.* She looked further into the box and caught her breath. The splendor of the gift silenced any further censure. Each shawl was exquisite, the patterns delicate and varied, textures rich and inviting, their colors ranging from muted grays and blues to creamy ivories, all perfectly suited to the season fast advancing upon the countryside.

Her fingers traced the edge of the top shawl, a shawl from Kashmir, the finest cashmere wool she had ever touched. The fabric was warm and light, the intricate paisley seeming almost to dance beneath her hand. Such pieces, she knew, were handwoven with exquisite care and often reserved for the wealthiest and most discerning ladies.

Beneath it lay an Indian shawl, of greater weight, with a rich pattern of gold and crimson woven through the wool and silk. Elizabeth imagined it as a gift fit for a lady journeying to distant parts, a piece that spoke of faraway lands and exotic beauty.

Next was a Paisley shawl, recalling the origins of those cherished designs in the Scottish town of that name. Elizabeth remembered reading that, though many shawls came from India, Scottish manufacturers had begun to imitate the prized patterns upon their own looms, making such luxury somewhat more accessible, though still costly and elegant.

Her hand brushed a shawl of fine Merino wool, imported from Spain or Saxony, its simple weave a contrast to the more elaborate. It was understated but undeniably genteel, its welcoming touch a promise of warmth on the coldest of evenings.

Next, a silk shawl caught the morning light, shimmering as if woven with threads of moonlight. Lighter than the rest, it was suited to evening wear—delicate and refined, embroidered with modest floral motifs.

Another bore embroidery of silk and gold thread over a fine muslin ground. Elizabeth pictured the hours of labor such a work required, the patient hand of an artisan breathing life into every stitch.

There was also a French cashmere-style shawl, fashioned upon Jacquard looms to imitate the prized shawls of Kashmir. More affordable, yet still beloved by the European elite, it testified to the blending of cultures and the shifting tide of fashion.

At the bottom lay an evening shawl of gauzy silk, edged with Mechlin lace and tiny metallic embroideries, the perfect finishing touch for a formal ball or intimate gathering. Elizabeth recognized the lace, prized for its airy delicacy, and thought it a choice of uncommon refinement.

Elizabeth smiled, torn between amusement and delight. "Nine shawls, indeed," she murmured, "each more exquisite than the last."

The rhyme might have faltered, but the thought behind the gifts was beyond doubt. She could feel the care, the affection, the deep attention to detail in each choice. More than the material worth, it was the gesture—the patience and imagination—that moved her heart.

She draped one of the shawls across her shoulders, a gentle silver-gray that would enhance the blue of a gown she much favored. The fabric slipped like water over her skin, light yet comforting, a shield against winter's bite.

She stepped before the looking glass, the shawl cascading in graceful folds, framing her figure with refined elegance. The thought of Darcy—of the man she suspected had chosen each gift so thoughtfully—filled her with a strange warmth that had little to do with wool.

"What a quiz," she murmured, "to send such treasures and yet remain so hidden." He had implied the night before that it was he. Why did he not speak? Surely he must know his efforts had borne fruit.

For a moment, she allowed herself to picture the shawls at the social gatherings to come—the rustle of silk, the murmur of admiration, the inevitable whisper of envy that attends a lady well-dressed. But more than vanity, the gifts made her feel seen, not merely as a gentlewoman, but as one worth cherishing.

I love him, Elizabeth realized, standing beside the table with a shawl gathered in her hands. As she folded them back into the bandbox, a tender hope took root within her. Perhaps this Christmastide promised more than just gifts and rhymes. Perhaps the dream with which she had awakened was a pledge, and the gentleman behind these tokens was prepared to reveal himself in the waking world.

She lifted the box and carried it to the window, where the frost-lined drive without echoed the imagery of the verse. A wistful smile played about her lips as she whispered, "Thank you, whoever you are." In her heart she saw Darcy's face, wreathed in gentle affection. Some sly-boots indeed, to hide himself thus, and yet contrive to be so generous.

It must be you…it simply must be you. No other will do, for my heart is now irrevocably tied to you.

Outside, the first pale rays of morning touched the rooftops of Hertfordshire, promising a day of new possibilities, and perhaps the beginning of a new chapter in her story. She had never been in love. This day was as fitting a beginning as she could desire.

The scent of tea and fresh bread lured Elizabeth below, her thoughts still fluttering like snowflakes from the dream she had left behind. Darcy's voice—so tender, so unguarded—had remained with her as she stirred from slumber. Even now, she could almost hear the whispered confession: *I love you. I am your secret admirer.*

She gave a small shake of her head and pressed her hand to her lips as she entered the breakfast room. The air held a crisp chill, the fire not yet having fully warmed the space. A hush lay upon the house, broken only by the occasional clink of crockery. Elizabeth took her chair and buttered a warm scone.

Moments later, Jane entered, her cheeks warmed by sleep and her eyes alight with curiosity.

"I overslept." She leaned near. "What did he leave you today?"

Elizabeth bit her lip to contain a smile. "A bandbox," she whispered. "But no hats. Nine shawls. Exquisite ones."

Jane gave a warm and easy laugh. "He grows ever more extravagant."

Mrs. Bennet's sudden exclamation broke their tempered merriment. "What are you two whispering about? Wedding details, I presume! Jane, my dear, you must set a date soon. It is not seemly to keep a gentleman waiting."

Jane demurred, mild as ever. "I shall speak to Charles this afternoon, Mama."

Before her mother could press further, Mr. Bennet lowered his paper. "Leave the girl be, Mrs. Bennet. You only experience the blush of first love once. Let her revel in it."

Mrs. Bennet gave a girlish giggle and colored, casting a coy glance at her husband. Elizabeth observed their exchange with wry amusement, recognizing beneath the playful sparring the deep—if at times bewildering—affection they bore each other.

The peace was soon broken by the boisterous arrival of Lydia and Kitty, who swept into the room like a pair of windblown leaves.

"Have we received any invitations for Twelfth Night?" Lydia demanded, her bonnet askew and her countenance bright with anticipation.

Mrs. Bennet answered briskly, "The Longs are to host a dinner party this evening. It is their turn, after all."

Elizabeth, sipping her tea, let her mind drift. She recalled a time, years before, when Sir William Lucas, newly knighted, had taken to holding such splendid Twelfth Night assemblies that others in the neighborhood felt compelled to compete. The divisions that followed had caused no small measure of ill-will. At last, in an effort to preserve civility, the families agreed to rotate the duty of host. It restored peace—though Kitty still lamented.

"I wish it were Longbourn's turn," Kitty said wistfully.

"I, for one," said Mr. Bennet dryly, "am grateful we have a few years yet to wait. Longbourn crammed with merrymakers is a trial I shall gladly defer."

Breakfast concluded, the sisters withdrew upstairs. Elizabeth led Jane to her chamber, and with a conspiratorial smile, opened her wardrobe.

"Look," she said, drawing forth the shawl she had chosen; the soft weave from Kashmir, pale silver threaded with lavender, shimmered in the morning light.

Jane's eyes widened. "How beautiful! And so fine—he must have spent a fortune."

Mary entered then, shutting the door behind her before joining her sisters. Her gaze lit upon the shawl, and even she could not restrain an exclamation, "Oh!"

"There are nine. Each lovelier than the last." Wonder threaded through her words, as though the gifts were less fabric than tokens of an affection she scarcely dared confess.

Mary ran her hand over the delicate fabric. "The embroidery is exquisite."

But their admiration was short-lived. The sound of a scuffle in the passage heralded the approach of Lydia and Kitty. In a flurry, Elizabeth and Jane tucked the shawl back into the press, Mary closing the doors with a swift, decisive snap just as the younger girls burst in.

"I want to stand up with Jane," Kitty said at once. "I shall look best next to her."

"No, *I* shall," Lydia interjected, pushing past her sister. "Everyone says I am the prettiest of us all."

Jane, gentle and composed, spoke with firm grace. "Lizzy will stand up with me."

Lydia pouted, then turned to Mary with a smirk. "Well then, I get to stand up with you if Sanderson ever comes to the point!"

Mary's face colored. "That is hardly appropriate," she muttered, discomposed.

"Do not look so prim, Mary; it is but a jest."

Elizabeth stepped between them, her tone light but firm. "If you will leave me in peace for the next hour, I promise to walk into Meryton with you later. You may flutter your lashes at every officer you see."

That seemed to satisfy them. With promises and a stream of chatter, Lydia and Kitty quitted the room. Mary followed more slowly, still flustered but curious enough to peer once more at the wardrobe as she passed.

As the door finally shut behind them, Elizabeth leaned against it and released a long breath.

Jane touched her arm. "You are very patient with them."

"I do love them, Jane. Even when they are at their most exasperating."

Jane nodded. "It is a gift to have sisters. I am grateful each day."

Elizabeth looked toward the window, the sun glinting off frost-laced branches. "So am I, especially now."

Her thoughts strayed once more to where nine precious shawls lay concealed, and a mingling of warmth and anticipation rose within her.

What will the morrow bring? And more pressing still—what will I feel when it comes?

Later that day, after fulfilling her promise to Lydia and Kitty with a stroll through Meryton, marked by giggles, glances, and endless talk of officers, Elizabeth was eager to escape. The streets, sodden with slush and rife with gossip, soon wore on her patience, and the call of solitude pressed upon her with familiar insistence.

Once returned to Longbourn, she quietly retreated to her chamber and readied herself for a longer walk. Donning her sturdy pelisse, she then wrapped herself in her warmest cloak and, with a breathless sort of anticipation, reached for one of her new shawls—the Merino wool, deep blue with simple yet elegant stitching. Of all the nine, it was the most sensible, suited to a walk rather than a drawing room. She concealed it beneath her cloak, unwilling to endure her mother's inquiries or her sisters' teasing glances. Only when she had passed beyond the hedgerow did she draw it about her shoulders. The weight of it, close and enveloping, was like the touch of an unseen hand. His hand. She clasped it closer.

The road to Oakham Mount was muddy, the melting frost sinking into the earth, but she pressed on, lifting her skirts and keeping to the firmer edges of the path. Her boots were soon damp, and her cheeks tingled with cold, but she did not mind. There was purpose in her step, a steady thrum of expectation beating beneath her layers.

As she began the ascent, her legs burned from the effort, but she welcomed the ache. It distracted her from the racing of her thoughts. She had walked this hill many times before—alone, with Jane, even with Charlotte—but never with such longing. Never with the possibility that her destination might hold more than a view.

When did I fall in love with Mr. Darcy?

The question rose within her, though she had already confessed the truth to herself. It had hovered in the background of her mind for days, perhaps weeks, yet she had resisted it—or perhaps she had not dared to give it name. But here, in the stillness of winter, with nothing but the wind and her breath for company, she allowed herself to examine it.

She had once believed him proud—no, worse than proud—cold, dismissive, arrogant. She had condemned him swiftly and thoroughly, taking pride in her judgment. How blind she had been! How easily deceived by wounded vanity and Wickham's false charm. It was not the poetry of his letters nor the grandeur of his gifts that had begun to alter her affections. Those only confirmed what her heart had already suspected.

No, it was his kindness toward her aunt and uncle. His eagerness to welcome them to Pemberley, to receive them with warmth rather than hauteur. And his defense of his sister—not with injured pride, but with honest vulnerability. It was the way he listened when she spoke. The way he challenged her, and allowed himself to be challenged in return. It was every conversation in the past several weeks, every shared glance at the evening soirees. It was the look he had given her when they danced, as though she were the only woman in the world.

When had it begun? She could not say. She was in the midst of it before she had known she had even started. Somewhere between the Meryton Assembly and Christmastide, her heart had changed its allegiance. It no longer beat against him, but towards him. Darcy, with his proud mien and unreadable eyes. Darcy, with his reserved manner and hidden soul—the soul she longed to know more deeply.

He had changed, yes, but more truly, it was she who had changed. She had seen clearly at last, and what she saw had undone her entirely.

Her pace slowed as she neared the summit. Her heart thudded, not from the climb, but from the sheer weight of her feelings. A word, a look, even a moment's carelessness, and she might have lost him forever. If it were not he—if she had misjudged the source of the gifts—what then? She would be made a fool, yes, but more grievously, her heart would break.

Do not presume. Do not indulge such expectation.

But it was too late. Anticipation had taken root.

She reached the crest; the wind tugged at the ends of her shawl, and she paused to catch her breath. The view stretched out before her: bare trees against a pale sky, frost glinting across the meadows, the village rooflines beyond the fields. It was beautiful in its wintry hush, and for a moment, it quieted her turmoil.

And then, as though conjured by her very longing, he was there.

At first, she thought it a trick of the light, an outline among the trees. But no; there he stood, not twenty paces ahead, set against the slate sky. Darcy.

Elizabeth halted, her breath suspended. He wore a great coat and leather gloves, hat in hand, the wind tousling his dark curls. His tall frame held rigid with surprise as he looked at her. But to Elizabeth, it was longing itself, laid bare in the stillness.

Chapter Twenty

January 2, 1812
Oakham Mount
Darcy

She wore one of the shawls.

He knew it at once: the fine Merino wool, light yet warm, its simple weave a contrast to the more elaborate patterns he had ordered from London. Its pattern he recalled from a shopping excursion with Georgiana, and he had recalled it when he began his task. It clung about her shoulders and shifted with the breeze like a second skin. She looked both elegant and steadfast, a figure of grace and resolute strength.

They stood in silence for a moment, the wind their only companion.

Then he spoke and bowed, his voice low and roughened by the cold. "Miss Bennet."

Elizabeth dipped into a graceful curtsy. "Mr. Darcy."

Their greeting was formal, almost absurd in its familiarity, and yet it comforted him.

"I had not expected—" He faltered, then smiled, truly smiled, not the reserved curl of formality but something unguarded. "I longed for it, but I did not expect to see you here."

"And I...wished to see you as well."

The wind continued to whirl around them, tugging at the edge of her shawl. His gaze fell to it.

"You are wearing a lovely shawl." His fingers brushed the wool at her shoulder.

"Yes. I chose it for practicality…and comfort. But I suppose beauty and sentiment factored in."

"You look very well in it. It suits you."

"I thank you, sir. It was a gift."

A pause.

There was a promise in her look that emboldened him to step nearer. His heart beat so fiercely he fancied it echoed in his ears.

"I worried I had left you discomposed or offended; the thought returned to me with unease all the evening, and even in sleep I was haunted with visions of your reproof."

Elizabeth met his gaze, steady and clear. "Only a trifle. But I did not object; you take too much upon yourself in supposing me so easily displeased."

The words warmed him more than the sun could manage as his breath misted in the air between them.

Some stubborn yearning had urged him to Oakham Mount that afternoon. When he espied her figure ascending the hill, shawl drawn close and bonnet tied snug against the wind, a rush of relief and awe filled his chest. He had pictured their meeting, but this—this unlooked-for moment—surpassed any expectation he had dared to indulge.

There was something in her eyes—encouragement, even yearning—that pulled him closer, though he did not move.

"I wonder if I might tell you more," he said. "About my sister."

Her head lifted. "Of course."

"She reminds me very much of your sister Jane."

Elizabeth blinked, plainly surprised. "You think so?"

"They are both gentle in their ways. Reserved, but not from indifference—only caution. Georgiana is painfully shy. She...she hides her heart behind timid smiles. But I believe they are alike in character."

He saw Elizabeth's pleasure in his words, the genuine smile that curved upon her lips stealing his breath. "Then I should like to meet her very much. It is only fair, sir, for you have met all four of mine."

Darcy laughed; a true laugh, rich and unguarded. "Yes, I believe I have been well initiated into the Bennet household."

Elizabeth joined in, her laughter bright as sunlight after a storm. The sound lingered between them, a fragile delight, until Darcy, aware of how near they stood, inclined his head toward a fallen log. "May we sit?"

"Gladly," she replied.

They seated themselves side by side. The log was worn but dry, and the wind, though brisk, had abated. The afternoon sun poured its mellow light upon them, and Darcy could not keep from studying Elizabeth. Curls had slipped from her bonnet, glinting with amber and chestnut. Her perfect complexion glowed in the golden rays, and every graceful turn of her head seemed to unman him.

He longed to take her hand, but instead folded his gloves in his lap.

"I have a confession to make," he said, breaking the hush. *If I wish for her to love me, I must be entirely honest.* Her reaction filled him with apprehension. Would she be incensed? Would all their hard-won accord be undone in a moment? *I once said that I had a resentful temper—that my good opinion once lost is lost forever. What if she feels the same?*

Elizabeth angled toward him, attention fixed upon him. "Go on."

"When Bingley was in town at the end of November, I...I encouraged him to remain. I did not speak falsehoods, only expressed concern. I thought Miss Bennet indifferent. But he would not be dissuaded. I returned with him only because he refused to stay away." He glanced at her, searching her countenance. "But now, having observed her more closely, I see my error. Your sister's affection is restrained, yet unmistakable to one who truly looks." Indeed, now that Bingley had declared his feelings, Miss Bennet's sentiments were plain.

Elizabeth studied him, her features unreadable at first. Then she nodded, grave but not angry. "I cannot fault you for loving your friend, or for wishing to protect him. But Jane...Jane feels things deeply. She conceals them even from me at times. Do not mistake her serenity for want of feeling."

Her words eased the tightness inside him. But then she added, almost hesitantly, "She received a letter from Miss Bingley. Right before you all departed."

His spine stiffened. He knew of the letter; he had suspected it contained something other than a farewell.

"She wrote implying that your sister was to marry Mr. Bingley, and that you supported it. I knew, of course, she wrote nothing but falsehoods, but knowing what I do now... about your sister..."

She trailed off, watching him.

His jaw hardened. "That is an abominable lie. Georgiana has never had any attachment to Bingley. She has not yet been introduced to society at all, and they have scarcely been in company together."

"I doubted it. Miss Bingley did not mean to spread the rumor widely—only to dissuade my sister."

"She had no right," he said sharply. "No right to use my sister's name in such a scheme." Darcy's heart contracted. What would Georgiana think, were she to learn her name had been tied to Bingley's? Good heavens, Bingley was now *engaged*. What a scandal that would be!

"I agree. But she did not succeed. Perhaps she might have, had you and Mr. Bingley not returned. And now—well, now it matters little, does it not?"

Darcy nodded, drawing a steadying breath to master his temper. "They are safely engaged, and I believe the marriage articles are signed. It will be well."

Elizabeth tilted her head, a teasing lilt to her voice as she spoke again. "Do you often find yourself managing other people's affairs, Mr. Darcy?"

He gave her a rueful look. "Too often, I fear. And seldom to good effect." He pressed an ungloved hand over his face, cool against his heated skin.

She laughed, and he allowed himself to watch her, wonder stirring at the ease between them. The moment felt natural—inevitable. His heart beat with a longing perilously close to desire.

"Has your sister settled on a date?" he asked, shifting just enough that his knee brushed hers. The contact sent a thrill through him, and she did not pull away.

"My mother presses her to decide daily. Jane, for once, means to do precisely what pleases her most. She refuses to name the day until she and Mr. Bingley have spoken and are of one mind. My mother has made no secret of wishing for a spring wedding, so that we might procure fresh flowers. I do not believe my sister will delay until April."

"Flowers may be purchased from a hothouse," Darcy concurred with a nod. "Bingley is an amiable, obliging man, but I have observed in him a curious impatience. I cannot think Mrs. Bennet will persuade either party to delay."

Elizabeth's laugh filled him with delight, her profile bright with merriment. "Whatever they decide, I trust they will choose what suits them best. Nothing less would content either of them."

Darcy quelled the impulse to declare himself then and there. She looked so beautiful—and with his gift resting upon her shoulders, she was the very image of perfection. He recalled his resolve of the previous night.

Only three days remain. Three miserable dog's days.

"Are there to be any more parties?" The question escaped him in haste, a desperate effort to divert his thoughts before he laid his heart bare.

"Only one," Elizabeth replied. "The Longs are hosting the gathering this year. Have I told you how the four-and-twenty families nearly came to blows over the vaunted Twelfth Night celebration?"

Darcy's eyes lit with curiosity. "No, I do not believe you have."

"You know, of course, that the festive season brings an unusual number of gatherings to our part of the country. Mr. Bingley once remarked it rather resembled town, in its own modest way. Many years ago, when Sir William was newly knighted and eager to display his consequence, he hosted the most extravagant Twelfth Night soiree Meryton had ever seen. The following year, the Gouldings, determined not to be outdone, planned a celebration to rival the Lucases'.

"Unfortunately, they were not alone in their ambition. No fewer than five families scheduled grand affairs for the very same evening, leaving the neighborhood in a quandary. How was one to choose? If Mrs. Long attended Lucas Lodge, she would offend her dear friend Mrs. Goulding, and if she favored the Gouldings, then the Miss Searles would certainly take umbrage. It was a social dilemma of the highest order."

Elizabeth paused, a spark of mischief lighting her eyes. "Naturally, no hostess could be prevailed upon to change her date. It was my father who proposed a solution. His voice, as I recall, was uncommonly grave when he said, 'Why do we not take turns? There are eleven other days in the Christmas season upon which to entertain, are there not?'"

She adopted his dry tone to perfection, and Darcy grinned, already anticipating the jest.

"The suggestion was agreed upon, and the only remaining dispute was how to determine the order. My father, ever the generous man, offered that Longbourn should host last. Sir William, having already had his moment of glory the previous year, accepted the second-to-last place."

She spoke dryly. "Though I suspect my father's true motivation had less to do with neighborly consideration and more to do with reducing the number of times he must endure a drawing room full of guests in December."

Darcy laughed, thoroughly entertained. "Your father's wit astonishes me once more. Tell me, was your mother very disappointed?"

"Oh, indeed, she was." Elizabeth grimaced. "We hear her complaints every year, except when it is Longbourn's turn to entertain. It has not curbed her delight in the activity, however, and as you may have noticed, my father's estate hosts a great many gatherings during the winter months. My mother claims there is nothing better to do, and so my father bears it as best he can."

"My mother was fond of entertaining," Darcy said, the words slipping out unbidden, carried on a breath of memory.

He rarely spoke of her. Even with Georgiana, the subject was broached with care and only in passing. The memories were too vivid, both beautiful and sharp-edged, and they had a way of carving into his heart before he could brace for it.

"I do not believe we have ever spoken of your mother." Her look was open, curious, but not intrusive. "Will you tell me of her?"

Darcy hesitated. His first instinct was to retreat behind reserve, to tuck away the ache and redirect the conversation. But there was something in her ardent violet eyes—gentle, unyielding—that made him feel as though he could not lie. Not by omission, not to her.

"My mother was..." He paused, unsure where to begin. "There are no words that quite do her justice. Georgiana resembles her physically; so much so that there is a portrait hanging at Pemberley, painted shortly after my mother's come out, which might as well be of my sister. But that is where their likeness ends."

He shifted slightly on the log, wincing at its cold firmness. The discomfort was oddly grounding.

"Lady Anne Darcy thrived in society. She was not bold, not loud, but she possessed a vibrancy...a way of making others feel at ease. I have heard stories of the balls at Darcy House and the summer parties at Pemberley—rooms filled with music, light, and laughter. My father adored her. We all did."

He paused, then spoke more softly, his voice shaded with pain. "Looking back, I believe she entertained in part to distract herself. From sorrow." His eyes fixed on the horizon. "Georgiana is more than ten years my junior. At the time, I knew only that she came late—an unexpected blessing, we said. But later, I learned the truth. My mother lost several children between our births."

Elizabeth's hand entered his sight, resting gently on his arm.

"My mama lost a child," she murmured. "A little boy. I was very young. I can scarcely remember more than a few hushed conversations. It was before Lydia was born."

Darcy turned toward her, her touch warming him more than any hearth. "I can imagine the devastation," he replied in a voice rough with empathy. He did not dare stir, lest she withdraw her hand. "A son to break the entail..."

She nodded, her fingers slipping away, and he felt the loss at once; his arm chilled not from the wind, but from the absence of her comfort.

"Yes. It was then she truly began to suffer her fits of nerves. Lydia's birth brought some joy, but she never wholly recovered from the loss of her son."

Darcy remained silent, absorbing the shared grief—the symmetry of their families' private sorrows. It was a strange solace to speak without reserve, to be understood without the need for explanation.

"The Bennet family is filled with secrets."

"That it is."

Then, after a pause, her eyes glimmered with mischief. "But I can promise you, sir, our secrets are not of the scandalous sort. I have no relations who have run off to join a traveling theater."

Darcy laughed, full and unguarded, and she joined him, their merriment mingling easily in the crisp winter air. There was comfort in laughter after sorrow—an unspoken acknowledgment that life, despite its losses, must go on.

They turned together to look across the fields, gilded by the sinking sun, the sky above brushed with strokes of amber and lavender. A tranquil silence settled between them.

Elizabeth started suddenly. "Mr. Darcy! I must get home at once. The time has quite escaped me. My family will be beside themselves. I shall miss dinner entirely, and my mother will never forgive such tardiness. I have never lingered abroad so late in the day, and certainly not alone."

Darcy rose at once, contrition sharpening his manner. "The fault is mine. I beg your pardon. I have detained you most selfishly. Pray allow me to escort you to Longbourn. I would not see you walk unattended, least of all at this hour. Forgive me."

"Not at all, sir. I enjoyed our time together."

He reached for his horse's reins, and offered his arm; she accepted, and together they descended the slope in measured step, Beau following close. As they walked in companionable silence, Darcy thought.

Three more days. Three more days until Twelfth Night. And then, if all goes as I most fervently wish, I might at last lay everything before her: my name, my home, my heart.

He glanced at her—cheeks flushed with cold and laughter, curls burnished like spun bronze in the fading light—and felt that longing swell within him. Yes. Three more days. And then, perhaps, forever.

Chapter Twenty-One

January 3, 1812
Longbourn
Elizabeth

> *On the tenth day of Christmas,*
> *By candlelight's glow,*
> *Ten lustrous pearls*
> *In a velvet pouch show.*

Elizabeth pulled the silver-tipped drawstrings that fastened the pouch. The rich blue velvet yielded with reluctance before parting, its contents dropping in a delicate tumble into her waiting palm. Another gift, another catch of her breath. There, nestled in her palm, was a pendant unlike any she had ever beheld.

Nine small pearls: perfectly matched, luminous, and creamy, encircled a tenth, larger pearl at the center. The heart of the pendant was wreathed in a halo of sparkling diamonds, set in finely wrought silver. Even the chain itself was a marvel: twisted links of silver, strong yet intricate, fashioned into a rope design. Such workmanship bespoke refinement; this was no trifle purchased in haste or without thought.

"I am spoiled forever for any other," she murmured, turning the necklace slowly between her fingers.

The giver of her treasures had not only been generous, but most deliberate. Every gift revealed thought, affection, and an understanding of her true nature. Pearls were no idle choice. They were said to be prized as emblems of purity, modesty and wisdom—gems formed in secrecy under the waves, shaped by time and patient endurance.

Am I fancying more than he intends? Something within her resisted such doubt. Whoever he was, this gentleman had studied what might please her. Learned, refined, and thoughtful. *Someone suited to me...*

Her reverie was interrupted by a gentle knock and the door easing open on its hinges.

Jane rushed in first, her cheeks rosy from the exertion, quickly followed by Mary, who carried a book in one hand and a small box tucked beneath her arm.

"You are up early," Jane observed, her gaze falling on the pendant. "Oh, Lizzy, what a beautiful necklace!"

Mary stepped nearer, her intent upon it. "That is no mere bauble. It looks an heirloom. See the settings, the stones. He must be certain of his success in his suit to bestow so costly a gift. Indeed, it is as fine as the locket."

Elizabeth smiled. "You sound almost as though you preach a sermon."

"I might be," Mary replied, but her lips twitched in amusement despite her attempt at gravity.

It was then that Elizabeth noticed a glimmer at her sister's throat. "Mary...is that new?"

A flush rose to Mary's cheeks. "Oh. Yes. Mr. Sanderson gave it to me."

Jane's eyes shone with delight. "Mary! How wonderful!"

Mary looked down, her fingers brushing the plain gold chain. "He has spoken no promise as yet, but...I believe he means to approach Papa soon."

Elizabeth grinned. "So, he courted you these last weeks, and Mama never suspected! Only think of her countenance when she learns the season has yielded yet another daughter engaged!"

All three sisters laughed together, their shared mirth enlivening the room.

Jane then turned to Elizabeth with a more subdued smile. She looked angelic, even in her night gown, with her plait falling over one shoulder. "Do you suppose your gentleman will soon declare himself?"

Elizabeth brushed the pearl pendant with her fingers. "There are still two days until Twelfth Night. I feel certain he will wait until then." She had given Darcy an opportunity to speak the previous day, had she not? *But what if it is not him? No—she could not believe it. It must be him. Her heart was already his.*

With care, she clasped the chain about her neck. The pendant nestled just below the edge of her bodice; fit for day wear, not ostentatious, merely elegant. She tucked it out of sight, as she had with the other tokens. This secret—her desires—were not yet ready for the scrutiny of the drawing room. Lydia and Kitty would be sure to spy it at once. Their exclamations would demand an explanation, and Mrs. Bennet would join them, demanding to have her curiosity satisfied.

Jane and Mary excused themselves to their chambers to dress. Before long, the three sisters descended to breakfast together. The fragrance of tea and toasted bread greeted them, along with the warmth of the fire. Mr. and Mrs. Bennet were already seated at the table, while Kitty and Lydia, unsurprisingly, had not yet appeared.

Mr. Bennet looked up from his paper. "Good morning, my dears." His paper rustled as he turned a page. "In consideration of your mother's nerves, I have an announcement. We are to expect Mr. Collins on Wednesday, the seventh. He will remain at Longbourn until his marriage to Miss Lucas on the ninth."

Mrs. Bennet dropped her spoon with a clatter. "He cannot come here! No, I shall not host the man who will throw us all into the hedgerows the instant you perish!" Her hands fluttered, and she fumbled with her napkin, pressing it to her lips. "You cannot ask it of me, sir. Such a trial I shall not allow my poor nerves to suffer! That gentleman has no place within the walls of this house!"

Elizabeth winced. Jane reached for their mother's hand and spoke soothingly. "Mama, please. I am to be married to a good man who would never see you without a home." The calm words did little to ease their mother's agitation.

Mrs. Bennet sniffled. "It would not be such a concern if Elizabeth had been a dutiful daughter and accepted Mr. Collins's offer when she had the chance." She dropped her napkin and raised her cup to take a sip of tea. "Willful, foolish girl! How could you? To throw away a chance at being the mistress of Longbourn? How ill you use me, Lizzy."

Elizabeth pressed her lips together, forcing herself to not to retort. Her hands rested motionless in her lap, though she itched to clench them. She would not quarrel. Not to-day. *I thought we had moved beyond this,* she reflected. Her mother's tirades had abated once Mr. Bingley had returned.

Never mind. Had I accepted Mr. Collins, I would never have known this...this wonder...this serene joy.

She looked down at the pendant kept secret beneath her gown. Her admirer—her *Darcy*, she dared to believe—loved her. That truth, however privately cherished, soothed the sting of her mother's reproaches. She toyed with her eggs, took a sip of tea, and nibbled at the corner of a slice of toast. Across the table, Jane, ever the peacemaker, smiled sweetly at their mother.

"Mr. Bingley is to call soon, Mama, to speak with Papa about wedding arrangements." Jane's diversion was subtle, and to Elizabeth's relief, they worked.

Mrs. Bennet brightened at once. "Oh! Then we must begin planning in earnest! I have already decided that lace shall adorn the sleeves of your gown: floral lace, and a scalloped edge…"

"No lace, Mrs. Bennet, I beg you," Mr. Bennet said dryly. "Allow me to eat my breakfast in peace before the wedding madness begins."

Mrs. Bennet cast him a knowing glance and laughed. "You are a tease, Mr. Bennet! What better time to speak of such matters than over breakfast?"

Elizabeth sipped her tea and allowed her thoughts to wander. *Perhaps Darcy will accompany Mr. Bingley.* She pictured him arriving, hat in hand, eyes seeking hers. Her fingers strayed to the chain about her neck.

Just then, Lydia and Kitty flounced into the room, all bustle and complaints.

"Mama," Lydia cried, "I must have extra pin money. I have seen a new bonnet in Meryton—light green silk with velvet trim. It will make me the envy of every girl at the Twelfth Night ball!"

Kitty tossed her head. "She does not need a new bonnet! She bought one but last week. The pin money ought to be mine; I saw gloves I *truly* require."

Mr. Bennet rose, laying his napkin on the table with studied calm. "I find I have an urgent need for solitude. Good day to you all."

He departed with his customary flair for theatrical exits, leaving behind a chorus of laughter, protest, and clinking china.

Elizabeth smiled into her teacup. The morning had been absurd, familiar, vexing, and yet she was content. Her thoughts drifted once more to Darcy. Soon, very soon, she might learn the truth at last.

Two more days. And her life, she knew, would never be the same.

The morning wore on with a restless kind of anticipation, each tick of the longcase clock in the hall tightening the expectancy in Elizabeth's breast. She would not name the emotion—could not—but her eyes strayed more than once to the window that looked upon the lane.

When the sound of carriage wheels reached her ears, she feigned indifference. She lifted her embroidery, long neglected in her lap, and deliberately set a few stitches.

Mrs. Bennet did not attempt pretense, but nearly upset her sewing basket as she leaped up. "Mr. Bingley's carriage! Oh, Jane, you knew exactly how it would be! What a devoted suitor! He calls upon you endlessly."

Jane's blush was immediate, though her composure remained unshaken. Elizabeth bent her head over her embroidery to hide a smile. Mary smoothed her collar. Lydia and Kitty, of course, scrambled for places at the windows like a pair of unruly puppies.

Moments later, the drawing-room door opened to admit Hill. "Mr. Bingley and Mr. Darcy, ma'am."

The gentlemen entered, and Elizabeth felt more than saw Darcy's eyes seek hers at once. She glanced up and was caught.

There was something in his mien—an intent gravity that made her breath falter. He bowed politely, of course, and exchanged the usual civilities with her mother; but Elizabeth sensed his attention return to her, even as Mrs. Bennet launched into her welcome.

"Oh, Mr. Bingley, how delighted we are to see you! And Mr. Darcy. How very good of you to accompany your friend. You are always welcome at Longbourn." Mrs. Bennet's warmth could not be mistaken.

At least she treats him kindly now. Mama did not like him at all before.

Darcy bowed again, murmuring his thanks, but Mrs. Bennet, carried away by the occasion, pressed on.

"And I must say, gentlemen, your visit could not come at a better, or worse, time. We are soon to be inundated again. Mr. Collins arrives on Wednesday to stay until his wedding. My poor nerves can scarcely endure it. Why Mr. Bennet insists on receiving the man who will one day cast us into the hedgerows, I cannot fathom!"

Bingley shifted uneasily, not quite certain how to respond to so lamentable a speech. Jane's cheeks reddened, and Elizabeth saw her sister draw a steadying breath.

Ever their mother's gentle guide, she interjected quickly, "Mama, shall I ask Hill to bring tea for our guests?"

Mrs. Bennet brightened. "Yes, yes—what a lovely idea. I shall go and speak to her myself." She bustled from the room, calling over her shoulder for Lydia to come and assist.

Elizabeth exhaled, grateful for the moment's reprieve.

She turned just as Darcy stepped beside her. "Miss Elizabeth," he said in that low, melodious voice she never mistook for another's, "might I sit with you?"

"Of course," she replied, drawing her gown close to allow space for him beside her on the settee. The embroidery lay forgotten in her lap as she regarded him. How handsome he appeared! His cravat was expertly tied, his coat admirably cut, and his waistcoat, dark green rather than his familiar black, became him exceedingly.

As he seated himself, warmth rose in her cheeks. His look was intent—steady, not bold, but she felt it as though it touched her. When his eyes fell to her neckline, she caught her breath, for he had fixed upon on the silver chain, visible just above the edge of her gown.

He sees it. He knows.

Her fingers moved instinctively to the spot, conscious of his notice. But he spoke not of the necklace, and she dared not mention it first.

Instead, he leaned nearer. "Mr. Collins is returning, then?" Curiosity...perhaps even amusement colored his words.

She folded her hands tightly in her lap. "Yes. He arrives on the seventh and marries Charlotte two days later." *Daft! I am repeating what Mama just said.* She wanted to sink into the settee, such was her embarrassment.

"Yes, I had heard. Miss Lucas spoke of it in December."

"Charlotte accepted quickly."

"She is a prudent woman. *You* would have been wasted on such a man."

He knows! He knows Mr. Collins proposed to me first. She could not fathom his design—he seemed to wait, intent upon her answer.

The words echoed in her mind. *Wasted? He thinks me fit for more.* From him, it could not be idle civility; Darcy was not a man to speak without meaning. If not Mr. Collins, then whom did he consider worthy? Could he be suggesting...himself? The idea trembled at the edge of belief, both thrilling and bewildering.

"My mother would disagree. She has spoken her sentiments often enough." Elizabeth shifted, turning more fully toward him. "I take it you have heard of my refusal?"

A shadow crossed his features. "Indeed. Miss Lucas revealed it. Tell me you are not angry." His beseeching look was so genuine that she smiled despite herself.

"You must think me rather foolish to refuse so suitable a proposal."

"Not at all." His protest warmed her heart. "The match might appear *suitable* from one perspective, but I believe I know you well enough to be certain you would have been wretched in such a union."

A thrill coursed through her at his words; he understood her so well. "Mr. Collins has his merits. He is…consistent in his absurdity. Charlotte is a sensible creature; she is content with her practical decision."

He let out a restrained chuckle, then grew more serious. "Collins is devoted to my aunt, Lady Catherine. That alone would deter most. I ought not to speak ill of my elders, but she is a formidable woman, determined to have her own way."

"I have only heard his account, and in his telling, she is a veritable goddess—wisdom, virtue, and elegance personified."

Darcy laughed outright. "Lady Catherine is imperious, commanding, and certain of her own infallibility. She assumes the air of discernment, but I fear little of it is genuine. Nothing escapes her notice—not the placing of forks upon a table, nor the manner in which a guest stirs their tea. My sister avoids her company whenever possible. Such is her perceived authority that she will even direct the butcher's orders on her parson's behalf."

Elizabeth began to laugh, but the sound faltered, her smile fading as an unwelcome recollection intruded.

Wickham once said something of Anne de Bourgh and Darcy…a betrothal. And had not Mr. Collins intimated the same? The first could not be trusted, yet the second?

She checked her spirits, touched with a desperation she prayed he would not perceive, and inclined away from him. "You surprise me, Mr. Darcy, that a man of your fortune and consequence is not yet married. Is it because you are already spoken for? What of Miss de Bourgh?"

His composure now shifted, just enough to betray surprise. "Anne?"

"I have heard from two sources that there is an attachment between you." *Please let it be false. I could not bear to lose him now.*

She noted his bearing scarcely altered; he was too disciplined for that. But something affected him—surprise, perhaps even hurt.

"An attachment?"

"Yes," she managed, forcing the words past the sudden tightness in her throat. "That you are to marry. Mr. Collins implied as much. And Mr. Wickham..." She pressed forward, fearful of being misunderstood. "He claimed it certain. I know that man's words are suspect, but my cousin? I do not know what to think."

Darcy drew a breath sharply, and for an instant, she feared she had overstepped.

He leaned a fraction closer, his words low yet resolute. "Miss Elizabeth, I give you my word: there is no attachment between myself and my cousin. Nor have I ever wished there to be one."

"I see." Relief broke from her in a breath she could not wholly conceal.

Folly, to have let their falsehoods prey upon me. How near I came to believing him lost, to thinking he belonged elsewhere. And now he is free. Free, and I am foolishly glad of it.

"My aunt would wish it so. She insists my mother desired it, and that the arrangement is of a peculiar kind, long intended since our infancy. Anne and I have never shared such inclination. She is a sickly girl, and quite shy; she is not at ease in large gatherings. We are simply cousins, nothing more."

She schooled her manner, though the impulse to reach for him was strong, so great was her relief. "I am sorry. I ought not to have credited them."

Darcy's reply was gentler still. "No, I am only sorry that you were given cause to doubt. As for him, suffice it to say that he will spread falsehoods no longer."

He reached for her hand, clasping it briefly before letting go. Their eyes met, and for a long, suspended moment, silence held. Her fingers sought the chain at her throat, but she dared not draw it forth. She wondered if he would speak, if he would declare himself at last.

No, he will wait until Twelfth Night.

The sounds of returning footsteps were heard, and the company's reprieve at an end. Mrs. Bennet bustled in, with Hill behind her bearing a tray of tea and cakes. At once came the chatter, Kitty and Lydia rushing headlong down the stairs in pursuit of sweets.

Darcy withdrew, his manner unreadable.

But Elizabeth's heart beat all the faster.

Chapter Twenty-Two

January 3, 1812
Longbourn
Darcy

MRS. BENNET WAS KIND enough to extend an invitation to dine. This suited Darcy exceedingly well, for it afforded him even more time in Elizabeth's company before returning to Netherfield. The hours between their meetings had grown into a torment, especially now, when he had gained some assurance that her feelings toward him had changed. If the warmth in her air, the lively sparkle in her eyes when they conversed, and her gentle teasing were any indication, she was no longer merely tolerating him. She was enjoying his presence.

Upon accepting the invitation, Bingley had dispatched his man to fetch a change of clothing for the gentlemen. They were shown to a pair of guest chambers, likely intended for a married couple, Darcy observed, for a single door adjoined the chambers. Longbourn, though elegant in its own modest way, did not boast an overabundance of accommodations for visitors.

In his chamber, Darcy stood before the looking glass, adjusting the folds of his cravat with precision. His fingers moved by habit, long-practiced in the ritual since he was at times obliged to travel without his valet, but his thoughts were far removed from the intricacies of linen and starch.

Her words echoed in his mind. *"You surprise me, Mr. Darcy, that a man of your fortune and consequence is not yet married."*

"I am only for you, Elizabeth," he murmured into the stillness. "No other lady is perfect for me, and I shall have only you, or no one at all."

That gentle probing, an observation far from indifferent, had stirred something within him. Her curiosity was not idle; her intent was plain when she inquired of Anne and the supposed cradle betrothal. By all appearances, she was testing the waters. The memory of her question stirred his heart, no less than when she bravely raised it. Had he only imagined her distress until he had calmly reassured her? He thought not. Surely she would accept him when he proposed. He fastened the cravat pin and took a moment to study his reflection, smoothing the front of his waistcoat with exact attention.

Not much longer now.

The days since Christmas had both flown past and yet seemed to lag, a contradiction he could not reconcile. Each day brought them closer to Twelfth Night, and the final gift. He dared not yet express his fervent hopes aloud, but he felt certain Elizabeth understood. And if she did not—well, all would be the sweeter when he declared himself.

A sudden knock and the creak of the adjoining door interrupted his reverie.

"Say, Darcy, may I ask for your assistance this evening?"

Bingley's genial face appeared around the edge of the door, furrowed in uncharacteristic agitation. The sight amused Darcy, for it was rare indeed that his friend displayed even a hint of vexation.

"Of course," He stepped away from the glass and motioned to the chairs near the hearth. "Come in, Bingley. You know I shall assist you in any way you require."

Bingley crossed the threshold, his movements quick and light despite his agitation. He held a small parcel wrapped in fine paper and tied with a blue ribbon, clearly prepared with care.

"I wish to give Jane a present," he began, taking the offered chair. "But it has been nigh on impossible to speak with her alone. Mrs. Bennet insists upon inserting herself into every conversation, usually with some urgent matter of lace, flowers, or guest lists. I mean no ill will toward my future mother-in-law, but if Jane and I are not afforded some privacy soon, I shall hie off to Scotland and wed her over the anvil at Gretna Green. At least there, I would be spared muslin samples. In truth, I begin to understand why Bennet locks himself in his study."

Darcy laughed, the sound warming the space between them. Bingley seldom let his feathers be ruffled, and it delighted him to see his genial friend unsettled by something so domestic. "Do not tempt fate. Mrs. Bennet might follow you to the border only to offer counsel on floral arrangements. Have you decided upon a date? Perhaps that would suffice to divert the lady."

Bingley grinned, though he pressed a hand to his temple in mock despair. "We intend to settle it this evening. I mean to give this necklace to Jane after we do."

Darcy sobered. "I shall do my best to secure you a few private moments. If necessary, I shall engage Mrs. Bennet directly and give her my full attention—though I warn you, I may never recover." He spoke in jest, for he had become rather fond of the matron.

"You are a true friend, Darcy" Bingley rose, clutching the parcel with renewed purpose. "Shall we go down? I daresay dinner should soon be served."

Darcy nodded. He cast one last glance at his reflection—sharp cravat, composed mien, expectant heart—and together they quitted the room, descending the staircase side by side to join the company in the parlor, anticipation mounting for the evening ahead.

The Longbourn dining room, though modest beside the great houses to which Darcy was accustomed, was warm and cheerfully appointed. A long table was laid with white linens edged in lace, silver cutlery polished bright, and delicate bone china plates painted with a rose motif. The aroma of roast beef with rich gravy and root vegetables filled the air, accompanied by the subtler notes of baked apples, stewed pears, and a currant-studded pudding kept warm near the hearth.

As the company gathered and the first course was served—a fine soup of parsnip and barley—conversation grew lively with the clinking of spoons and the rustle of napkins.

"Mrs. Long has promised mistletoe and several kissing boughs at her Twelfth Night party!" Lydia announced from her place with excessive animation, nearly knocking over her glass of small beer. "I expect I shall be kissed a dozen times before the night is out."

Kitty huffed, flicking a crumb off her sleeve. "That is nonsense, Lydia. Everyone knows the officers like me best. Denny paid me two compliments in one evening!"

Lydia rolled her eyes and scoffed so dramatically that even Mr. Bennet looked up from his plate. "Kitty, you are absurd. It is not only the officers—it is everyone. I am the liveliest girl in Meryton. Why, even Colonel Forster's wife said so; she ought to know, being the colonel's wife and all."

Darcy, seated beside Bingley, gave no outward sign of his opinion, though inwardly he reflected that both Miss Lydia and Miss Kitty wildly overestimated their own attractions. Such was the way with very young ladies—undisciplined, indulged, and wholly unaware of the weight of their words in mixed company. He found himself wondering how Elizabeth and Miss Bennet bore it with such grace.

When the first dishes were removed and a fragrant lamb pie with a golden crust was brought in, Darcy addressed Mrs. Bennet with civility. "I must say, madam, this is a remarkably fine meal. I have rarely enjoyed a dinner more than when dining at Longbourn."

Mrs. Bennet, already beaming from the distinction of having two wealthy gentlemen beneath her roof, flushed with pleasure. "Oh! Mr. Darcy, you are too kind! But I must admit, it is all owing to my mother's receipts. I never stray from them—not for meat, nor pie, nor jam. Even the plum preserves are prepared just as they were when I was a girl."

Darcy smiled as he took a sip of wine.

"They are closely guarded secrets, of course," she went on, leaning toward him to speak as though sharing a confidence. "Mrs. Goulding has tried above twenty years to get the way of making my syllabub from me, and Mrs. Long is forever pestering me for my pie paste receipt. But I always say, 'Some things are not to be shared, even among the friendliest neighbors.' Why, if I let those ladies know how Cook contrives my lemon tarts, they would be passing them off at their tables as their own!"

"You are wise to keep them to yourself," Darcy returned with sincerity. He set down his fork and met her gaze with composed gravity. "Your puddings and pies would not be out of place in the finest dining rooms of London."

Mrs. Bennet fairly fluttered with delight.

Elizabeth, seated opposite, had paused in her own conversation to regard him with astonishment. Her cheeks flushed prettily, and her striking eyes glowed with warmth and amusement. He allowed himself a brief glance, and when their eyes met, an unspoken understanding passed between them. She was pleased. And that meant more to him than the approval of any London hostess.

After the meal, the ladies adjourned to the drawing room. Darcy tarried but briefly with Bingley and Mr. Bennet over a glass of port, but his every thought pressed toward Elizabeth. When the gentlemen joined the ladies, she had seated herself upon the settee with needlework in her lap, though the needle moved but little. She glanced toward him once, almost in invitation.

Before he could cross to her, Bingley caught his eye and raised his brows meaningfully. The plan. Of course.

Darcy altered his direction, approaching where Mrs. Bennet was expatiating to Miss Mary and Miss Bennet on the superiority of goose over turkey for Christmas Day. He bowed slightly. "Mrs. Bennet, may I beg your counsel on a rather personal matter?"

"Oh! Of course, Mr. Darcy, anything at all." She clasped her hands eagerly, her attention entirely his. Miss Bennet rose and slipped away from her mother's side.

Darcy continued, intent on his assignment to keep the matron's attention engaged until the pair returned. "I wondered; do you have any notion of what a young lady of sixteen might like for her birthday? My sister's is soon, and I confess I find myself at a loss."

This was not wholly accurate, nor was it the full truth. He did feel somewhat baffled and unsure when it came to presents, but he knew Georgiana would treasure whatever he chose. However, Mrs. Bennet must be talking. And staying.

"Oh, bless me! Sixteen? The most difficult age, to be sure! Not quite a girl, and not yet a woman. But I can tell you this, sir: ribbons and hair combs are always admired. Perhaps a small writing desk? Or lace-edged handkerchiefs? My own girls all wanted keepsake boxes and smelling salts at that age. And if she is musically inclined, a new set of music sheets; you London folk have the finest publishers already…"

Darcy listened with courtesy while edging himself subtly toward the door. Five minutes had passed. Where was Bingley?

Mrs. Bennet rattled on. "And then, of course, if she is fond of horses, perhaps a new riding crop—oh! Or something truly special, like a miniature portrait of her dearest brother. Though that would require a painter, and I dare say you have little time to sit for that sort of thing—"

Her words faltered, trailing off as her attention was drawn elsewhere.

Darcy turned and beheld Miss Bennet and Bingley returning to the company. She now wore an exquisite emerald necklace, the stones setting off her fair skin and golden hair to great advantage.

Mrs. Bennet squealed. "Oh! What is this? Jane! My dearest girl! Is that new? Where did you—? Oh, it is beautiful! Mr. Bingley, you are too generous! I declare, it is the finest gift anyone has ever received in this house!"

She hurried toward her daughter in a fuss of ribbons and gratitude, abandoning Darcy mid-sentence, all her daughters following to admire the gems and share in Miss Bennet's joy.

Elizabeth was the first to reach her. "It suits you, Jane. I have never seen you look more elegant."

Bingley passed Darcy with a triumphant smile, leaning close to murmur just loud enough, "I thank you."

He returned a discreet nod. The mission was accomplished.

Another screech came from Mrs. Bennet. "February? No, that will not do at all!" The couple, it seemed, had at last settled upon a date for their wedding.

Freed at last from diversion, he crossed the room to where Elizabeth had resumed her seat, her work lying idle in her lap. As he approached, she watched him with amused curiosity.

"You appeared much engaged with my mother. May I ask what engrossed you so thoroughly?"

Darcy took the seat beside her. "A strategy," he replied. "Involving emeralds, evasions, and an exhaustive list of birthday gifts for a girl of sixteen."

Elizabeth laughed, her eyes dancing. "You must tell me more."

"I should be happy to; however, I warn you, it is a rather long list."

"Then I must ask: was it a true inquiry? Or merely a noble sacrifice to the cause of young love?" She nodded toward her sister and Bingley, both now seated with Mrs. Bennet in earnest discussion.

"You are too clever by half, Miss Elizabeth. It was the latter, I confess. I needed no counsel for Georgiana. She is easy to gratify and would value whatever I chose with thought. But your mother is wonderfully *zealous* on such topics. I trusted her advice would require several uninterrupted minutes."

Elizabeth nudged his shoulder and laughed heartily, a warm, spontaneous sound that struck him through. He was glad that she had not missed his playful reminder of their Z-word contest only days before.

"You used my mother's love of birthdays and baubles against her? You are more devious than I imagined."

"I prefer to call it strategic delegation." He rubbed his shoulder in mock injury.

She chuckled again, shaking her head in feigned disapproval. "Well, I cannot fault your methods. Jane looks happier than I have seen her in days. My mother's attentions can at times be...excessive."

He studied her beautiful countenance, radiant with humor and affection. Her laughter, light, natural, wholly genuine, was unlike anything he had ever known. It was warmth; it was music. And in that moment, he thought, *I want to hear that sound every day of my life.*

He leaned closer to her and spoke only loud enough so she could hear. "Your laugh, Miss Elizabeth...it is a song so sweet it gladdens the heart."

Her breath caught—in the twinkling of an eye—but he saw it: the subtle lift of her bountiful lashes, the deepening of her blush.

She wagged a finger at him, her smile betraying her jest. "Careful, Mr. Darcy. You will make me vain."

The gesture, light though it was, stirred a sharper desire than he dared reveal. *How am I to endure the days remaining before Twelfth Night when I long to seize that mischievous hand and press my lips upon it?*

He mastered himself and inclined his head. "I should think it impossible. You remain unspoiled, despite every cause to be otherwise."

Elizabeth glanced down, clearly moved; when she met his eyes once more, he sought to convey his sincerity in his gaze.

"Thank you."

The company bustled about them, full of holiday cheer and familial chatter. Miss Mary entertained them with songs on the pianoforte, while the two youngest Bennets were bent over an embroidery frame in the corner, one helping the other with a difficult stitch. But for Darcy, all else receded. What mattered was the woman beside him—and the growing certainty that she might become the very heart of his world.

Chapter Twenty-Three

January 4, 1812
Longourn
Elizabeth

THE MORNING BROKE CRISP and cold, the kind of biting chill that turned breath to mist and tempted one to linger beneath a counterpane. Frost glistened upon the glass, painting delicate arabesques with nature's unseen hand, and obscuring the world without. And within Elizabeth's chamber, the fire had burned low in the night, and the air now held the sting of winter against her cheeks.

Still, curiosity overpowered comfort.

Elizabeth stretched, her arms reaching toward the bed curtains before she tossed the coverlet aside and slipped from the bed. The chill met her skin with a nip, and she gave a startled squeak as she padded across the rug in haste to the table where a new parcel awaited. Another gift: large, ornate, and gleaming in the early light, it rested beside a folded slip of paper bearing her name in that now-familiar, strong hand.

With tingling fingers, she opened the note first:

> On the eleventh day of Christmas, in a
> jewel box divine,

> Eleven sapphires of deep, steadfast shine.

Her breath caught. Sapphire? She reached for the box.

It was unlike any she had ever seen. Made of rich rosewood with inlaid panels of ivory and mother-of-pearl, it was shaped like a miniature chest, the lid curved and edged in gilt filigree. A delicate clasp of bright sterling silver caught the light. Upon the top lay a marquetry design: a bouquet entwined with musical notes, carved with precision into the glossy surface. When she lifted it, a lining of plush ivory velvet was revealed, against which rested eleven sapphire hairpins, each crowned with a faceted gem set in fine silver stems, their brilliance heightened by so pure a ground. The stones shone with the brightness of twilight.

Her heart thudded as she took one in hand, the gem catching the light. "To match my fine eyes, I imagine," she murmured with a smile.

The door opened, and Jane and Mary entered, both wrapped in shawls.

"Oh, how beautiful!" Jane exclaimed, stepping nearer to admire the box and pins. "They suit you perfectly."

"Your gentleman has exquisite taste," Mary observed, touching the edge of the box reverently. "Are you prepared to learn who he is?"

Elizabeth hesitated, her smile wavering. "I...I do not know. What if he never comes forward? What if it ends as a riddle never solved?" She bent over the pins, her fingers gently brushing one gem. "He could vanish, leaving his identity a mystery forever."

"To think he has shown such devotion," Jane mused softly. "Eleven gifts already."

Elizabeth, in true Bennet fashion, turned the subject before her emotions could take root. "And speaking of devotion, Mary, should we not be speaking of Mr. Sanderson?"

A rush of pink stole into Mary's cheeks, her hand flying to her mouth. "Elizabeth!"

"Well, he is expected at tea, is he not?" Elizabeth continued, recalling her sister's mention of it the previous evening. "And from what I have observed, he has every intention of declaring himself soon."

"I have every expectation of a proposal," Mary admitted, cheeks still flushed. "And with the militia possibly relocating, we may not wait long after that to marry."

"Then you will be the second of us wed," Elizabeth teased.

At this, Jane gave a soft laugh.

Mary turned to her eldest sister with interest. "Mama monopolized the conversation yesterday; we never heard the tale of the necklace. Is it new? Did Mr. Bingley commission it?"

Jane's hand lifted to her throat, touching the ornament. "No, it belonged to his mother. She left it to him, intending he should one day give it to his wife."

"How romantic," Elizabeth said sincerely. "It is truly lovely."

"And Mama was not pleased with the date. We have settled on the twentieth of February. She spent the rest of the evening trying to convince us to delay."

"I cannot imagine why," said Elizabeth.

"She fears it is too soon, that there will not be enough flowers. But we do not wish to wait any longer." Jane's tone held firm resolve. "There is no reason to."

Mary nodded. "Your wedding day ought to be precisely what you and Mr. Bingley desire. Mr. Sanderson and I shall likely wed quickly too; there is no telling when his regiment will receive orders."

Elizabeth was all-a-mort, caught by the image of another man—Darcy, upon one knee. Her name upon his lips, spoken with solemn intensity. His eyes, so intense, so full of restrained longing, lifted to hers as he asked the question that had hung between them for days.

She drew in a breath and pushed the thought aside. *No sense dreaming. Best to be realistic. Best not to build dreams upon silence and glances.*

The moment passed. With mutual smiles, the sisters gathered their things and went to their separate chambers to dress for breakfast, the morning light and warmth of the fire beginning to melt the frost-touched glass, and the jewel box gleaming like a promise.

After breakfast, the Bennet household dispersed to various corners, but Elizabeth felt too restless to remain indoors. Bundling herself in her warmest pelisse, she secured the Paisley shawl about her shoulders, its vivid pattern a welcome comfort against the encroaching chill. She tugged on her fur-lined gloves, tied the ribbons of her bonnet, and stepped outside. Though the morning sun had broken clear, a bank of clouds now drew across the sky, dimming the light. The air hung heavy, promising snow before long, and the ground crunched beneath her half boots with frost that had not yet lifted.

She had scarcely set foot upon the drive when Kitty and Lydia burst from the vestibule.

"We wish to walk with you!" Kitty declared, shrugging into her own wrap.

"Yes, as far as the lane. We want to visit the haberdasher's," Lydia added, her expression bright with anticipation. "Do you think it is too late to re-trim my sleeves for tomorrow's celebration?"

Elizabeth smiled. "If you sew all day and all night, you might finish—if you enlist the maids to help and forgo tea."

"I shall settle on new shoe roses and that blue ribbon Pratt gave me," Lydia said with a dreamy sigh. "I cannot decide which officer I shall allow to fetch my punch cup first. They are all so charming."

"I want a new fan," Kitty chimed in. "A white one with painted blossoms."

As her sisters skipped ahead, Elizabeth followed at a measured pace, the breeze teasing tendrils of hair from beneath her bonnet. Their laughter and chatter carried back to her, full of ribbons and admirers.

Her own gown, ready and waiting in her wardrobe, rose to her thoughts: cream muslin with a delicate blue sash and fine ribbon trimming the sleeves and hem. Modest yet elegant. And perfect with the sapphire hairpins. One of her shawls, perhaps the ivory with the embroidered border, would suit well. And mayhap she would wear the pearl necklace as well.

Would Lydia or anyone else remark upon it? She trusted not.

But even if they did, it would hardly matter—*not after tomorrow*. A private smile touched her lips. If all went well, there would be no more need for secrets.

At the fork in the lane, Kitty and Lydia turned toward Meryton, waving gaily.

"Do not let your cheeks freeze, Lizzy!" Lydia called with a grin.

"We shall be back before dinner!"

Elizabeth waved in return, then took the path toward Oakham Mount. It steepened, winding through bare trees whose branches clawed at the leaden sky. Her breath rose in small clouds, the cold stinging her nose and ears, but the steady climb warmed her limbs and cleared her mind.

By the time she reached the summit, color had risen in her cheeks and her pulse beat fast—not from exertion alone.

But the hilltop was still and silent.

No tall figure silhouetted against the sky. No trace of Darcy.

The wind caught at her shawl, and she pulled it close, struggling not to yield to disappointment.

She had dreamed—perhaps too much. Had she conjured what was not there?

No. He will come tomorrow. He must.

And still, she lingered, her gaze sweeping the horizon. The bare hills stretched into the distance, stark and cold beneath the January sky. She drew in a long breath and closed her eyes, gathering her thoughts as neatly as the shawl drawn close about her shoulders.

Tomorrow. It will all be clear tomorrow.

Then, with resolution, she turned and began the descent toward home, even as she held back tears of disappointment.

The fire crackled cheerfully in the drawing room, casting a golden glow upon the assembled guests. The tea service had been set out with delicate china cups and plates of ginger biscuits, seed cake, and sugared walnuts. Elizabeth poured a cup for Jane and had just taken her seat when the butler announced their visitors.

"Mr. Sanderson, Mr. Denny, and Mr. Pratt, ma'am."

Lydia and Kitty perked up at once. "Oh! Pratt, do come sit here," Lydia called with a coquettish tilt of her head. Kitty followed suit with a coy smile toward Denny, and the four soon gathered near the hearth, deep in talk of ribbons, the Meryton assembly, and the scandal of Miss Carter's ruined slippers.

Sanderson, however, approached Mary with purpose, and with a gentlemanly bow, asked leave to join her in the window alcove. Mary, cheeks tinged with color, nodded shyly and led the way.

Elizabeth caught her eye briefly, then moved to intercept her mother, who was about to follow. "Mama, will you sit beside me? I was just about to ask your opinion on the color of the new ribbon I received."

"Oh yes, dear. Let me see. Was it the one trimmed with lace? Or the one with the narrow border?" Mrs. Bennet seated herself eagerly, and thus began a prolonged discussion on trimmings, lace widths, and which colors best suited which complexions.

Time passed. Elizabeth kept one ear for her mother, the other attuned to the window, where Mary and Sanderson sat deep in conversation. She noticed with some satisfaction that neither had touched their tea. At length, he rose and offered his hand. Mary accepted, and together they slipped discreetly from the room.

Mrs. Bennet remained oblivious, still discoursing upon the superiority of embroidered muslin over plain, when Jane entered, a small, knowing smile playing on her lips.

"Elizabeth," Jane murmured, coming to her sister's side. "Papa has a visitor, and I have been expelled from the study. I was in the midst of making a fair copy of Mama's receipts, but apparently, they may only be transcribed under supervision."

"That is true!" Mrs. Bennet chirped. "They are for daughters' hands only, and only when I or your father may oversee. We cannot have them slipping into just anyone's possession. But who is visiting your father?" she added, setting her teacup down with a light clink. "Surely one of the officers? Oh! They are surely asking for Kitty's or Lydia's hand!"

Before Elizabeth or Jane could reply, Mr. Bennet entered the drawing room, spectacles still perched upon his nose and a rare smile playing at the corners of his mouth. Mary and Sanderson followed. Elizabeth caught Mary's eye; her sister said nothing but gave a slight nod, her pleasure evident.

"My dear," he said to Mrs. Bennet with theatrical calm, "a very proper young gentleman has just asked for our Mary's hand in marriage. I was so startled by the novelty of such a request that I nearly refused him outright, but in the end, I gave both my consent and my blessing."

Mrs. Bennet's eyes widened. "Mary?" she gasped. "Mary engaged?"

"Indeed," Mr. Bennet replied, clearly relishing the moment. "They will wed before the militia quits the neighborhood. He has already secured lodgings, and, as it happens, his term will end this summer. They shall remove to his family's estate afterward."

Sanderson pressed a brief kiss to Mary's hand.

At this, Mrs. Bennet shrieked with joy. "Oh! Mary! Engaged! Oh, I knew it. I always said she was the most serious of my girls. A paragon of virtue! Oh, how clever she is!"

Later that evening, as the house settled into calm, Mary and Jane joined Elizabeth in her chamber, each clutching a warmed brick wrapped in cloth to keep their toes from the chill.

"Well?" Elizabeth asked as she began to plait her hair.

Mary looked uncommonly pleased. "He is a younger son, but his father has a small estate set aside—one he shall inherit after his militia service ends. It brings in nearly a thousand pounds a year. And it is in Cheshire. Oh sisters, I am sorry to leave all my family behind!"

Jane's manner warmed with approval. "That is quite respectable! But never fear, Mary. Charles has been searching for an estate in the North. Perhaps we shall be neighbors."

This appeased their sister, and she relaxed. "There is more," Mary proudly continued, almost whispering. "His mother left him a modest inheritance when he was a boy. It has remained untouched in the four percents for over a decade."

Elizabeth gave a low whistle as she moved to join her sisters upon the bed. "Well then! That is a fine, prudent arrangement."

"I shall be very comfortable and very happy," Mary said. "He is often overlooked because he is reserved and does not mix like the other officers. But as it turns out, he has more consequence than all of them."

Elizabeth couldn't resist. She clasped her hands dramatically and mimicked Lydia's lilt: "*What a good joke!*"

All three gave way to laughter, warm and unchecked, echoing against the bedchamber walls like music.

"If only everyone could be this happy," Jane mused, resting her head upon Elizabeth's shoulder.

"Perhaps you will be next, Elizabeth," Mary murmured. She shifted closer, and Elizabeth wrapped an arm around her. "Tomorrow is Twelfth Night. Only a few short hours and you will have your answer—if Providence is kind." Mary yawned. "I do not believe you will be left in suspense. This gentleman of yours has shown his admiration sufficiently to dispel any doubts."

Elizabeth did not reply, praying silently that her sister would be proven correct in the morning. *And if she is not?* Whispered the contrary voice in her mind. *Well,* she answered, *then I shall face that when it comes.*

Eventually, they kissed each other goodnight and withdrew to their own chambers. Elizabeth extinguished her candle, the embers in the grate casting a flickering glow across the ceiling as she lay back upon her pillow. Shadows played along the walls, soothing as her eyes fluttered. She tucked one arm behind her head as she rolled onto her back, staring upward at the dark canopy above.

Tomorrow, she thought, her heart thudding as the image of Darcy filled her mind—tall and silent, eyes searching hers, his words weighted with feeling. Tomorrow, *it all ends. Or begins.* She smiled to herself, her eyes drifting shut. *Please,* she prayed. *Let it begin.*

Chapter Twenty-Four

January 4, 1812
Netherfield Park
Darcy

MATTERS OF BUSINESS DETAINED the gentlemen at Netherfield through the morning, the drawing room transformed into a temporary study. Papers lay stacked upon the sideboard, maps unfurled, and a fire blazed cheerily in the hearth. Bingley, seated near the writing desk, held a letter in one hand and frowned over a sheet of parchment.

"Darcy," he said, setting the papers aside, "I have resolved to make one more alteration to the marriage articles before the final draft is prepared. Only a small clarification regarding the jointure."

Darcy nodded with approval. "Prudent. 'Tis best to have everything set forth clearly now."

"I have also received a packet of correspondence from an agent in the North; he sends word of five estates, all within fifty miles of Pemberley. I thought I might settle nearer to you."

Darcy regarded Bingley with interest. Such a choice would certainly aid his own cause with Elizabeth; being so near her dearest sister must prove highly agreeable. "Let us look at them."

Bingley spread the papers, and Darcy read each aloud:

Ashbrook Hall — Located in Cheshire, this estate comprises a modest manor set on 520 acres, with twelve tenant farms and a gently sloping park. The house is in fair repair, though the dower house requires renovation. The nearby village provides both a school and a church.

Windmere Grange — Set in Derbyshire, only twenty-five miles from Pemberley, Windmere Grange offers 700 acres, fifteen tenant farms, and a late Tudor manor with substantial stables. The estate includes a well-kept dower house and excellent roads. The library is reputed to be impressive.

Netherby Downs — In Nottinghamshire, this estate encompasses 470 acres with ten tenant farms, and a rather grand Queen Anne manor. The house is beautifully maintained and boasts a small ornamental lake. There is no dower house, though a detached guest cottage might be converted.

Highmere Park — Near Bakewell, also in Derbyshire, Highmere consists of 610 acres, thirteen tenant farms, and a weathered but dignified manor house dating from the reign of

Charles II. The estate includes a mill, and the dower house has been recently reroofed.

Rosegate Manor — Situated in southern Cheshire, Rosegate features a modern Palladian-style house, 450 acres, eight tenant farms, and extensive flower gardens. The house is in excellent repair, but the estate lacks woodland and has no dower house.

Darcy studied each summary carefully. "Windmere Grange and Highmere Park are both strong candidates. Ashbrook has promise, but the work required may not justify the cost."

Bingley tapped his fingers. "I agree. And Rosegate is charming, but lacks substance. It has too many gardens, and too few fields."

"Then let us set aside Ashbrook, Rosegate, and Netherby Downs. I shall accompany you in touring Windmere and Highmere, and together we can determine which suits you best."

Bingley gave a grateful smile. "Your help means more than I can say."

Just then, the butler entered with a tray. "A letter for you, sir," he said, presenting it to Darcy.

Darcy recognized the hand at once. "From Georgiana," He excused himself and withdrew to his chamber. There, he sat by the window and broke the seal.

Dearest William,

It has been far too long since I have written you anything of length, and I am determined to amend that now. Mrs. Annesley encouraged me to sit and take my time, and so I do, with her smiling at me from across the room as I begin this letter.

My days have been quite regular, though not unpleasant. Aunt Matlock has been most attentive, taking me to visit acquaintances and lending me books from her library. I am presently studying Italian with renewed interest and have even begun composing short pieces anew.

I have been practicing some particularly challenging works—Dussek's Grand Sonata in F-sharp minor *has tested my patience, and Haydn's* Andante with Variations *continues to elude perfect execution. But Mrs. Annesley says she sees progress, and I must trust her ear.*

My companion has been wonderfully patient. I cannot express enough gratitude for her guidance. She knows how to lift my spirits without flattery, and though I still struggle with moments of melancholy, they are fewer now.

Aunt has also expressed her approval of my diligence, and last week she brought me a folio of sonatas by Clementi. They are light and pleasant, and I find them a welcome contrast to the more demanding pieces. I played one for her yesterday, and she declared I had improved since Michaelmas.

The household here is kind and orderly. Evenings are spent in reading or music. I have begun copying passages from Richardson into my commonplace book. As Aunt says, it will improve my penmanship as well as my moral sensibilities. I believe she means it affectionately.

The garden is dull this time of year, but I have taken to walking the gravel paths after breakfast. The hellebores have begun to open in the south corner—such brave blooms.

I am eager to hear more from you, dear brother. Your last letter was so short that I feared you were unwell or troubled. Please tell me what occupies you. I long to know how your days are spent, and whether you are happy.

With all my love,
Your devoted sister,
Georgiana

Darcy folded the letter and held it a moment, his heart full. He drew out his own paper and began his reply.

My dearest Georgiana,

Your letter was balm to my soul. I cannot express the joy it gave me to read your thoughts at such length. I must first apologize for my recent neglect. My days have not been idle, but I ought to have written more faithfully. You are very dear to me, and though you are well attended by those who care for you, I should never let distance become an excuse for silence.

You asked what occupies me; dearest sister, I continue my visit with Bingley, and I believe, with every certainty in my heart, that I am in love.

It has been twelve days since I began giving small gifts to the lady who has captured my heart entirely. Each day I have chosen something thoughtful and personal—tokens meant to delight her and to discreetly convey the depth of my admiration. A fan of painted silk, a length of violet ribbon, a volume of poetry, a finely embroidered shawl, silver combs, a pearl necklace, a diamond locket that belonged to our grandmother... To-day, I sent her eleven sapphire hairpins. To-morrow, the final gift.

Her name is Miss Elizabeth Bennet. I have mentioned her in my letters before, if you recall. She is clever and lively, her wit sparkling yet tempered with wisdom. Her eyes—oh, Georgiana, her violet eyes—lovely and luminous, seem to speak volumes when her words fall still. She walks with dignity, converses with elegance, and holds to her principles with steadfast resolve. There is a light in her that makes the world itself seem warmer.

What astonishes me most is how she perceives the truth of character. She has not been dazzled by wealth or name. She has teased me, challenged me, and perhaps unknowingly, healed something within me.

We have not spoken of these things openly yet, but I feel a certainty growing between us. I confess I began these tokens in secret, for I was not certain she would welcome such attentions. Yes, my dear sister, she is singular, caring not a jot for being Mrs. Darcy of Pemberley unless she felt sincere attachment to my person. Now, however, I hope—I dare to hope—that she may return my affection, and I intend to make my offer before I quit Hertfordshire, though I find myself more anxious than when engaged with her in our sharpest exchanges of wit.

I wish you could meet her. I believe you would find her a kindred spirit. Her devotion to her sisters is admirable, and she speaks of music and novels with great pleasure. She once spoke so warmly of a sister who plays the pianoforte, and I longed to tell her of you. I restrained myself, but only just.

Pray that I may soon bring her into our family, to call her not only my wife, but your sister. I think she would love you very well, and you, her.

On another note, a certain person will no longer trouble us. I will tell you more, but do not wish to mar this missive with thoughts of him.

I will write again soon—with good news, I trust. And if all goes as I desire, my next letter may contain not merely my wishes, but the beginning of a new chapter for us all.

Ever your loving brother, William

He closed the letter, signed it with a flourish, then sanded and sealed the missive. It would go out with the post, and when he wrote again, it would be to announce success. Georgiana would not wait patiently; she had longed for a sister and would wish to know immediately when he knew success.

The dining room at Netherfield was unusually subdued that evening. The fire crackled in the grate, and the candles glimmered upon the silver. Only two places were set for dinner; he and Bingley sat across from one another, each sunk in thought. The footman served a hearty fare: a roast saddle of mutton with red currant jelly, buttered turnips, and a game pie, the repast concluding with a custard tart.

Bingley glanced around the room as he sipped his claret. "I must confess, Darcy, I find I miss the chaos of Longbourn. Meals there are never tame."

Darcy allowed a rare smile. "Indeed. Lively does not begin to describe it. I own I am quite fond of their company."

"Fond? I see you are less rigid with the Bennets, but *fond?* I never thought to hear it from you."

"You are not the only one surprised, They have a way of endearing themselves, almost unawares. I believe, above all, they are genuine, which is more than I can say of many in the first circles."

After dinner, the gentlemen retired to the billiard room with a decanter of port. The table was already prepared. Bingley chalked his cue and leaned against the edge, his manner contemplative.

"I intend to marry Miss Bennet in February, as you know," he said of a sudden, "and I have no plans to inform my sisters until it is already done."

"Truly?" Darcy was hardly astonished. The Bingley sisters had made no secret of their disdain for Hertfordshire society.

Bingley scoffed as he sent a ball smartly into a corner pocket. "I have had no fewer than ten letters from them. Each demanded my whereabouts, speculating wildly. I had my post forwarded, yet they persist in sending everything to your house in town."

Darcy's amusement faded as Bingley grew serious.

"Darcy...how would you handle disapproving relatives when taking a wife? Especially after a proposal has been offered."

Darcy rested his cue, thoughtful. The question struck deep, for it was not fancy. He had already considered it—agonized over it—on countless solitary walks and sleepless nights. At length, he replied.

"I would remember that the woman I marry must become my foremost duty. No other opinion, however loudly voiced, should outweigh hers. A gentleman's charge is to protect his wife, not only from hardship, but from insult and disdain. He must shield her from those who would belittle her, even if they bear his name."

He paused, the weight of his words settling between them. His thoughts turned unbidden to his aunt, Lady Catherine. She would be livid, unyielding in her condemnation, should she learn that he had chosen anyone but her daughter. Her pride, her expectations, her imagined influence over him would all be shattered. But the thought no longer dissuaded him. If Elizabeth accepted him, he would face his aunt's fury with resolute gladness.

"I think often of Lady Catherine. She will not be pleased with my choice not to marry her daughter. In truth, she may do all in her power to oppose it. But I have come to understand that love must not bow to pride, nor affection to pedigree."

Bingley absorbed this in silence, his cue idle in his hand.

Darcy spoke on, more firmly, his words edged with protectiveness. "If you mean Miss Bingley and Mrs. Hurst, I will offer this: Miss Bennet is gentle, and your sister is...formidable. You must not allow your wife to be made uncomfortable in her own home. Miss Bingley will seek to dominate, as she always has. She is clever with her tongue, subtle in her slights. Miss Bennet may not call it out, but she will feel it. It is your duty, Charles, to prevent that—to be her advocate, her shield, her safe harbor."

"And you, Darcy? Would you apply the same measures with your family? You have always spoken of duty. Would it not weigh against your own sense of obligation?"

Darcy's reply was steady, without hesitation. "My duty will be to my wife—whoever she might be; above all others. That is the lesson I have learned. A man may inherit title and fortune, but it is love and loyalty that render him worthy of both. The family name is nothing if preserved at the cost of his heart's happiness."

His eyes turned distant. "I once believed it my task to uphold every expectation, to see the Darcy name remain unblemished. But I have come to know my truest duty lies not in pleasing my relations, but in cherishing the woman who will stand beside me for all my days. In her happiness, I shall find my honor."

Darcy stood at the window of his bedchamber, one hand resting against the cold glass as he stared into the inky blackness beyond. The candles flickered, their glow casting long shadows across the walls. Behind him, the fire crackled low.

He had spoken the words to Bingley readily enough, but now, alone with his thoughts, he considered them more deeply.

He had never truly examined his stance—at least, not until Elizabeth. From his earliest years, he had been taught that family was everything. Respect, obedience, and loyalty were the pillars of a Darcy's life. One deferred to the wisdom of one's elders; he was to uphold the dignity of the family name at all costs.

It was that creed which had driven him to leave Hertfordshire the first time, to walk away from the possibility of love because it did not accord with the standard imposed upon him.

But now...now he knew better. Love, true and abiding, did not disgrace a name. It honored it.

Elizabeth had altered everything.

All that mattered was winning her regard. And if he did, if she accepted him, they might build a life together that would withstand the disapproval of any who objected. Together, they could weather all.

Darcy turned from the window, conviction steady within him. He snuffed the candle by his bedside and lay down. As his eyes closed, it was her face he beheld—the radiance in her eyes, the charm of her smile, the memory of her laughter.

The morrow. On the morrow I shall speak at last.

Chapter Twenty-Five

January 5, 1812
Longbourn
Elizabeth

The morning dawned differently than Elizabeth had expected. She had retired with a heart full of anticipation, her mind circling without cease. Sleep had not come easily, and when it did, it was filled with visions of Darcy—tall and steadfast, with his attention fixed upon her alone. In a dream he had taken her hand and spoken words she could not recall upon waking, only the echo of warmth and certainty that they had been uttered in love.

But now, in the still grey light of dawn, her eyes fluttered open. The fire in the grate had long since gone cold, the air in the chamber biting as she drew the covers close about her shoulders. She rubbed the sleep from her eyes, willing herself to wake, and turned her head instinctively toward the small table beside her favorite chair.

Empty.

Her heart plummeted. Surely not. She threw back the counterpane, pulled on some wool socks, and crossed the cold floor, her breath catching in her throat as she reached the table. Still nothing. No ribboned parcel, no folded note, no surprise. Eleven days of wonder, of tokens so carefully chosen, each one feeling more like a secret avowal of devotion, and now, on the final day—nothing. A chill deeper than the room's cold settled upon her as she sank into the chair.

What had changed? Had she mistaken everything? Her thoughts raced, doubt seeping into the fragile hope she had nurtured. What if Charlotte had been right? What if *he* were not her Darcy, but rather, a gentleman already bound by marriage, and all this merely some cruel amusement at her expense? She choked back a sob. What gentleman would woo with such care, only to withdraw at the last? Surely *not Darcy!* And if it had not been he—then who?

Anger rose, but it was fleeting, soon giving way to sorrow. She had wanted it to be him—had *believed* it was he. His presence these past weeks, his steady attentions, the way he regarded her when he thought himself unobserved—it had all seemed so real. She pressed a hand against her heart. The ache was more bitter than she expected. She had dared to hope.

A knock on her door startled her.

She turned in haste, brushing her eyes as the maid entered with a small curtsy. "Pardon, miss. I have a note for ye."

Elizabeth blinked. "A note?"

"Yes, miss. I am terribly sorry. I overslept and—" The maid looked down and fell silent.

"You have been delivering the gifts?"

The girl nodded. "They were brought to me from the village, and it were my task to place them in your chamber when I tended the fire."

"Then you do not know who the sender is?"

The maid shook her head.

Elizabeth sighed. *So much for that.*

The maid stepped forward and held out a folded paper. Elizabeth's breath caught the moment her eyes fell upon the hand—*his* hand. The same bold, orderly script that had graced the card with the locket. The ache that had held her so motionless gave way to relief, and her fingers trembled as she broke the seal. Two words.

Oakham Mount.

She was filled with a sudden exhilaration that set her whole frame in motion. Elizabeth clutched the note tightly and moved without hesitation, calling for her morning things. She dressed swiftly, choosing a dark green wool gown that flattered her figure and held warmth. Over it she slipped a shawl—one of *his*—and wrapped her red pelisse close, fastening the buttons with careful fingers. She tied her bonnet, then donned the fine gloves he had given her. Last of all, she took up her fur muff.

The sun had not yet risen above the horizon when she stepped outside, her boots crunching through the crust of snow that covered the path. The world before her lay hushed, small branches and hedge rows weighted by their wintry burden. It must have fallen in the night. Longbourn's garden was transformed into a winter kingdom, and she, a solitary pilgrim, went forth in search of her fate.

Her pace was brisk, urgent. The cold stung her cheeks, but her blood ran warm with possibilities. Her breath formed clouds before her, and behind her, the eastern sky kindled with a faint golden wash.

At the base of Oakham Mount, she slowed. The snow lay deeper here, and the climb was steeper; she paused, not from weariness, but wonder.

The landscape stretched in frozen stillness around her, painted in pearl and silver. On either side of the path, the bare trees rose like sentinels, their branches laden with snow. The air was crisp and pure, the whole scene a harmony of repose. She marveled that she could behold nature's beauty.

Just before gaining the summit, Elizabeth set a gloved hand on the rough trunk of a tree and stilled herself once more to master her feelings. At length, when she stepped forward to continue, she halted for an entirely new reason.

There on the rise above her, silhouetted against the paling sky, stood a man.

Waiting.

In that instant she knew him, and a thrill of certainty swept through her; no distance could disguise him from her. Not waiting another moment, she hastened forward. The crunch of her steps in the snow betrayed her presence, and he turned.

What he had long kept hidden from her was revealed to her at last. Love—deep and unguarded—was laid bare. Longing too, and reverence. He regarded her as if she were the answer to a question he had carried for a very long time.

"Elizabeth," he greeted, his voice warm despite the cold air. Then, almost shyly, he advanced a pace, holding a long, ribbon-wrapped package in his gloved hands.

"For the most *tolerable* lady of my acquaintance." A familiar wry smile played about his lips.

A warmth spread through her at his first use of her given name; it was at once disarming and exhilarating, yet she reached for the parcel, unable to resist a playful retort. "Am I then tolerable enough to tempt you?"

His smile deepened, amusement giving way to something more tender. "More than enough. Entirely, wholly, and irrevocably. It has been many weeks now since I considered you the handsomest woman of my acquaintance."

"High praise, considering my sister is Jane Bennet." She cradled the gift, the weight light, yet laden with meaning. The corners of her mouth lifted as she studied him.

"I believe, sir, since those first moments at the assembly, you have improved upon further acquaintance."

"I have had an excellent teacher in humility," he replied, stepping closer, "and in hope."

A gust swept past them, scattering snowflakes through the air like falling diamonds in the rising sun. Elizabeth's eyes flicked to the package in her arms, then back at him.

"Shall I open it now?"

"If you please. Though the words I mean to speak matter more than anything within."

She lowered her eyes and untied the ribbon slowly, her fingers deft despite the cold. Inside lay twelve silk roses, each a perfect imitation of nature, yet unfading. Their colors ranged from the palest blush to the richest crimson, the petals curled with exquisite workmanship. Their stems, she thought, were wood, wrapped with green ribbon, and even the leaves were of silk, embroidered and stitched with care. Beside them lay a small card, handwritten in his now-familiar hand:

> On the twelfth day of Christmas, twelve silk roses lie,
> Unfading, eternal—as steadfast as I.
> With treasures so lovely, yet none half so dear,
> As the vow that I whisper for only you to hear.

When she looked up, he was no longer smiling; his features were serious now, his eyes searching hers.

"Elizabeth, these last twelve days have been the most meaningful of my life. I dared to hope that you might guess the heart behind them. But hope is not enough. I must speak plainly."

She grew utterly still. The roses trembled in her hands.

Darcy steadied himself, his eyes fixed on hers, the winter air between them suspended, as though time itself had ceased its course.

"I love you. With all that I am. And I know—*I know*—that your love cannot be bought with wealth or flattery. Not at all. You are not a woman to be impressed by gold or titles, nor swayed by grand houses or fine carriages."

Elizabeth's lips parted, but she said nothing. She felt overcome, as though every nerve had awakened at once.

He continued, stepping closer, his gloved hands open at his sides as though offering all he had. "You value what is *real*. A man's honor. His principles. The content of his character." He paused, his gaze earnest. "That is why I chose each gift not for its worth, but for what it might convey. The meaning behind the object—the intention—was what I wished you would see."

Elizabeth blinked, her composure wavering as her mind traveled backward. Yes. She *had* seen meaning. The books, the combs, the locket, the hairpins... She had wondered, suspected. Her eyes swam with rising tears as she gave a slow, silent nod.

Darcy took another step, the snow crunching beneath his boots.

His words came quieter now, but she knew he was no less certain.

"I love you, my dearest Elizabeth. And if you can love me in return, even a little...I beg you to end my suffering and consent to be my wife."

He swallowed visibly, his features taut with the effort of restraint. "But if you cannot…if your affections are already set against me, then still—*forever*—I shall love you. For the rest of my life, I shall love only you. There is no one else, dearest, loveliest Elizabeth. There could never be another. You have my heart, my devotion, which I now offer freely, and without condition."

Elizabeth could no longer meet his eyes without her own feelings welling within her. Her throat tightened. She pressed her fingers to the roses in the box, as though they might anchor her. His gifts were not trifles; they were pieces of him—of his very soul. And he had waited. Hoped. Believed in her.

She looked up, and in his eyes dwelt a tenderness that banished the last of her trepidation. Elizabeth held the box of silk roses close, as if they could steady the tumult within her. Her eyes met his once more—so open, so achingly sincere—and for a moment, she simply drank in the sight of him. The man before her was not the proud, distant gentleman who had once slighted her at a ball. He was something else entirely—something more.

"I *did* see the meaning in your gifts." The words slipped forth, scarcely more than a whisper. "Each one seemed to speak—to say something you dared not put into words. I saw your thoughtfulness in them…your care. But more than that, I have seen the change in you."

Darcy stilled, every nerve taut, intent upon her every word.

"You are no longer the man who looked down his nose at a country assembly. You have become someone kind. Considerate. Humble and welcoming." Her voice wavered. "You are a man worth knowing…and worth loving."

She watched the tension in his frame break, his shoulders lowering as though her words had lifted a great weight. For a moment his lips parted, yet no words came to answer what hers had just bestowed.

"I did not know for certain my admirer was you. But I *wanted* it to be you." Her eyes brimmed with tears she refused to shed. "I *prayed* it was you."

Darcy stepped forward then, as if he could bear no more distance between them. The box of roses pressed lightly between them as he lifted one gloved hand to her face, the leather cool against her skin. His fingers brushed her cheek with reverent care, trailing down to her chin. He tilted her face up to his, and with exquisite gentleness, lowered his lips to hers in a kiss that spoke all he could not say.

It was a kiss filled with unspoken promises. Tender. Chaste. Filled with meaning. The roses did not so much as bend between them.

When he drew back, her eyes fluttered open to find his gaze still fixed upon her—intense, searching, full of awe.

"Yes, sir," she whispered, her lips tingling with the echo of his. "I will marry you. How could I not after such exquisite delight?"

Darcy's laughter rumbled low in his chest, rich with relief and joy. She gently set the box of roses on a nearby tree stump, and he gathered her into his arms. She pressed her cheek to the fine wool of his coat, breathing in the scent of sandalwood and cedar, a fragrance she would forever after associate with home.

His arms tightened around her, steady and sure.

"Shall I speak with your father?" He pulled away just enough to look at her once more.

Elizabeth smiled up at him, her eyes bright. "Yes. But I warn you—informing my mother might provoke a fit of nerves. Three daughters engaged at once is enough to unbalance even the steadiest of women."

Amusement lit his eyes. "Perhaps Bingley and your sister would not mind sharing their wedding day," he said with mock solemnity. "I find I have not the desire to prolong my agony."

Elizabeth laughed, the sound carrying clear in the crisp winter air. "We can ask them—and perhaps even Mary and Mr. Sanderson would join us. Imagine! Three weddings at once."

His look held a shade of doubt. "Is Hertfordshire prepared for such felicity?"

She kissed his cheek, rising on her toes to reach him. "With the right groom, it most certainly is."

They remained there atop Oakham Mount as the sun climbed in the sky, casting gold and rose across the fields below. The snow sparkled, and a hush lingered, broken only by the soft breath of the breeze and their hushed conversation. Darcy held Elizabeth's gloved hand in his own, his thumb brushing over her knuckles with idle affection.

"I cannot believe it is real. That this morning began in disappointment and has ended in...this." At his puzzled look, she explained the delayed delivery of his note.

He nudged her shoulder. "What a beginning! To think your faith in me was almost undone."

She laughed. "Yes, but all has come right in the end. And with such a treasure—beautiful silk roses. I feared the last gift was not to come after all. And now I can openly display all the tokens of your affection."

"I noted you were careful to conceal some of the gifts."

"Yes. Many were so fine, I dared not show them lest *someone* find a way to relieve me of my treasures. But the locket—" she placed her free hand over her heart "—I wore close. Every day."

He took her hand and entwined their fingers.

"And the pearls," she continued. "I wore once or twice, beneath my gown, where no one could see. The risk was too great."

His lips twitched. "Miss Lydia?"

Elizabeth gave him a knowing look. "Precisely. She would either steal them outright or make the most ridiculous assumptions. I had no wish to explain myself. Mama would have been hysterical, raving about lost reputations and ruined daughters."

"It grieves me that I could not be more open, but I trusted you would understand. You see, I firmly believed you would have turned me away had I spoken too soon."

"You are correct. I did not love you then so well as I do now. And tonight, at the Longs' Twelfth Night celebration, I shall wear your gifts—all of them—in a manner of speaking. It would not do to come draped in nine shawls."

He laughed, his eyes searching hers, a question lingering unspoken.

She smiled. "The sapphire pins..."

"And the necklace?"

"And the necklace," she confirmed. "Though which I have yet to decide. I believe the pearls will go best with my gown."

He lifted her gloved hand to his lips and brushed it with a kiss.

"Perhaps...we might even announce the engagement tonight?"

At her words, she saw joy kindle in him, bright and unrestrained. "If your father consents, then yes. Let the world know I have won the hand of the finest woman I have ever known."

It was difficult to say whether her cheeks were blushed by his declaration or the the cold air as they stood together in the hush of the morning, but Elizabeth suspected it was both. The world slowly awakened around them, as love bloomed steady and sure—enduring, eternal, like twelve silk roses kept in a box of red.

Chapter Twenty-Six

January 5, 1812
Longbourn
Darcy

THE MORNING SUN FELL softly upon the windows of Mr. Bennet's study. He looked up from his desk to find Darcy standing at the threshold, composed yet visibly resolute.

"You asked to speak with me, sir?" Mr. Bennet prompted, setting his spectacles aside.

Darcy stepped forward, posture as upright as ever, yet his address was more earnest than Mr. Bennet had ever heard from him.

"I am come, sir, to request your consent to marry your daughter, Elizabeth."

The words hung in the air. Mr. Bennet gestured to the chair opposite; his surprise was plain. "Sit down, Mr. Darcy; let us talk as men."

"Pray call me Darcy, sir."

"And I am Bennet."

Darcy took a seat, clasping his hands before him.

"You must know, Darcy," Mr. Bennet began, studying him closely, "that Lizzy is very dear to me. She is headstrong, opinionated, and entirely too clever for her own good. But she is also tender-hearted, fiercely loyal, and deserving of a husband who sees her worth—not as a possession, but as a partner."

"I know it well." Darcy's manner was firm. "And I cherish every one of those qualities. She has altered my very course in life. I came to Hertfordshire proud and blind. It was she who opened my eyes—and my heart."

Mr. Bennet leaned back, folding his arms. "What of your family? The ton is not always kind to those they deem beneath them. How do you intend to shield her from the inevitable disdain?"

His regard was unwavering. "I will love Elizabeth with all that I am. That love will be her armor. My family may disapprove, society may scoff, yet I shall stand firm. She will be mistress of Pemberley, and no one—*no one*—will ever make her feel unworthy."

Silence settled between them as Mr. Bennet studied the young man. At length, the stern cast of his countenance yielded, a smile suffusing his countenance with paternal joy.

"I had wondered if any man might truly deserve her. His words trembled with feeling. "But now I find that I could not part with my Lizzy to anyone less worthy, sir."

Darcy exhaled, the tightness in his shoulders easing. "Thank you, Bennet. You have gifted me my heart's greatest desire, sir."

Mr. Bennet's chuckle held both fondness and resignation. "She is full of surprises, my Lizzy. I suspect you will never be bored."

Joy broke through his reserve, and a true smile spread across his face, unguarded and bright. "I should hope not."

As he rose, Mr. Bennet followed and extended his hand. "Welcome to the family, Darcy. Heaven help you."

He clasped the offered hand with contained pride. "And heaven bless us all."

He made to depart.

"Send Lizzy in, will you? I wish to speak with her."

Elizabeth

Elizabeth entered her father's study smiling, the promise of her future shining in her eyes. He gestured to the chair Darcy had so lately occupied, and she sat, folding her hands neatly in her lap.

Her father regarded her carefully, his features unreadable.

"So," he began, drawing out the word, "Darcy has just left my study after a rather earnest appeal. He wishes to marry you."

"Yes, Papa."

He leaned forward. "You are determined to accept him?"

"I am."

He rose and moved toward the window, clasping his hands behind his back. He stood in thoughtful silence before speaking again.

"I must confess, I once thought him the proudest, most disagreeable man I had ever met. I disliked him greatly. But he has changed; anyone can see it. He was not always kind in his manner, Lizzy, and I know too well what can happen when respect between husband and wife is lost."

He turned and faced her, his eyes gentle but searching. "Are you certain, my dear? Truly certain? Marriage is a long journey. You must be very sure of your heart and your regard."

Elizabeth rose and came to stand beside him. "I am sure, Papa. He is no longer the man we first thought him to be—he is better. Darcy is generous and principled, and above all, he is kind. He wooed me not with grand speeches or flattery, but with care and understanding. I found myself in the middle of it before I knew what had happened. And now I love him with my whole heart."

Mr. Bennet studied her for a long moment; then the sternness of his countenance gave way to tenderness.

"Then I am satisfied. And I dare say, you may yet prove that a sensible man with a good fortune is not always so rare a find."

Elizabeth laughed and hugged him tightly, and Mr. Bennet, blinking back the tide of feeling that pressed too near, held her as though he knew she would not be his much longer.

"Shall we delay telling your mama? If she is informed now, she will have half the neighborhood invited to dine before the day is out. Perhaps Mr. Long can be persuaded to allow the announcement this evening, when her triumph may be shared with the largest audience possible."

"That suits me perfectly, Papa."

"Off with you, then. Go to your betrothed."

She did as she was bid, eager to be with Darcy once more.

Darcy

The drawing room at Purvis Lodge glittered with light and laughter as the Longs hosted the annual Twelfth Night gathering. The guests were resplendent; the fire crackled merrily, and the fragrance of wassail and roasted chestnuts lingered in the air.

Darcy stood near the hearth, surveying the company with composed interest until Bingley leaned close and muttered, "I declare, I have quite had my fill of holiday events. Who knew the Hertfordshire countryside would be as busy as town?"

"Yet none in town offer such lively company."

Then she entered—Elizabeth, radiant in a gown of cream and blue, sapphire pins glinting like starlight in her hair. The pearl necklace lay gracefully about her neck, the embroidered shawl draped over her arms, and the evening gloves fitted her hands with elegance. A selection from nearly every gift he had given her was on display.

He crossed the room and bowed. "The sapphires suit you."

Elizabeth's eyes gleamed with mischief. "As well they should. I am told they were chosen by someone with exceptional taste."

"You are remarkably composed." He drew nearer, unable to resist.

"Someone has been sending me rather romantic tokens. It flaunts propriety, I dare say, but I cannot refuse them. It would be a slight to the gentleman who chose them with such care."

Their eyes met, and for an instant, the very air seemed suspended about him.

"That would not do at all. No, you had much better flaunt propriety. Causing offense is best avoided."

Her laugh was low and merry. "Very well, sir, I shall do as you suggest." She paused. "I was right to conceal them before. Lydia remarked upon my pins and shawl the moment I stepped into the drawing room before we departed."

"Did she? You know your sister very well, then. Did your mother have anything to say?" He guided Elizabeth's hand through his arm, intent on keeping her close all evening.

"She did not. Mama told Lydia to cease her complaints and prepare to depart. Kitty wisely kept silent, though she examined my attire more closely before we boarded the carriage."

"I am pleased you managed to reach the gathering without conflict." Darcy regarded her with wonder, marveling that he had won her heart and her hand.

Moments later, came a call for dancing. Mr. Long cleared the floor, and Mrs. Long, full of mirth, declared, "We shall have a waltz!"

Gasps rippled through the room—how scandalous! But Darcy was ready. He turned to his beloved, her arm still linked with his.

"Shall we dance, my love?" He spoke in low tones, the force of his anticipation unmistakable.

"It would be my pleasure." Elizabeth's smile warmed him to the core. "Though you may be required to compensate for my errors. I have not danced the waltz in public. It is not the done thing."

"I have only paired with Georgiana. I promise I shall not fail you."

They stepped onto the floor. As the waltz began, the world beyond them ceased to matter. Her hand rested lightly upon his shoulder, his on her waist, and they moved as one. Her eyes searched his face, filled with love. Bliss carried them through the measure; her perfume surrounded him, her nearness intoxicating. When the music ebbed, Darcy bent close. "I love you," he breathed for her alone.

Before Elizabeth could answer, Mr. Bennet's voice carried across the room, "Ladies and gentlemen, if I might have your attention. Mr. Long has graciously allowed me to make an announcement in his home. My daughter, Miss Elizabeth Bennet, has consented to marry Mr. Fitzwilliam

Darcy. My wife and I are very blessed. Three of our lovely daughters have secured their happiness this festive season!"

A hush fell. Mrs. Bennet gasped audibly and clutched the back of her chair.

"My stars," she cried. "Three daughters engaged! All at once! I shall swoon!"

But Elizabeth only laughed as Darcy swept her into another graceful turn, his heart steady and full. For on this twelfth day, she had become his.

Forever.

Elizabeth

The air inside the drawing room brimmed with lively spirit. News of the engagement had spread swiftly, traveling to the card room and the retiring room, and well-wishers from Meryton and the surrounding area clustered around the newly betrothed, offering congratulations, blessings, and the occasional speculative glance. The warmth and laughter of the company was as heady as the punch.

Elizabeth stood at Darcy's side, her arm lightly brushing his. Though she had often felt on display at such gatherings, this evening she did not mind in the least. Not with him beside her.

Mrs. Long's eyes twinkled. "Miss Elizabeth, I will have to remember to say Mrs. Darcy soon. My dear, what a splendid match! I am honored to have it announced at my gathering."

More neighbors came to wish them joy. A few young ladies whispered of their envy at Elizabeth's elegant accessories, while others admired the romance of the evening, declaring it the perfect close to the festive season.

Just then, Jane and Bingley approached, their expressions alight with mirth.

"You sly thing!" Jane's laughter belied her reproach. "Not a word, not a single hint! And you—" she wagged a finger in mock reproof—"you spent the whole day being perfectly composed. I had forgotten entirely about your secret admirer!"

Elizabeth grinned, feigning innocence. "It was all very mysterious, was it not?"

Darcy inclined his head. "I had the distinct impression Elizabeth enjoyed being mysterious."

Bingley clapped Darcy on the back, laughing. "And you! Keeping silent when I have been agonizing over invitations and estates and managing my sisters. I demand a forfeit, Darcy." He paused. "Oh! Caroline will be furious when she hears what the season in Hertfordshire has produced: your betrothal to Miss Elizabeth, my own happiness secured, and even a match for Miss Mary. She long wished for a closer connection between our families. She will have it, though not in the manner that she intended. That alone is prize enough, I think."

At that moment, Mary and Sanderson joined them. Her cheeks were flushed, her hand snug in her betrothed's.

Sanderson tipped his head toward Darcy and Bingley. "It seems congratulations are in order for us all."

Mary added primly, though her eyes betrayed delight, "It is a remarkable thing that all three of us should become engaged within such a short time."

Elizabeth caught Jane and Mary's hands. "Shall we marry on the same day? We would cause quite a stir, the three of us entering the church together."

Mary and Jane agreed at once, and Bingley lent his ready assent. "There is wisdom in that. We ought to consult your father; he will appreciate one wedding breakfast instead of three."

"I dare say he will approve on account of the expense." Jane's smile held a wry twist. "Though Mama will likely suffer a fit of nerves."

Darcy's amusement deepened. "Shall we have her salts at the ready?"

Sanderson chuckled. "We shall simply keep the window open; the air will revive her."

The three couples stood close, a triangle of affection and resolve, laughter threading easily among them.

Darcy leaned nearer, his subdued fervor unmistakable. "We gentlemen have waited long enough. I, for one, do not intend to delay in claiming my bride."

Bingley raised his glass. "To haste—blessed haste."

Sanderson echoed, "To our brides—and a joyful union for us all."

Their glasses met in perfect accord, the sound clear against the soft hum of merriment. Elizabeth found Darcy's eyes, her smile blooming once more.

It was a new beginning, and it would be a very happy one indeed.

As the Bennet carriage rumbled along the lane toward Longbourn, Elizabeth sat nestled beside Jane, her gloved hands resting upon the sapphire shawl Darcy had given her. Mrs. Bennet chattered happily from the seat opposite, praising Providence in loud and effusive tones. "Three daughters well married! It is a blessing indeed. God has been very good to us, and just wait until I order the lace—"

"No lace, Mrs. Bennet! Let that wait until morning." Mr. Bennet checked her with sly humor, and the conversation shifted.

On arriving home, Lydia cast a speculative look at Elizabeth's attire and gave a dramatic sigh. "Lizzy, you look far too fine. All those beautiful things. 'Tis positively unfair!"

Mrs. Bennet turned to truly take in her daughter for the first time, eyes widening as they swept over the pearl necklace, the gloves, the pins. "From your betrothed? Indeed, Mr. Darcy is very generous. A fine man! I always said he had good sense."

"You said he was proud and disagreeable!" Lydia protested. She folded her arms; jealousy, coupled with a sulky pout was writ large upon her countenance.

"Hush, Lydia." Mrs. Bennet swatted at the air. "That was before I knew how very generous and very attentive he could be. Your sister is most fortunate to have secured such a man. Who would have thought he should prefer an impertinent miss?"

"I only meant," Lydia huffed, "that I would not mind borrowing a few of Lizzy's things."

"Absolutely not." Mrs. Bennet regarded her daughter intently. "That would offend Mr. Darcy, and we must be very respectful. Very respectful indeed."

Elizabeth felt nothing but relief at this. Her mother would not permit Lydia's usual pilfering when it came to her future son-in-law. That meant Elizabeth could display her gifts without fear.

Both Kitty and Lydia clamored to know whether they might stand up with their sisters at the wedding, talking over one another until Jane interposed gently.

"We can discuss it in the morning, dears," she said. "Let us all rest for now."

Elizabeth rose and bid her sisters good night, and retired to her chamber. As she laid her head upon the pillow, her heart overflowing, she closed her eyes and dreamed of Darcy—of his steady regard, his tender words, and the life awaiting them. Her future was no longer uncertain, for it was secured in love, and it was hers.

Epilogue

March 1, 1812
Longbourn
Elizabeth

THE FIRST DAY OF March dawned bright and clear, a rare gift for an English spring, and so began the marriages of three Bennet sisters—Elizabeth, Jane, and Mary—joined in holy matrimony to three good and worthy men. The decision to share the day had been born more of necessity than design; to contrive three separate weddings lay beyond the resources, or patience, of any one household. Still, the joint celebration proved joyful, bustling, and memorable, with guests proclaiming it the event of the season.

Mr. Collins had arrived at Longbourn on January seventh, only to be thoroughly astonished. On hearing of Elizabeth's betrothal to Darcy, he hastened to write to Lady Catherine, convinced she would wish to interfere. She did. The ensuing uproar thoroughly exasperated his future bride, Miss Lucas, and thenceforward he ceased to meddle in the affairs of others.

Descending upon Netherfield in high dudgeon, Lady Catherine demanded an audience with her nephew. But Darcy was not to be found; he was at Longbourn with his future wife. Undeterred, she swept there directly, intent on tearing Elizabeth from his affections. Her scolding manner and lofty airs were met with unshaken resolve. Darcy stood firm, declaring he would not see his aunt again until she offered his betrothed a sincere apology. Mr. Bennet was delighted, remarking that it was abundantly clear Darcy would protect his daughter from every quarter—even the titled ones. Lady Catherine was removed from Longbourn and sent unceremoniously on her way. With no offered lodgings, and disdaining the local inn, she traveled to London to air her grievances to her brother, Lord Matlock.

A week later came a letter from Lord and Lady Matlock. Though politely worded, it was Lady Matlock's postscript that revealed the true sentiment: Lord Matlock was inclined to approve of the match, if only to spite his sister. Darcy and Elizabeth were amused and content. Lady Matlock assured Darcy of her support for Elizabeth as she entered London society, and her patronage would ease the way for the new Mrs. Darcy.

Darcy's sister, Georgiana, joined him and his future bride shortly before the wedding; he scarce recognized her, so great was the change. Timidity and her wounded sense of consequence were replaced by confidence, warmth, and grace. Mrs. Annesley's companionship had aided her recovery, and five new sisters completed it. She and Elizabeth grew close, and together they influenced Kitty and Lydia. In turn, the younger Bennets shared with Georgiana some of their liveliness, while adopting much of her polish. Many remarked upon the transformation in all three girls, often attributing it to Elizabeth's steadying presence.

As for Bingley, he carried out his plan not to inform his sisters of his marriage until he could present it as a *fait accompli*. His letter was brief and unapologetic; their reply was anything but. Miss Bingley, incensed, accused him of ruining her prospects, and relations between them cooled irrevocably. Mrs. Hurst said little, but likewise withdrew. Bingley felt no loss.

Miss Bingley remained with the Hursts until she at last consented to wed a wealthy tradesman. Her acerbity and haughty sense of superiority had driven away gentlemen of higher station. Once her estrangement from her brother—and by extension the Darcys of Pemberley—became known, any who might have considered her soon drew back. She was compelled to look elsewhere, and after her marriage, she removed to her husband's home in Liverpool.

After a brief wedding tour through the North, the Bingleys settled at Windmere, one of the finer estates he and Darcy had inspected. Situated conveniently near both Pemberley and Sanderson's property, it offered proximity to their dearest family and friends. With minor repairs underway, they would spend the remainder of their lease at Netherfield. In time, Windemere became a lively and loving home, filled with laughter and light, blessed with three children: one strong, good-natured son and two sweet-tempered daughters.

Mary and Sanderson first visited his family's estate after the wedding, where Mary was received warmly. His family, having attended the wedding, had grown quite fond of his young bride. That summer, the couple went to Brighton, an indulgent farewell to Sanderson's service in the militia. By autumn, they returned to his estate, where Mary assumed her new role with calm assurance. Their household soon rang with the laughter of four children: two sons followed by two daughters. In an unexpected turn, Sanderson's elder brother never married; upon his death, the principle estate passed to Mary's eldest son. The younger inherited the smaller property, but due to prudent improvements and sound management, it yielded a respectable income of two thousand pounds a year.

And the Darcys? They were blissfully happy.

Each Christmas, the family gathered at Pemberley, where Elizabeth would read aloud the poem her husband had written—the one that began with a diamond pendant and ended with twelve silk roses and a whispered promise on Oakham Mount. Their five children—three boys, tall and intelligent like their father, and two girls as lively and lovely as their mother—knew the story by heart, yet begged to hear it time after time. And always, Elizabeth obliged, holding the worn paper in her hands and glancing over it to meet Darcy's eyes—still steady, still full of love.

For theirs was a love not merely immortalized in verse, but lived daily, joyfully—and, when life was done, eternally.

The End

I hope you enjoyed Darcy's 12 Days of Christmas! It was an adventure to explore this alternate path for our dear couple. Be sure to check out my other books. I have a soft spot for redemption stories, so if that's a favorite trope of yours, take a look at my other books! Find them at Amazon.com!

<u>MJ Stratton Books</u>

Thank you for reading!

Mr. Darcy's Twelve Days of Christmas Poem

On the first day of Christmas, a memory restored,
A token once cherished, from a heart long ignored.
Your true love came softly, with hope to reclaim—
A locket he gave you, on a gold chain.

On the second day of Christmas,
With his beloved in view,
Two silk gloves,
Stitched delicate and true.

On the third day of Christmas,
Wisdom and beauty combine,

Three pearl combs
To grace thy locks so fine.

On the fourth day of Christmas,
Wrapped in satin so rare,
Four velvet ribbons
To adorn thy hair.

On the fifth day of Christmas,
I penned thee a line,
And presented five quills,
Gilded and fine.

On the sixth day of Christmas,
In crystal so clear,
Six vials of scent,
From London brought here.

On the seventh day of Christmas,
With flourish and pride,
Seven painted fans
From lands far and wide.

On the eighth day of Christmas,
With words soft and sweet,
Eight books of verse,
Their gilt edges neat.

On the ninth day of Christmas,
Through streets touched with frost,
Nine silken shawls,
Lest thy comfort be lost.
(Woven with care,
From a Bond Street display,
To warm gentle shoulders
In winter's cold gray.)

On the tenth day of Christmas,
By candlelight's glow,
Ten lustrous pearls
In a velvet pouch show.

On the eleventh day of Christmas,
In a jewel box divine,
Eleven sapphires
Of deep, steadfast shine.

On the twelfth day of Christmas, twelve silk roses lie,
Unfading, eternal—as steadfast as I.
With treasures so lovely, yet none half so dear,
As the vow that I whisper for only you to hear.

Other Books by MJ Stratton

Note: Books with an asterisk are redemption stories

Darcy and Lizzy Variations:

A Far Better Prospect**

When Given Good Principles**

No Less Than Any Other

The Lake House at Ramsgate

Thwarted

To Marry for Love

Love Unfeigned

Character and Countenance

Body and Soul

Shadows of the Past

Look on the Heart

Strange Happenings at Longbourn

Other Stories:

The Redemption of Lydia Wickham**

Catherine Called Kitty**

Mary, Marry? Quite Contrary!**

Charmed

Charming Caroline**

<u>From Another Perspective</u>
<u>Crossroads</u>
Variations from Jane Austen's other works
<u>What Ought to Have Been</u>**
Collections
<u>Quills and Quandaries</u>
Thank you for reading!

Acknowledgements

Acknowledgements

Special thanks to my lovely line editor, Ree. I *know* my books are so much better after you're done.

Thanks also to Tish, Rebecca, and Gratia for the proof work! You are all fabulous!

A special thanks to https://regencyromancecovers.com/for the cover design!

Thank you, Summer Hanford, for helping me with the blurb. Someday I'll figure those out!

And, as always, thank you to my darling husband, who has supported me through it all, especially when it came to finding time to write while still being a wife and mom. Throw in a doctoral degree, and we are a load of crazy around here! I couldn't do it without you.

About The Author

MJ STRATTON'S LOVE AFFAIR with Jane Austen began at sixteen, thanks to a much-beloved aunt who introduced her to *Pride and Prejudice*. That fateful moment led to an insatiable passion for Austenesque fiction, sealing her destiny as both a reader and a writer. After nearly a decade of beta reading and editing for others, MJ took the plunge into publishing her own works in 2022.

A lifelong enthusiast of reading, learning, and all things bookish, MJ balances her time between crafting Regency tales, tending to her garden, and sewing her way through creative projects. She shares her small-town life with her husband, four lively children, and cats who firmly believes they are the true masters of the household.

When she's not writing or wrangling her feline overlords, MJ can usually be found lost in a book, researching obscure historical facts, or daydreaming about her next story.

Printed in Dunstable, United Kingdom

74928788R00163